JYNA
MAENG

A QUEEN
OF
WHISPERS

Copyright © 2026 by Jyna Maeng

All rights reserved.

No portion of this book may be reproduced in any form without written permission from the publisher or author, except as permitted by U.S. copyright law.

This is a work of fiction. Names, characters, places, and incidents are products of the author's imagination and are used fictitiously and are not to be construed as real. Any resemblance to actual events, locales, organizations, or persons, living or dead, is entirely coincidental.

Cover designed by MiblArt

ISBN: PB: 979-8-9882773-2-3; eBook: 979-8-9882773-3-0

To learn more about this author go to www.jynamaengbooks.com

DEDICATION

When you make a mess of everything
You still deserve love
Especially from yourself

CHAPTER 1

Everything moved in slow motion.

Wet mouths stretched open like caverns on blurred faces, as pudgy fingers pointed from one person to another. Their voices garbled, as if they were underwater, and in their fervor, flecks of spit arched into the air, landing on long gray silken robes.

The twelve council members rallied in a frenzy, climbing over each other's speech, trying to get their word in before the other.

"We need to secure our relations with Kethrendel and Cheacia's trading routes first!" one of them shouted.

"Have they already received news of her Highness' ascent?" another yelled.

Their loud shouting was piercing to all but Arla, because although her body was there, her mind was not.

I killed him.

Cold sweat slicked her palms as she gripped the edges of the throne chair that was too tall for her short frame. Her nails dug into the polished wood, leaving permanent moon-shaped grooves.

Her stomach twisted, pushing acid up her esophagus, forcing her to remember the horrid bumps bubbling on her father's skin when she held his wrists. He had screamed so loudly she saw his tonsils in the back of his throat, shaking in utter pain.

She remembered how desperately she tried to wrench her hands off of him, but *her* grip stayed firm. Unrelenting.

The voices in the room kept rising.

She had no control.

Her body was a shell she had lost to another. *The Woman.* Someone she thought was on her side, but ended up betraying her, stealing her Whispers to murder her fa–.

Arla squeezed her eyes shut.

It wasn't me.

But it *was* her.

In the end, it was her hands that did it.

This is all your fault. You stole his throne.

Darkness squeezed around her heart, which thrummed in irregular, desperate beats, threatening to pop. They would execute her for treason if they found out the truth.

And what about the other truth? The one you truly fear.

"What do you think, Queen Arla?"

Slowly, Arla emerged from her tangled thoughts. An older man, bald as a baby and as well-fed as a cow, looked at her expectantly. Docannon, advisor on her father's council, was one of twelve sets of eyes that all gazed up at her.

Arla's mouth went dry.

Hearing herself addressed this way, it felt so wrong. *Queen* and *Arla* should never have been a combination that existed, and yet here she was: Queen Regent of Ulsana. Until her infant brother turned sixteen, all the responsibility of running the largest kingdom on the continent was on her inexperienced shoulders.

"U–um." Arla desperately searched through her memory in hopes of finding a hint of what they were discussing, but there was nothing but hot ash. "I think... there should be... we can..."

No more words came.

Docannon's face fell in slight disappointment, but he didn't look surprised. None of them did. Because many didn't believe Arla could do this. Why would they? Unlike most royal first-borns, she wasn't trained for this. No one would have thought the talentless daughter of Mathus Seojin would become Queen.

And yet, here she was.

Norendra cleared her throat beside her. Just as she held the position of First Advisor to her father, Norendra retained the title for Arla. "What her Highness meant to say was, we will prioritize solidifying her current rule here, before reaching out to the other kingdoms."

The other council members accepted this answer, relieved that at least they had Norendra around to guide the new Queen.

Arla wanted to melt into her chair until she disappeared. She felt like a child wearing a crown too big for her small, oddly shaped head.

Norendra gave her a cursory glance before addressing the council again. "It has been a long week. Perhaps we can reconvene tomorrow when –"

The doors flew open.

Ametha stood underneath the ornate doorframe. Her blonde hair, usually perfectly curled and cascading down her back, now clumped in odd places and looked dull and dry, like crisped edges of yellow hay. Her makeup was only half-done, and without her usual black eye-liner, Ametha's sparkling ocean irises looked more like stagnant pond water.

Arla's heart ached seeing her step-mother look like a snuffed out star, because she knew she was responsible for it.

"Lady Ametha." Norendra gave the former queen a sharp, condescending look. "This is a private meeting."

Ametha's voice came out like a croak. "I have waited a week and nothing has been done, so I have been forced to come here to address you all directly." Ametha scanned the room, making sure to hammer the guilt into each council member, until her eyes fell on Arla, the guiltiest of all. "Why after so long has Leo Treterra not been executed?"

Arla's lungs stopped taking in air.

Ametha's nostrils flared in rage. "He needs to pay for what he did."

Arla remembered the punch, the crack of bone, how fire overtook them as her father raged at the man who dared to defend her. The room remained silent, with each person looking to the other in indecision.

"That bastard killed the king!" Ametha shouted, charging toward Arla, stopping just at the foot of the platform. "Doesn't everyone see that? He tried to do it once, and the second time he succeeded! He killed the King!"

The smell of burnt flesh filled Arla's nostrils.

"No, he didn't." Arla tried to keep her composure as her breathing threatened to stop.

I did.

The Woman did.

She wanted revenge. Arla wanted revenge. Against King Namkil. Against her father. For killing *her* lover. For hurting Leo. For hurting her.

Norendra shot Ametha a warning glance as her gaze fell from Ametha's foot to the edge of the platform, indicating that she should not step any further. "We've already determined that the undercroft's collapse crushed the king."

It was the only theory that made sense to them. The only way their great and powerful king could have died was to be surprised and overcome by a force that no human could combat, a ton of stone so heavy, it would crush any living thing under it.

"And you believe that?" Ametha hissed.

Arla's eyes darted from one council member to the next.

They did not know her true magic.

In the chaos of the day of Leo's planned execution, everyone was so busy looking out for their own survival that no one noticed what Arla was doing on that balcony. Besides, no one suspected that the weak, obedient daughter of the great King Mathus Seojin could do any harm to anyone.

Well, no one except one man.

Lingering near the back of the crowd, Simion's dark brown eyes locked onto hers. His lips curved into a hideous, crooked smile that made Arla cringe.

"It is the most logical explanation," Norendra replied dismissively. She was not one to take pity on anyone, even the grieving.

"Then why can't we find his body?" Ametha turned to the other council members, whose expressions were now shifting into something dangerously close to agreement. "That Low-Born filth killed Mathus! He deserves to die!"

A middle-aged councilwoman whose name Arla did not yet know, chimed in. "We do not have evidence of this, but regardless, I do believe we should complete King Mathus' orders and execute this soldier."

Arla's heart dropped. She remembered how the blood splayed out from Leo's back. How he screamed in agony at the open sky. It hurt her to even think about it again.

Another nodded in agreement. "Yes, and those other soldiers that helped him escape. They must be punished too."

Slowly, they started nodding in unison.

Seeing the tide turn, Norendra gave a small sigh like she couldn't be bothered with this trivial argument anymore. "Regardless of this unbelievable rumor. We can proceed with the execution. Send guards. I believe the captain is still in the infirmary. The other two are in the soldier barracks."

Arla leapt to her feet. "No!"

The entire room went silent.

Arla hesitated from the instant effect. Never had her voice silenced others like this before. The last time a crowd of nobles looked upon her like this, she was holding back tears as she ran from the room in utter embarrassment, as they held back their ridiculing laughter. Now they were looking up at her with focused attention.

She curled her fists. "Captain Treterra will not be executed, and neither will the others. They will be pardoned."

A rush of disagreement flew through the council members.

"How can this be?!"

"It was King Mathus' last orders!"

"It is the least we can do in memory of your father!"

"Unbelievable!"

The Whispers tumbled into her head, urging her to speak them.

The hairs on Arla's arm stood on end. Was The Woman here? She pushed the Whispers behind a mental door. She could not let The Woman take over.

"I am Queen Regent!" she shouted.

They stared at her in baffled silence. Never before had they heard Arla shout. They probably believed she was not capable of it.

"It's within my power and my power alone to give royal mercies to anyone I believe worthy of it. And Leo Treterra is worthy of it."

Sunlight and shadow shifted along the wall, which bent slightly around a tense Norendra. "Is that an official royal decree, Your Highness?"

"It is."

"Then it will be done." Norendra replied rather bitterly. She bowed, and the others followed as they barely tipped their heads down.

And just then, Arla realized the extent of her power.

She had used her crown to save her friends. She could do that *because* she was the ruler of Ulsana. If Ametha were still Queen, Leo, Uro and Rose would be dead by now. For days she had wrestled with whether she wanted this new title and what she would do with it, but now it seemed so clear.

If this was her fate, then she would take it. If not for her sake, then for the people she cared about. She would be queen.

A cry rang out against the walls.

Ametha bent over herself, holding her stomach, like someone had kicked her, but it was just the crumpling of a woman whose pain reverberated outside of herself. No one came to soothe the widow, whose disheveled hair fell over her face as she shed tears of loss, of her husband, her title, and the life she used to have.

Arla wanted to comfort her step-mother, but she knew it would only be met with hatred. So she sat still on her throne as the guards picked up Ametha and carried her back to her chambers.

Arla knew from this point on, for her and everyone else, nothing would ever be the same.

CHAPTER 2

Town criers were sent to every corner of Ulsana to spread the news that Leo Treterra, Uro Paek and Rose Ogada were wrongly accused of treacherous deeds and were pardoned on all accounts, returning them back to their lives in the army.

No doubt, the rumors would follow fervently afterward, speculating why their new Queen would do such a thing.

Arla hoped that whatever stories the townspeople wove would unravel quickly in the upcoming weeks.

The sun had not yet risen when Arla snuck out of her bedchambers. She made sure to step lightly down the hall and the various flights of stairs so as not to draw attention. Her royal chambers were in the northern part of the castle with fewer crumbling walls, so her access to the secret inner-tunnels were limited here.

Today was the day she would finally reunite with her brother.

Saving him was the reason this whole journey started, and she had never been able to even hold him, not once.

And Norendra would not stop her this time.

Between the unending history, geography, and social lessons Norendra put her through in addition to her routine royal duties, it was hard to get away. It was as if her advisor was purposefully stuffing her days to constrain her.

Every time Arla tried to sneak away, Norendra appeared from the shadows and turned her around to complete another lesson.

But this morning would be different, because Arla had memorized Norendra's comings and goings and she knew which halls her advisor would stalk and when, but more importantly, when she would not. Besides, who was awake at such an early hour?

In hindsight, she really shouldn't have asked that question, because as her bad luck would have it, the moment she stepped into an open courtyard, a roar of laughter echoed across the marbled square from the opposite corner. Arla practically dove headfirst behind a pillar to avoid being seen. Was it Norendra?

Daring to take a peek, she observed a group of men jabbing each other in light humor as they stumbled across the open plaza. Their cheeks were flushed pink and their steps were wobbly, no doubt returning from a long night at the taverns. And right in the middle was Simion.

Arla inwardly groaned. *Simion*.

Being a councilman suited him. In the last weeks, he had made himself comfortable with his new colleagues. Wherever they were, he was too. Arla did not know the specifics of what they spoke of, but she knew they were always laughing with him, patting him on the back and lauding his wit.

Did they know how much of that wit he used to bring her to tears as a child?

She couldn't understand why the nobles loved Simion so much. What was it like to be charmed by such a snake? He was so different with them than with her.

'No one cares that you disagree. No one cares about your opinion at all, Princess.'

Every word he had ever spoken to her was meant to belittle her. If there was anyone Arla could say she truly hated, it was Simion.

She hurried in the opposite direction.

"Queen Arla."

Simion shimmered into existence right beside her with his hands intertwined behind his back, like a creepy old man except he wasn't old at all. Actually, he was only a few years older than her, with a dark complexion and soft features that made many ladies fawn over him.

Arla did not startle. She wouldn't give him the satisfaction of her surprise. Instead, she kept walking as if he were not there.

Unfortunately, he kept her pace with ease. "I was hoping to run into you here." He kept her pace with ease.

How could you possibly hope to run into me here of all places at this early hour?

"I have something important to speak to you about," he continued, clearly in a jolly mood.

"What do you want?" She quickened her strides, hoping to lose him in a few turns, maybe even jump into a hidden tunnel that she knew would be coming up in a few minutes, if she hurried.

"I humbly request that you make my presence mandatory at every one of your meetings."

"And why would you want that?"

Two lefts and then a right would get her to the tunnel opening. She just needed to figure out how to do it without Simion seeing her. She didn't want others to know about her hidden passageways.

Simion hiccuped from his stupor. "Despite what you believe, I aim to do my job well, and I can only do that if I know exactly what is going on in your day-to-day affairs."

"You are not my First Advisor," she reminded him. "You do not need to be in all of my meetings. That role belongs to Norendra."

"I hope you don't forget how very useful I am, Your Highness." He playfully tapped his head with his forefinger. "My mind holds all the information Ulsana can offer."

Arla readied herself to argue, when Simion's next words cemented her.

"There is nothing in this kingdom that happens without me eventually finding out... as you know."

Arla ground her teeth.

'I know you killed your father.'

That was what he was really saying.

She glared at him with all the hate-eating fire in her soul. "Fine. I will invite you to every meeting I have. Happy now?"

Simion's wide grin made Arla want to scrape it painfully off his face. "Yes, Your Highness. Thrilled. You are a constant joy in my life. A gift that just keeps on giving."

Arla would have said something so biting, so harsh that it would have made Simion tear up in shame, she was sure of it, if she had the time to respond, but there was no time, because with one Whisper, Simion evaporated into thin air.

CHAPTER 3

The solid oak door loomed in front of Arla, a heavy and impenetrable barrier between her and the person she wanted to see. Carvings of ivy bordered its edges and almost mirrored the ivy carvings of her own bedchamber doors, but her stepmother owned this one.

Arla gave three quick and careful knocks. Loud enough to be heard, but quiet enough to signify it was coming from someone friendly.

Ametha's voice came through the bottom slit underneath the door, coated in suspicion. "Who is there?"

"It's Arla." She was supposed to say *'Your Royal Highness'*, as Norendra kept reminding her every day. She softened her voice. "I'm here to see Jun."

"I will not allow my son to be seen by anyone," came the reply.

Ever since the coronation, Ametha had hidden Jun away in her bed chambers with her, which was uncommon for royals to do. Often, royal children had their own separate rooms, cared for constantly by wet-nurses and servants while the Queen fulfilled her duties, but Ametha had become quite protective (or possessive) and would allow no one else to tend to Jun.

"He is my brother. I have a right to see him."

"Is that so?" Ametha mused.

"Please open the door." She drew a deep breath. "Your Queen commands it."

There was a pause, a quiet defiance, but it lasted only a second before the door pulled wide open to reveal Ametha, who was still in her nightgown, even though it was well into midday. Her blonde hair looked even more tangled than before, resembling more and more like a bird's nest.

"You are no Queen," Ametha snarled, her cracked lips pursed and spread like the desert floor. "The outdated laws of this kingdom put you somewhere you don't belong. Don't fool yourself because you wear a sparkling crown on your head. You are still the weak little girl your father always said you were."

Etchings of Whispers crawled along the inside of Arla's skull. Arla blinked hard trying to clear them, but they skittered in earnest.

Weak?

There was a time when Arla would have agreed with her, but she had gone through too much to believe this about yourself anymore. Ametha was not there in the tunnels or the arena. She had never seen Arla fight against the death of The Forest. If there was something Arla knew she wasn't, it was weak.

The Whispers piled on top of themselves now, pushing against her tongue, ready to show how *weak* she was.

She pushed them back.

Ametha gave her a smug look, believing her words had made Arla cower in her own skin, like they used to.

"Where is Jun?" Arla asked in a controlled manner.

A small light gurgle bubbled from a crib in the back corner of the room, far from every window so the sun could not touch him. A chubby pinkish-pale hand reached toward the ceiling, barely surfacing above the white embroidered edge of the crib, fisting and unfisting nothing.

Arla wanted nothing more than to go to him and reach for that inviting hand, but Ametha still stood in the way.

"I'm going to raise our new king to be the leader we need," Ametha said. "Once Jun turns sixteen, he will sit at his rightful place upon the throne and bring Ulsana into its golden age." She gave Arla a long glare. "Let us hope you don't do anything to ruin it before he has the chance."

"When Jun turns sixteen, I will gladly give him everything," Arla responded. "But until then, the crown sits on my head."

Arla stepped past the boundary of the door, but Ametha still did not budge, not making space.

She could have made Ametha move. She could have ordered it, just as she did in the throne room, when she ordered her friends' pardons. Guards would have pulled Ametha from her chambers, kicking and screaming, and Arla would have waltzed in and scooped up Jun in her arms. She could have separated Ametha from Jun forever. Linuth would help raise Jun instead, and her baby brother would grow up without ever knowing his mother at all, just like Arla.

But...

Arla took in the woman before her.

Ametha looked like she was trapped in a storm on the edge of a cliff where anything could set her on a tumbling fall downward. Arla remembered all those nights she wondered who her mother was, wishing she was there to comfort her when everyone else tossed her aside.

She could not do that to Jun. Her baby brother had already lost his father, *their* father, he should not lose his mother too.

Arla stepped back from the doorway.

Ametha grinned at her perceived win.

As the door slowly closed on Arla's face, she took in another deep breath, trying to quell her own storm from deep within.

Only she knew the truth.

Ametha had not won, she was spared.

CHAPTER 4

Arla's fingers thrummed along the throne chair's arm as the next nobles shuffled to their designated spot on the long velvet carpet in front of her. Nothing about judgment day had changed since the last time she partook in it, except for the fact that she was now the one to determine who would win or lose in High-Born quarrels.

The bearded middle-aged nobleman stood alone in his spot, the others waiting patiently behind the doors for their turn.

"My uncle has gone missing." Lord Yeen held his chin high, a strange juxtaposition to his quivering lip. "He had a lot of unpaid debts, and I'm afraid those he owed will finally want repayment."

Her interest piqued. "How long has he been missing?"

"Five days."

"So you want to send a search party to find him?"

"No." Lord Yeen quickly responded. "I want protection. A couple of soldiers to follow me around and make sure I am well."

"You believe that whoever took your uncle is going to go after you to collect his debts?"

"Yes."

"And you don't want a search party?" she asked again.

"No."

She paused. It was strange that he was asking for protection, but not a search party at all. "Aren't you worried about your uncle?"

Norendra violently cleared her throat beside her.

Arla had said something wrong again.

"He should have worried about *me*," Lord Yeen said defensively. "He's not one to think things through, and now I could pay for it."

Norendra took over the conversation, trying to push past Arla's rude response. "Everyone knows your uncle notoriously wanders, especially when spring is in bloom and the cranes have returned for the season."

Lord Yeen flushed pink at that statement. For some reason, Arla felt there was an underlying message in that phrase she did not understand.

"I am sure he has just wandered too far and will be returning soon. There is no danger to you," Norendra said.

"It's true that my uncle has been known to disappear, but this feels different. He did not pack any of his things, and his usual… contacts have not seen him either. There is something strange going on."

"Unfortunately," Norendra said. "There are not enough soldiers to spare for your protection."

Lord Yeen frowned. He was from a high-ranking family in Ulsana, so he was the type of man who was used to getting what he wanted. "There would be enough soldiers if we enacted a mandatory draft for the Low-Borns. Pull them into the army."

Arla's face twisted in distaste. "What did you say?" Arla could not believe what she was hearing. It was already illegal to leave the army once you entered, now he wanted Low-Borns to be forced to join?

"I *said*," Lord Yeen repeated himself with annoyance. A tone he would have never taken up with her father if he were still sitting on this throne. "We should start a draft and make Low-Borns join the army."

Norendra responded before Arla could. "An interesting idea for sure. We will take that into consideration."

"You cannot be serious." Arla blurted out to both of them.

Norendra threw her a look to be quiet, but Arla could not contain herself.

"We are not going to issue a draft." Arla replied. "We cannot force Low-Borns into the army just because you want more guards."

"But I am in danger, Your Highness," Lord Yeen said, appalled. "Does my safety mean nothing to you?"

"Not in exchange for all the Low-Borns that would be affected by a draft."

His lordship's mouth hung open. "Your Majesty,–"

She raised her hand to stop him. "Thank you for taking the time to come all the way here. This is my final judgment."

A short snicker echoed from across the room.

Norendra threw an annoyed glare at Simion, who remained close to the wall in his silver council robes, and then pointed that same annoyance to Arla. Norendra was not happy to hear that the former scholar was going to join them during judgment day. Usually, this was an event meant only for a monarch and their First Advisor. It was only one of the two things that annoyed Norendra that day. The other was what Arla had added to the decor.

Arla patted the middle head of her statue that had once belonged to the Endezee Garden. Her large stone creature, with three snake heads and the body of a lion, possessed the talons of the largest birds that Ulsana ever had before hunters drove them to extinction.

Lord Yeen flushed in embarrassment. He looked to Norendra for help, but received nothing but a neutral expression. And so he marched out in a huff.

Exhilaration filled Arla. The power of the crown was truly remarkable. She sat at the edge of the throne seat, eager for the next one, but no one stepped into the room. Instead, Norendra commanded Simion to leave, which he did rather reluctantly.

"I thought we had another hour of judgments," Arla said, confused.

Norendra's tight shoulders expanded, releasing all her pent-up frustrations. "That was the most tactless, irresponsible, foolish thing I have ever seen in this room."

Yes, leave it to Norendra to criticize. It was one of her many talents.

Arla smugly stood up and walked the few steps to Norendra's level. "I thought it was great."

"I cannot believe you openly told Lord Yeen that his safety was less important than a Low-Born's livelihood."

"I wasn't going to force Low-Borns to join the army just so he could have more guards. It's ridiculous and unfair."

Norendra rushed up to her with a hiss. "You sound like a Low-Born sympathizer, Arla."

Arla leaned back, struck by how close Norendra was. Her advisor's eyes were dangerously sharp, like a cobra's, ready to strike. "Low-Borns are not as important as nobles. *We* are the ones with magic. *We* are the ones who need to be protected and preserved. It is what kept Ulsana strong for centuries. If you forget that, you endanger yourself."

"How would that endanger me?"

"You are a new Queen, whose power is not yet solidified. An abrupt transition like yours... Do you know how fragile your claim to the throne is? The nobility do not know if you can lead them, and in that doubt others can take advantage and find a way to remove you. In your first real act as Queen, you pardoned soldiers that were labeled traitors to your father. Do you know how that makes you look? There are already rumors among the High-Borns that you are a Low-Born sympathizer, and your words today will only fuel them. You're someone they would never support. And a Queen with no allies is open to be *removed*."

Arla did not like the sound of that.

"And don't think just because you pardoned your soldiers means they are safe. Disgruntled nobility have ways of removing annoyances if they want."

Arla did not like the sound of that either.

Arla lengthened her spine, trying to match Norendra's height. "When my father was king, everyone treated him like a deity. No one would question him even when he burned and tortured people right in front of their faces. He was untouchable."

"Because he was ruthless." Norendra snapped. "You are not, and they know that. Your father was a great leader because he knew how to control people. That is the only way to keep the peace."

"He used fear and violence to keep people in their place." Arla argued.

"That is what power is!" Norendra shouted, exasperated by Arla's naivete. "This is why you are so stupid. You–"

"I'm not stupid."

One strand of black hair from Norendra's perfectly pulled back bun snapped out of place. "What did you just say, child?"

"Norendra," she said in a calm, steady voice. "If you are going to continue to be my First Advisor, I suggest you stop insulting me."

Norendra remained transfixed on Arla, unblinking, unbelieving.

"Can you do that?" she asked softly.

Norendra smoothed back her hair, her sharpness returning. "You cannot afford to be soft. Ulsana needs a strong leader now more than ever and a strong leader does not buckle under harsh words."

CHAPTER 5

Someone was screaming again.

Bent fingertips permanently frozen toward the darkening tree tops which turned a colorless gray. Thick blood moved like cooling molten lava across the grass, and the dirt drank it in like bitter wine. And once the earth got its fill, it shook, bloated and furious. The grass keeled and died, only to be shocked back to life in glistening obsidian, standing straight like steel needles.

Arla stood in the middle, her feet cold from the blood. Ulsanan soldiers drew their weapons nervously, not noticing her.

The trees shed their leaves and twisted unto themselves over and over again until their limbs were just as sharp as the grass along their roots.

The Forest was turning.

The tremors of its sorrow and anger vibrated across her bones.

It screamed something again.

What was it?

The sound garbled and rang until Arla found a pattern. It was screaming, *Wynera*.

Wynera.

A name.

You killed my gift.

The Forest caved in on itself, taking the light with it. The trees ripped through the soldiers and horses with their branches.

She tried to wake up, but the blood endlessly pooled around her ankles and rose higher and higher. The iron stench of it made her gag.

It's only a dream, she tried to remind herself. *It's only a dream.*

And then a voice came. Not The Woman. Something else. Something older. More ancient and terrifying than any sound Arla had heard in her entire life.

'This is the end.'

It yanked her under the blood. Arla tried to scream, but choked on iron-tinged crimson instead. She flailed her arms out, desperate to grab anything to pull her up, but there was nothing.

It pulled her down, down, down.

It got into her lungs and her eyes, drowning her.

'Wake up!'

The maroon haze drained away and the starless night burst above her.

In one great gasp, Arla stopped in her tracks. Bending over, she choked back hot liquid from her throat that was not really there.

And that's when she noticed her bare feet were covered in cold mud.

What?

Soft edges of lavender billowed around her ankles.

That's when she realized she was in her nightgown.

And she wasn't in her bed.

In fact, she was no longer in the castle at all.

She was on the main road outside the city limits.

How–?

A high-pitched shriek sent knives of pain behind her eyeballs.

'He's here!'

Before Arla could even react, five hooded figures appeared from the darkness ahead of her, and they were coming for her.

Everything went cold.

Don't freeze, she told herself. *You have to move.*

She scanned the road.

A scattering of rocks along the edges of the road. No trees. No homes. Nowhere to hide. Nowhere to get help.

The group was getting closer, taking their time, as if they knew she had no escape.

She looked behind her, trying to judge how fast she would have to run to get away. When she turned back, they were already in front of her. It was unnatural how fast they caught up.

A low male voice vibrated from beneath the hood of the central figure. "Good evening, Arla. I've been looking for you."

The others moved around her in a circle.

She turned on her heel and ran for the city walls.

"*Dem'an'al'i un seol.*"

A streak of black lightning struck the ground beside her, sending her flying to the side. She landed roughly on her shoulder, sending a jab of pain through the joint.

Did he just conjure lightning?!

Pulling herself to her feet she ran again, but there was already someone there. A heavy body wrapped around her, squeezing her arms tight to her side and swung her back to face someone. She kicked out, but the attacker knocked her to her knees, preventing her from moving completely.

A hand grabbed her chin, forcing her to look up at the hooded figure that spoke before.

He reached up and removed his hood, revealing an older man with murky mud-colored eyes that held all the intensity of someone Whisper-bent on getting what he wanted.

He wrapped his right hand around her throat, squeezing so tight she could barely breathe. Whispers scurried to the tip of her tongue. Flashes of fire took her vision, but it was no time to worry about The Woman now.

Arla tried to squeeze the Whispers through her teeth, but there was no space. No air.

Arla thrashed against the large one holding her, but it was no use.

"*Yul-andef fuy-ara.*"

She screamed as something tore into her like a hound clawing into every crevice of her being, hunting for something. Her Whispers scampered to the back of her skull, trying to hide themselves.

The hound kept ripping through her, trying to get to its prize. Tears blotted her vision as the pain crescendoed.

"*Ne-eri len-the.*" The hound flung itself sideways, shattering her thoughts. "*Rhu-dthra-a-.*"

The creature stopped, turned around and stalked up to the base of her skull, locking in.

And that's when Arla realized, whatever this thing was, it was *listening* to its wielder. Just like her monsters did to her. He was speaking to it in the full language of The Forest. A gift that Arla thought only she had until this moment.

The man's expression twisted in satisfaction the way a hunter's did when he found his prey. "*-- sum-nahi*"

Claws impaled something within her and then yanked it backward. She let out a soundless-scream. It was like her insides were flipping out, ripping blood vessels and muscle along the way.

Her skull threatened to collapse in on itself.

"*No.*"

The Woman's voice rang in her head. And then a force stronger than she had ever known blasted the creature away, freeing her from its claws.

The man snapped his hand back. Hot streaks of pain cut across her throat as his nails ripped through skin as they separated.

Arla wheezed out a gasp as everything inside her snapped back into place.

She could barely understand what happened.

He held his hand like it had been burned. "It's not possible."

A small blade flew.

Hot blood burst onto her hair and back.

The person holding her screamed and instantly let her go.

The hooded figures around her shouted, lunging for someone, who kept disappearing and reappearing behind them. In the darkness, his lean frame moved quickly, silently sinking blades into the backs of his opponents. And with one graceful spin, his amber eyes flashed at her.

Simion gleefully dodged more attacks, unable to be touched by anyone as his Whisper teleported him unpredictably around the others. One by one, he plunged daggers into their backs. The man who held her throat did not move, only observed undisturbed as he watched Simion kill his companions.

And then he raised his arm in Simion's direction. "*Dem'an'al'i un seol.*"

"No!" Arla tackled the man to the ground, jostling his aim.

Black lightning shot from the tip of his finger and crackled a few feet from where Simion stood. The scholar whipped around, eyes wide at the two of them on the ground. Arla frantically rolled out of the man's reach, in case he were to snatch her throat again.

Another scream. Arla looked at Simion as he drove his final blade into the back of the neck of the last attacker standing. And when she turned back, the man was gone.

Four cold bodies lay motionless on the road, and it happened in mere seconds. Arla's heart was still racing even though the road was eerily quiet again.

Looking at his bloody dagger, Simion tsked and dropped it to the ground the way one frivolously discarded something no longer useful. "A little rude of him to leave so early, don't you think?"

Was that all he had to say in a situation like this? She noticed all the hooded figures had bleeding backs. Of course, Simion would not fight directly.

She held her tender throat, barely able to speak. "Simion." Her voice, hoarse. "What are you doing here?"

Of all the people she thought would help her, Simion was not on that list.

With a single shrug, he replied, "Can't let my greatest asset die."

"How did you even know where I was?"

Simion brushed the dirt from his sleeve as if it were offending him. "I told you, I make it a point to know everything." He flashed her a sickly grin. "Which is annoying if you want to be hidden, but very appealing if you want to be found, and I'm guessing this time, you wanted to be found."

"I did..." She was still shocked that he, of all people, had arrived to help her. "Thank you."

It pained her to say it, but he *did* deserve a thanks. He did save her after all.

Simion rolled his eyes. "A bit shaken up, my Queen?"

Oh, how much she wished she could swap out her gratitude with a slap instead. She startled at such an aggressive thought. Since when did she start wishing to harm others?

A strong breeze lifted the edges of her nightgown, fluttering it in all directions, reminding her how exposed she was. Simion unashamedly absorbed her image from her muddied bare feet to her disheveled hair, which made Arla instinctively cover herself the best she could. Thankfully, she wore her long-sleeved gown, which covered her scarred arms.

Simion snorted dismissively. "Don't worry, my Queen, nothing I see entices me. Especially with all that mud, blood, and rocks in your hair."

Scowling, Arla crossed her arms. "I am never concerned about what you think, Snake."

"I think you have forgotten that my name is Simion."

"I think you are forgetting you are speaking to your Queen."

She glared at him so hard he should have melted on the spot, but unfortunately, he did not.

The throbbing in her neck was slowly turning into a high-pitched flare as the adrenaline wore off and the rest of her bruised body was aching worse and worse. She needed to get to a physician.

"Can you teleport us back to the castle?" she asked.

"I can only teleport myself, my dear Queen, remember?" Simion cooed, clocking the distance between them and the castle. "Speaking of which, I should get back. It's quite unpleasant out here."

"You're not going to–?"

"*Tre'lehen.*"

And with that, Simion was gone. She huffed in irritation. He would rescue her from a violent end, but then leave her to walk the streets alone back to the castle? Why was she surprised? Grumbling, Arla picked up the bottom hem of her dirtied nightgown and started the hike back.

CHAPTER 6

The balm immediately soothed the abrasions on Arla's neck, making them throb a little less.

Norendra was already pacing in a perfect, repetitive circle in Arla's bed chambers, going the exact same route at the exact same speed over and over again. Her eyebrows were furrowed, deep in aggravated thought.

It had taken her an hour, but Arla had finally made it back to the castle, drenched in sweat and mud, which sent Norendra into a frenzy. She wasn't sure if her concern was more over her injury or the fact that Arla was in a nightgown in public. The shame her advisor must have felt on her behalf, but Arla was just glad she was back in her own room where the elderly physician was carefully wrapping her neck with a cool cloth.

"And there were how many?" Norendra asked again.

"Five."

Arla had told Norendra mostly everything that had happened on the road, from the sleepwalking to Simion to the man whose magic she did not understand. Except for what The Woman said. Norendra did not know about her. No one did.

Thinking of The Woman, brought the memory of the dream. The ringing of a name.

Norendra remained pacing near the door. "You were lucky that Simion was there."

Was she? Was Norendra not listening to the part where Simion had abandoned her on the road afterward?

And how did he even know where to find her? He never did give her an answer... And then a thought entered her mind.

Maybe Simion knew to be there because he had orchestrated the entire thing and was using this as an opportunity somehow. She wouldn't put it past him. Simion was a power-hungry bully who only cared about making himself look important. She remembered his cruel words. *'No one cares about your opinion at all.'*

Those were not the only cruel things he had said to her. Years ago, he told the other noble children that she had no magic because she was too dumb to hear them.

'The Whispers are probably talking to her, but she is much of an idiot to understand them or even know what they are.'

She remembered how they surrounded her and pushed her like a dog from one boy to the next. Simion shoved the hardest, making sure she hit the ground. She remembered the moist rag hitting her in the face.

"You might as well start learning how to clean and cook like a Low-Born. If you can even do that."

The ring of their laughter had sent her crying to her room that day where she boarded herself up for a week.

Rage flared within her from the memories.

But honestly, she could not think of a reason why he would create such an extreme ruse.

The physician finished wrapping her neck and put his supplies back in his bag. "Her Majesty has been through a lot tonight. She'll need time to heal and calm her nerves."

The physician made it sound like Arla was some fragile bird whose hollow bones would break from a simple gust of wind. The attack was a surprise, but Arla was not as frazzled as they thought she was. The Forest had made her accustomed to all sorts of people and things trying to kill her. This was not new. If anything was unnerving, it was the fact that she was sleepwalking. She had never done that before, and that dream... It felt like a message.

Regardless, fear was not the emotion she was experiencing now; it was curiosity.

When the physician saw himself out, Arla turned to her advisor in a serious manner. "Norendra. The other day you said that this was a dangerous time for me. A shift in power is the perfect time to strike a monarch down. Do you think that is what happened tonight?"

Norendra's mouth opened slightly in shock, probably because Arla had not collapsed into a puddle of tears.

"Someone is obviously trying to kill me. Most likely because they want me gone."

Norendra's lips closed into a thin line. "What I feared has come true. This assassination attempt is proof that you are not solidified in your power, which endangers Ulsana even more. Your enemies will use your weaknesses against you."

Arla had remembered Norendra's earlier warnings. *And don't think just because you pardoned your soldiers it means they are safe. Disgruntled nobility have ways of removing annoyances if they want.*

Was this another warning? If this attacker was going after Arla's weaknesses, then she had three glaring ones, and they all lived in the soldier barracks.

"And you have so many weaknesses." Norendra just had to add.

Arla threw Norendra a warning look. "Can you say that nicer?"

Norendra scoffed. "Nicer? My job is not to be nice. It is to steer you onto the right path. To keep the peace and prosperity of Ulsana that has reigned for hundreds of years. To–"

"If you want to criticize me," Arla pushed. "Then, make a sandwich."

"Excuse me?"

Arla placed her palms together, her fingers flat out like a sandwich. "Say something nice about me, then something you want to criticize and then something nice again. Like a sandwich."

Norendra stared at her, incredulous, and Arla innocently blinked back, waiting.

Her advisor recoiled, as if the thought of saying anything kind was going to make her sick.

Arla waved her hand toward Norendra in support. "You can do it."

"You..."

Arla leaned forward, hopeful. "Yes?"

"You..." A vein in Norendra's neck pulsed wildly. "You... are... You are good at... eating." She blew out a breath, like she had finished lifting a heavy weight. "So good you have gotten fat."

Why was this so hard for Norendra? Arla shook her head and chose to move on. "We need to find this assassin and get answers."

She thought of how her father would have retaliated after an assassination attempt. He would have started a relentless hunt and taken no mercy. When the assassin was caught, he would have made his death long and torturous, but was that what she wanted to do? Did she really want to be that cruel, even if this man tried to kill her?

"I think you were right before. I can't ignore the High-Borns or anger them too much right now." If someone was disgruntled enough to send an assassin after her, it meant Arla had a lot further to go to win the nobles to her side. Norendra was right; her reign would be more stable if she had their support. "I need them to believe I am their Queen too."

Norendra eyed her suspiciously, like she wasn't quite sure who this person was in front of her. She was always telling Arla to be quicker about things, if only she took her own advice in adjusting to the new version of her Queen.

"In the meantime," Norendra said. "Your security will need to be doubled."

Somehow, Arla felt that would be more restricting. Another opportunity for Norendra to keep an eye on her and control her. "I don't think that is necessary."

"You found yourself in the middle of the road because you were sleepwalking. You are in no position to refuse protection. You can't even control your own body."

Those words hit Arla harder than her advisor even knew. Everything felt so out of her hands right now. Her schedule belonged to Norendra. Her body belonged to The Woman and now this mysterious sleepwalking. And even Simion was manipulating her to do what he wanted. Was there not one thing she could have control over?

"Maybe you're right…" Arla said softly.

She had felt so powerful only a day ago, but now she wondered how strong the crown really was on her head.

CHAPTER 7

The smooth wooden edge pressed firmly into her abdomen as Arla leaned forward on her vanity facing the mirror. She traced her finger lightly on the side of her bandaged neck until she got to a sensitive spot and then pressed. Sucking in a breath of pain, Arla's mind jolted awake.

Good. She needed to stay up. But it was only a mere twenty seconds before her head grew heavy again and her body slumped.

This wasn't going to work. She needed something harsher. She jabbed the tip of her nail into her arm, right over a raised scar underneath the cloth. Yelping, she curled away from the bright sting, tears blotting the edges of her eyes. She wondered if scars from Whispered fire would ever stop hurting.

With a frustrated sigh, Arla breathed through the pain and the scurrying drowsiness. Eventually she would fall asleep against her will. There was only so much pain that could keep her up without permanently damaging herself.

And there was no one to distract her either. Norendra had left almost two hours ago.

But she could not let herself sleep. Sleeping meant losing control now too. Who knew where she would wake once she shut her eyes.

Through the mirror, Arla studied her round pale face, which used to make her look younger than she was, but it was balanced nicely now with the haggard tiredness of her eyes, which aged her enough to look a little older than her sixteen-year-old self.

Glancing at her bed behind her, she wondered if she should tie herself to the posts on each corner. That way, when she did inevitably fall asleep, she would be constrained. But how could she tie all four limbs on her own? Maybe she could get Norendra to do it.

Distracted in her thoughts, Arla did not take heed of the shuddering of wood and glass behind her, blaming it on the wind.

But then she saw the shadow.

Leaping from her chair, Arla grabbed the nearest object. Unfortunately, that object was a small hand-sized porcelain bowl. It was made to hold rings, which meant it was too light to do any actual damage of any kind.

The window shook again.

She had to run. This useless bowl would not help her.

Just as she turned to escape, a voice whispered through the glass.

"Arla."

Her feet cemented.

In a flash, she was at the window, unlatching it. The shadow tumbled into her room like a stone, landing hard on his shoulder before rolling up into a standing position like a stage performer.

Arla could only gasp. Standing in the middle of her bedchamber was Leo, drenched in sweat so thoroughly, she could see through his partially torn cream-colored tunic.

Her thoughts tumbled at the sight of him.

Hello. Are you well? Have you eaten? Did you notice the clouds today? I saw a very cute horned beetle crawling over a pile of smooth pebbles and thought of you. I think you're much more a horned beetle than a snail. Don't you? Oh. I also found a new spice the cooks are using. I'm not sure what it is, but it blends the perfect balance of sweet and sour. You should try it.

She opened her mouth to say all of those things, but she accidentally inhaled a ball of her spit instead and started choking. Unfortunately, it was not the type of choking that could be done away with a small harrumph. It was more the type that required manic heaving and arm flailing to survive. A completely unattractive ordeal.

"Are you alright?" Leo made a move to help her, but Arla swung her arms around in protest to keep his distance. This was beyond embarrassing.

After a final violent cough and gag, Arla hoarsed out, "Leo." Another croaking cough. "How did you get in here?"

Leo gave her a playful smile as he loosened his shoulder with a few circles. "A lot of climbing. Bribing. And some... obstacles, but I managed."

Ah, that smile. It was so... warming. His loose, wavy dark hair was a little longer than when she saw him last, falling mostly to the right side of his face, making him look even more ruggedly handsome than before. There was one loose strand floating over his sweaty forehead, and it needed to be moved back into place. She reached for it and then stopped herself, realizing what she was doing and where she was.

Leo was in her room. Alone. With her. In the castle.

Panicking, she ran past him to the window, looking below. "Did anyone see you?"

"No," he assured her as he wiped his sweaty forehead with his sleeve. "Your security is terrible, by the way."

His arm jerked for a moment before falling back to his side. Of course. His back was still healing from the whipping a month ago. She had sent the best physicians to him, whose Whispers sped up the healing process of any injury, but magic could only do so much.

Red marks were slowly fading from his fingertips and forearms. Whatever he did to get here took a lot of physical effort and a lot of foolishness. What was he thinking, risking so much?

Shutting the window quickly, she turned to him. "Why are you here?" Realizing the question made it sound like she was irritated at him, she added. "Not that I'm not happy to see you. But you know it's dangerous for you."

Leo's grew serious. "I heard what happened, and I had to make sure you were alright with my own eyes."

He is worried about me?

A slight blush warmed her cheeks.

"I'm fine, really." She unconsciously touched her wrapped neck. "It was just some scratches on my neck and bruises on my arms."

Scanning the wrapped neck, Leo asked softly. "And it doesn't hurt to talk? You can breathe alright?"

She nodded.

His carob eyes moved onto her arms. "Did the physician do something for the bruises?"

"No." Arla reddened in embarrassment as she tugged her sleeves down past her wrists. "I didn't tell him my arms were bruised."

Leo didn't need an explanation. He had seen what was underneath her sleeves.

"I bruise easily," she tried to explain it away. "So it doesn't hurt or anything. It wasn't worth checking."

Lies. They hurt. Especially there. Any touch hurt there.

Leo offered his hand. "Can I see?"

Arla wanted to refuse. She didn't want anyone to see them ever again, but his pleading expression made Arla give in. Slowly, she pulled up her sleeves to reveal the scarred skin where the attackers had grabbed and held her.

Leo cradled her left wrist in his palm as if he was holding delicate glass.

A flicker of fury crossed Leo's face as his fingers traced over her arms, littered in raised burn scars that healed in such ugly ways that made Arla want to pull her arm back from him in shame. But she did not move, wanting his touch more than she wanted to hide.

His jaw tightened as he visually counted each patch of purpling skin.

She remembered how her father would get angry too. How he held her wrists. How fire seeped under her skin. Her scars started to heat from the memory.

And then they flashed in sudden pain. She needed to wriggle free from his grip. From *his* rage.

Don't hurt me. Don't hurt me.

Something bellowed in the darkness of her heart.

I won't let you hurt me. I am not that girl anymore. I can hurt back.

And then Leo's face changed. From anger to quiet sadness.

"This can't happen again," he muttered. To her or to himself? She wasn't sure. "I should have been there."

Her entire self relaxed, and she felt like she was walking into the sunlight again. It was strange the places her mind went. It was like being dragged underwater, where all you can think of is survival. An animal with no conscious thought. Leo would never hurt her. She knew that. But sometimes, her body did not.

"Don't blame yourself. There was no way you could have been there."

Leo pulled Arla's sleeve slowly down her arm, centimeter by centimeter, careful not to let the cloth rub her scars. It was so gentle. Arla was surprised he was even capable of it. The same rough hands that held a sword most of the day did not seem like the ones that now smoothed out the edge of her sleeve over her wrist.

"I wanted to see you sooner," he said. "But I knew you were probably under a lot of stress with your new... role. I didn't want to make your life harder."

Guilt was written all over his face, which made Arla's heart weaken.

"I wanted to see you too."

Leo gently placed his thumb and finger underneath her chin, tilting her face up toward him. "It's not right. Why do they keep trying to hurt you?"

It was like a knife nicked her vulnerable heart, letting it bleed ever so slightly.

"Maybe I'm just someone no one wants around."

She had all but disappeared in her childhood, and no one seemed to mind. And when she tried to make herself known, she was ostracized and put down. No one seemed to want her. Even Leo.

'*You are a Queen. And I am a soldier.*'

He had made it clear that they should keep their distance.

"That's not true," he said.

His eyes glazed over, lost in hers. She felt herself being pulled to him once again. Wanting to –

An echo of stone clattered along the hall. They pulled away from each other and froze in instant stillness.

A minute or two passed, and the noise did not return. Arla let out a breath of relief.

Whatever moment they had was gone, leaving a lingering uncertain space between them.

"How are things at the soldier barracks?" she asked, trying to push past the awkwardness.

Leo reluctantly peeled his eyes from the door. "When you come back from an execution alive, it tends to make you the center of attention. I'm not exactly fond of it, but that doesn't matter. What matters is your safety."

"And yours." Arla argued, not liking how he was brushing off his own problems. "Norendra said that whoever this assassin is, they are going to try to use my weaknesses against me. And my biggest one is you."

Leo blinked at her.

"AND Uro and Rose." Arla quickly added. "Weaknesses, in that you are my friends and someone could hurt one of you to hurt me."

"We'll be alright."

He was doing it again, making his dangers smaller than her own. Why did he do that?

"Well, I *am* worried. I want you all safe and, honestly, we'll probably be safer if we are together." And then the idea hit her. She grabbed Leo's sleeve in excitement. "What if you were to be my personal guard? To ensure my safety and escort me wherever I go? We can find this assassin together. And–oh." Arla released Leo's sleeve. "Right. It's not a good idea to be around me. I understand that. I'm sorry. It was a stupid idea. I should have–".

"I accept."

Arla's heart leapt, but then quickly dove into doubt. The answer was given too fast.

"It's not an order..." she carefully said. "You don't have to accept it if you don't want to."

Leo cocked his head to the side with a slight smile. "I know. I am not the type to follow orders just because they are given to me."

This was true. The first time she saw Leo, he was bad-mouthing Wilkins, something no soldier would do in the first place, and even attacked Wilkins to his detriment.

Arla started pacing the room in excitement. "You think Rose and Uro will agree to join too?"

Giving it a contemplative thought, Leo replied, "Rose will accept because she doesn't like being far from us."

Arla remembered the last time she saw Rose. She had placed the tip of her steel sword on Arla's chest with a threatening warning in her eyes. Now that she thought about it, she didn't know if having Rose around was actually safer or more dangerous.

Leo frowned. "But Uro might be a problem."

Arla tilted her head. "Why would Uro be a problem? This position will bring him closer to all the interesting gossip and parties he loves."

Leo sighed. "He's been difficult lately... You'll see."

Steps echoed outside the room, this time coming straight for her door. And then Arla remembered that Norendra wanted to send guards to her room to stop her from sleepwalking.

"I should go." Leo started toward the window.

Completely agreeing, Arla opened the window for him.

She watched Leo climb out, keeping her eyes on him to make sure he did not fall as he painstakingly climbed down the stone edge. His fingertips turned white from gripping the barely jutted out pieces of rock that stopped him from plummeting to his death. She was stressed just watching him. It must have taken him hours to get here, and it would take him probably the same to return.

She felt guilty that he went through all that just to see her for five minutes.

A harsh knock came to her door. "Queen Arla, there have been some reports of a break-in. Some guards have gone missing. We were ordered to guard you for the rest of the night."

"Thank you!" she called out to them. "I am quite safe and about to go to bed."

Leo's arms rippled in muscled effort as he climbed faster down the rock wall. She did not slink back into her bed until she saw him land on the roof of an adjacent tower and disappear around the corner.

CHAPTER 8

The halls of the castle were bustling with activity that morning. The end of the spring rains had washed away most of the pollen and dust, leaving a crisp sense of newness in the air. The energizing atmosphere sent the servants into a cleaning frenzy, straining to get to every nook and cranny of every room with their straw brooms and goose feather dusters.

The High-Borns were in their latest fashions, boasting to each other of their new resolutions in the upcoming summer season. Four ladies-in-waiting, including Linuth, and two guards accompanied Arla past the nobles, who paused their conversation to give her a slight obligatory bow.

"First, she pardons traitors, and now they are her guards?"

"I heard she was attacked the other night."

"Oh, really?" another responded with curiosity. "Do tell."

Clearly, they were more curious than concerned about the assassination attempt.

The guards split up and flanked either side of a humble wooden door. Familiar voices spoke on the other side.

Instead of opening the door, she leaned her ear to it, catching slivers of the conversation.

"You have to learn to adapt." It was Leo's voice, stern and slightly annoyed. "All creatures learn to adapt to their surroundings; that is how they survive, and you are no exception to that."

"I want to live my *one* life the way I want to."

That was Uro's voice.

She had never heard the young boy sound so defiant before.

Linuth cleared her throat behind Arla. The elder was not a supporter of eaves-dropping. With a sigh, Arla entered the room.

The study was a former storage room, filled with random trinkets and memorabilia before Arla cleaned it up and set a small desk and bookshelf in there. She did not want to occupy the same study as her late-father. In fact, she really did not want to occupy any of the rooms where her father had lingered for all his forty-five years.

The bed chambers her father once dwelled in were shut away with his belongings. The only thing she shared now with the late king was the throne.

Leo and Uro stood in the center of the room while Rose leaned against the bookshelf, arms crossed.

"Arla!" Uro ran toward her, arms open.

In one swift motion, Leo planted himself between them and bowed to Arla. "Your Highness."

None of them moved for a moment, confused, and then it dawned on her.

The door was open.

Her ladies-in-waiting and guards were watching. No Low-Born soldier should ever greet their Queen in such a casual way.

Arla turned to the guards. "You are relieved of your duties. The captain is here now." She shut the door before getting a response from them. There was a slight shuffling before everyone outside decided to leave.

With a wide smile, Arla finally embraced Uro. Arla slightly tilted her head up to hook over Uro's shoulder. He was getting taller.

"I'm so glad you're safe!" Uro peeled away from her and immediately dove into the million-questions game he loved to play. "How is Queendom? You must be so busy! Is it any different than before? I can't believe you pardoned us!" He smacked his hand against his head. "I really thought they were going to hang us. That was scary. Leo told me not to be afraid, but that's just something someone says when they think they are about to die, right? It brings no comfort at all!" Uro puffed up. "And now we're your royal guard. Who would have thought?!"

Watching Uro's round face flush in excitement sent Arla into a small chuckling fit, which Uro readily joined her in.

Leo cocked his head toward the door. "These doors are not completely soundproof, you know."

Leo was being more uptight than usual. His protective nature was ramped up to a level that made him wary of everything. Uro threw Leo a different expression she had never seen before. One of disdain.

What had happened between these two?

"I hope I wasn't interrupting anything..." Arla treaded carefully. She wanted to know what the issue was, so she could help solve it, but pushing the subject too far could bubble up emotions that would worsen whatever was bothering them.

Uro brought himself to smile again. "Nope. Leo was just being his usual stubborn self."

"How so?" she asked.

"He thinks drawing is a waste of time."

"Drawing?" She was not expecting that answer.

"I have drawn here and there since I was a child, but have been really focused on it the last month or so."

"Instead of joining the daily drills like he's supposed to." Leo added.

Uro brushed off the comment. "I am really good at it."

"Well, I must be very lucky then." Arla said. "Because I can definitely use an artist right now."

Uro perked up at the same moment Leo frowned.

"I was thinking it would be helpful to have a sketch of what my assassin looks like. That way we can post it around the city and offer a reward for anyone who has any information about him."

Uro clapped his hands together in excitement. "What a great idea! Do you have a brush or quill here? Charcoal will also do."

Arla nodded, pointing to the desk. "There should be some in the drawers. And paper too."

Uro zipped to the desk, rummaging through the drawers.

From the corner of her eye, she could see Leo glowering.

"It *is* a good idea," she said softly to Leo. She couldn't understand why he was so disagreeable about this. Looking at Rose, it didn't seem like she agreed with Uro's new hobby either. Arla did not try to address the silent soldier. She was slightly afraid of what Rose would say if she did.

"Whether it's a good idea or not is not the problem," Leo sighed, his disgruntledness easing into a tiredness.

"But he's so happy."

What was so bad about making Uro feel good about his new skills?

Uro returned with a few loose papers and a writing quill in hand. Plopping himself on the edge of the wooden desk, he dipped the quill into a jar of ink. "Describe everything you can remember."

"A middle-aged man, probably in his forties. Shoulder-length brown hair..." Arla continued to list off the assassin's attributes as Uro drew hunched over his paper, like a turtle.

"It's strange that the assassin showed his face," Leo said. "A noble who openly kills other High-Borns is rare enough that he will be found quickly."

"Maybe he doesn't care whether he is caught or not," Arla replied.

"Then he is not a good assassin," Rose chimed in.

Uro's eyebrows furrowed in concentration. "Did he have any scars? Or other unique features?"

"No, nothing unique. He looked like any other normal man. But his eyes were wider set and his chin was pointy. Like a triangle." She was close enough to notice this when he was choking her to death.

Arla turned to the other two. "The faster we find this assassin, the faster we can get answers."

"Why were you even alone outside the city that night?" Leo asked.

"I was sleepwalking. And he found me there. Like he was expecting me."

Leo grew suddenly concerned. "Sleepwalking?"

"Is this him?" Uro turned the paper around to reveal his drawing, and Arla gasped. It was quite good. So good that Arla thought it could be real.

"Uro, your talent is amazing."

Uro blushed. "Thank you."

"I think this is enough for anyone to be able to recognize him if they see him on the streets. I am sure of it." Arla said. "Do you think it's possible for you to draw a few more?"

Uro beamed. "Of course!"

Uro went to work right away, hunched over his paper again, putting his finished drawing on the desk next to him.

Arla picked up the drawing. "Tomorrow we will post these up in the market with a reward for information. Someone is sure to have seen him."

It had not taken long for Uro to sketch another copy. Much faster the second time than the first, but he needed at least a day to get a handful of copies.

"You can have the study today and leave the drawings in the drawer. I have to attend more lessons for the rest of the day, but I will make sure to look at them tonight." Arla moved to leave.

"Arla, wait." Leo stepped closer to her so as not to have the other two overhear. "How long have you been sleepwalking?"

"This was the first time."

He paused as if trying to find the right thing to say. "That must be frightening."

It is. Arla wanted to say, but instead she said, "I'm okay."

Leo didn't buy her answer completely, but chose to let it slide. "If you were sleepwalking, how could you have walked out of the castle past city walls without anyone seeing you?"

He was right. It would have been nearly impossible for her to stay out of sight the entire time.

"It might be better if we protect you from a closer distance. Guarding just your doors may not be enough. We need a line of sight."

Rose scoffed. "Are you suggesting we guard her in her room? Watch her while she sleeps?"

Leo responded with utter seriousness. "Yes."

Arla blushed at the thought of Leo standing in her room again, just the two of them. The things they could do... She stopped herself, aghast at the direction of her own mind.

Oblivious to her scandalous thoughts, Leo waited patiently for her response, which made her feel even more guilty. To subject any form of Leo (even the mental image version of him) to situations he did not agree to seemed wrong. Even if images of his toned chest leading up to his sharp jaw and melt-worthy eyes were quite pleasing to think abou–she shook herself to scatter the image.

Stop that!

Lately, she had felt almost a stranger to herself. The sudden changes in her life were bringing about equally large changes to herself. Or was it more of an awakening?

"I don't think it's necessary..." She half-heartedly responded as she forced herself to look deeply at a small crack in the floor.

"There is no room for failure in this type of job. We cannot afford to be nonchalant with our duty. If we are going to protect you, then I intend to do it to the best of my ability and that means knowing where you are at all times and being ready for anything."

Anything?

Her mind began to form images again.

She shoved them down. "Alright, if you insist."

CHAPTER 9

I magine the most organized shelf on your bookcase, each section dedicated to its own purpose and products, neatly displayed in order of size so you could see everything clearly. That was what Ulsana's city market was like. A perfectly curated and extremely large array of tables and carts of all shapes and sizes in their designated rows and columns, each filled to the brim with vegetables, cured meats, collectibles, leather bags, jewelry, and much more. Think of any good, and it was most likely sold at a marked-up price here.

Arla drank in the splendor in front of her. If there was a place she loved most in Ulsana, it was here.

But today, the market was buzzing with more than just haggling and familial gossip. It was buzzing with curiosity over one thing. Indeed, almost every person locked their eyes on Arla and the guards that surrounded her.

Leo marched in front, separating the crowd like the bow of a ship through water. A few guards along with Rose walked beside her while Uro lingered behind. Moving with so many guards made it hard to stay inconspicuous, but Leo had refused to let her enter such crowds without complete protection.

It was the compromise they had come to, since she insisted on speaking directly to the people to ask what they might have seen on the night of her attack.

Linuth had dressed her in a high-neck dress to hide her bandaged neck, and long-sleeves were of course covering her bruises and scars as always. Heavy makeup covered the bruises and cuts on her face. No one could have guessed that Arla was attacked only a few days ago just by looking at her. Of course, no one had to look at her to know, news spread fast here in Ulsana.

She brushed her fingertips along a nearby cart of purple yams, picked one up in her hand and basked in the joy of its rich color and smell. Name any variety of produce, and most likely Ulsana's farmlands grew it. It was what made Ulsana so powerful. They did not rely on other kingdoms for resources and had enough to feed their large population.

Rose gripped her stack of drawings. "I will post these on each corner pole with the most traffic." She motioned for Uro to take her place before disappearing into the crowd.

Uro remained vigilant, scanning every face that walked by.

Women in elegant dresses showed off their new jewels to friends. Boisterous men in flashy-colored jackets chatted along with beers in their hands while chewing on baked goods. It was a world of plenty here. If one bought an item such as a flaky, buttery pastry and decided its flavor was not to their taste, they could simply throw it away and find another completely different pastry that might suit them. That was how abundant the Ulsanan market was.

The light spring breeze brought the smells of fresh strawberries and ripe peaches along with salted and sugared meats. Arla had an overwhelming urge to taste everything.

She noticed the sticky rice sticks immediately and the merchant second. His hair speckled with gray, his back curving the way people do at a certain age when the number of wrinkles on their skin outnumbered the remaining years of their life.

He looked like he had been here for ages. So he was a natural candidate to ask. Plus, she was dying to eat at least a dozen of the sticks. And it looked like, so did he.

A murky gray outlined the seller's pupils as he hungrily looked at the pile of sticky rice on his own wooden table. A tall man dressed in gold and black pointed at five of them, handing the old merchant a handful of coins, who took it with a bow and a wide smile. In exchange, the rice sticks were wrapped in leaves and handed over.

As soon as the noble walked away, the merchant's smile faded back into a tired, hungry expression.

Low-Borns grew the crops, picked them, prepared them, carted them to the market and sold them, but could not take from the supply themselves, because they did not own any of it. Instead, at the end of the day, this merchant would pack up the remaining goods, push his heavy cart down the hilly streets of the city and trek back to the farm he came from. He would be expected to return the leftovers in exchange for being allowed to continue to live on the High-Born's land.

But he still has enough wages to feed himself, right? Arla pondered to herself.

"Excuse me." She stepped into the merchant's view-line, followed closely by the other guards. "Have you seen this man before?" She dangled the drawing close enough so that his old eyes could see. The merchant squinted, taking in the drawing and then he shook his head. "I'm sorry, Your Highness, I have not."

She lowered the illustration, disappointed. "I see. Well, if you hear of anything, please let me know."

"I will, Your Highness."

She watched the merchant's eyes return to the food on his table.

"And can I get three of these?" Arla dropped the coins into the merchant's hands.

"Of course, Your Highness."

He handed her the rice sticks.

Instead of eating them, she kept them outstretched. "For you."

The merchant paused, wide-eyed. He waved his hands out in front of him in refusal. "Oh no, Your Highness. I cannot."

It was just a rote polite refusal, the type one does as a courtesy not to seem desperate.

Pushing the sticks closer to him, she repeated, "I insist."

"No. *Please*."

Something in his voice made her pause.

She looked around and noticed the nobles watching. That was when she wondered if the merchant took the sticks and ate them, what would happen to him? Would word get around to the High-Born that employed him? Would the merchant be punished for this?

His eyes were not wide with gratitude; they were wide with fear.

"Queen Arla!"

A few feet down the way, Lesandres and his rotund frame came marching toward her, his face red from excitement and physical exertion. "So good to see you here this fine afternoon!"

She groaned inwardly. The problem with public places was that you tended to run into people you did not wish to see.

"Lesandres," she begrudgingly addressed the nobleman. "Hello."

Her gaze flicked to Leo, whose sharp eyes targeted the High-Born like a wolf. She wasn't sure if it was because he was half covered in shadow, but Leo suddenly appeared... menacing.

Years ago, Lesandres had beaten Leo's father so badly, he passed away soon after. How horrible it must have been for Leo to see his father's killer roam free while Leo had to stand in obedient silence. Arla wondered if Jun would look at her the same way if he ever found out what she did to his father.

But isn't it better this way? Now Jun will never have to know what a terrible person his father really was.

Arla blinked, surprised at her own thoughts. *Better this way?*

"Queen Arla! Good day!" Lesandres straightened his jacket. "I am looking forward to developing a new repertoire with you as I did with your father. You are welcome on my land anytime. I can host another grand feast!"

There is no world in which I will ever dine with you again.

"As you know, I have done really well in yield this year." Lesandres continued. "So much so that I had to bring extra help today. Come. Come. Let me treat you to my finest fruits."

Lesandres pointed only a few feet to his stall and, just like he said, it was overflowing with produce.

Workers unpacked piles of vegetables and fruits in various stalls, most of them tanned and wrinkled from hours of work under the sun and... thin. Thinner than Arla had remembered them being the last time she was there. Or were they always this thin? It was the first time she had truly stopped long enough to pay attention to them.

An older woman lost grip on a heavy pallet box of peaches, sending them tumbling to the ground.

"Useless woman!" Lesandres shouted.

It was no wonder she dropped the box; those skeletal arms could not lift any heavy object. Leo stepped forward and lifted the frail woman from the ground. When she stabilized herself, he still did not let go of her.

Leo ashened in horror. "Why are you so thin?" Leo stopped as he noticed bruises on the woman's temples near her hairline.

Lesandres pointed a pudgy finger at the woman. "I warned you that if you dropped it again, I would–"

Leo shoved Lesandres back so hard, the nobleman tripped over himself and fell straight on his back.

"What did you do to her?!" Leo stalked toward Lesandres, death in his eyes.

Onlookers stopped what they were doing and stared at the commotion.

"What business is that of yours, soldier?" Lesandres spat, still on the ground.

Leo pressed the heel of his heavy boot on Lesandres hand, eliciting cries of pain from the nobleman.

"Leo!" Arla didn't know what sparked such a rage. The last time she saw such fire in his eyes, it was when he attacked Mathus. Arla looked at the old woman, whose eyes were wide in shock.

Arla paused.

She knew those eyes.

She looked at this woman with more attention.

The same eyes. The same wavy brown hair.

And then it dawned on her.

This was Leo's mother.

Leo stood over Lesandres, who was shaking now. "*Ena–*"

Leo slammed his palm over Lesandres' mouth, hard enough to force Lesandres to choke on his own tongue. The nobleman gagged as he desperately tried to pry Leo's hand off his face.

"I should have killed you a long time ago." Leo snarled.

Leo slammed his fist into Lesandres' face, sending a sickening crack of knuckle to mouth. Blood sprayed across the rust-brick road. Lesandres screamed as he watched two of his teeth roll across the uneven ground.

"You bastard!" he screamed wildly. His fists clumsily swung at Leo's sides, which Leo didn't even bother to block as they landed on his shoulders and arms.

Leo's next blow was harder.

Lesandres stopped speaking, only wailing incomprehensible words as he reflexively moved his hands to cover his face.

Leo brought his fist down again and again and again. He was going to keep smashing Lesandres' face until there was nothing left.

"Stop!" Arla grabbed Leo's raised fist in mid-air, pulling back enough to stop the momentum. "Don't do this," she whispered, trying to make eye contact, but his focus was entirely on Lesandres, who was crying now.

Leo's chest heaved, sucking air in and out in heaving motions. He was like a bull in the middle of trampling his enemy. Could he even hear her?

"This is not you." She tried to remind him.

Leo tightened his fist, his knuckles turning white.

Arla put her other hand on his cheek and forced him to look at her. "Leo."

She locked her gaze to his, using herself to anchor him back to this world.

And for a moment, she was afraid it wasn't enough.

And then, he lowered his fist and placed his hand over hers.

Arla inwardly sighed in relief. He was back. The rage within him simmered down, replaced by exhaustion and a deep sorrow.

It was only then she realized how many people in the market were looking at them. They both dropped their hands and stood up, far apart from each other.

Leo's mother stood shivering with a group of other malnourished workers. Her eyes were wet from weeping. Leo looked at his mother apologetically before turning his attention back to Lesandres, who was helped up by a few passing High-Borns.

"This man needs to be detained!" Lesandres screamed, pointing a finger at Leo. "He attacked me without cause! Or warning!"

Leo curled his fist again, his knuckles dripping with Lesandres' blood.

"My captain did only his duty," Arla said. "He thought you were a threat and so protected me."

Lesandres puffed bright red as more blood streamed down his nose. "How could that possibly make any sense?!" He winced. The yelling was stretching out his wounds. And then, a look of recognition crossed Lesandres' face. "I know you," he said as he looked at Leo with a keener eye. "You are the captain who was pardoned." He looked at Arla. "He is violent and treacherous, and you defend him?!"

"You should see to your wounds, Lesandres," Arla advised. "Before they scar. I will send you our best physician."

"What kind of queen lets her own people get attacked and abused?" Lesandres spat out, spraying more blood on the ground. The High-Borns in the crowd nodded in agreement.

Arla looked at Leo's mother, who continued to shake in fear. *What kind of queen indeed?*

Standing tall as a queen should, Arla walked over to Leo's mother. She hoped she seemed as unattached and judgmental as a High-Born would in front of a Low-Born. "This servant will be coming with me."

Leo looked at her in surprise, but she pretended not to see. Leo's mother looked from Arla to Lesandres to Leo before looking back to Arla. *What are you doing?* she seemed to say.

"But she is my servant!" Lesandres shouted.

"You will be compensated generously."

Lesandres gaped, the blood from his nose slowing. To have his worker taken from him like this in front of all these onlookers stripped him of his pride. She knew this. But she would not leave Leo's mother with Lesandres any longer.

Arla gently touched Leo's mother's elbow and pulled her away from the others, who looked at Arla with begging eyes. They were equally thin. Equally desperate to leave. Arla's heart constricted. Maybe she could take them all with her...

High-Borns in the crowd glared at her with contention. If she took all of them, the High-Borns would think she was a threat, out to steal all their workers from them. All their sources of wealth. No, she could only take one.

She looked down in shame as she continued to pull only Leo's mother toward the circle of guards. Despite herself, she looked up one more time and met the eyes of someone she didn't know. A Low-Born, only slightly younger than her with fiery red hair. Her expression was different. It wasn't dread or even hope or gratitude at what Arla did for Leo's mother, instead it was raw, unfiltered hatred.

She looked away, unable to face such a powerful expression. The guards tightened the surrounding circle.

Suddenly, the market was not an abundant dream of joyful choices, instead, it had become a painting, whose lifting, dry edges revealed the darkness underneath.

It was strange how one's perspective could change so drastically in a moment. The mind saw what it wanted to see, and when it realized something different, the entire world felt... off.

Maybe it could be rebalanced, she hoped. Maybe she could change it. As her feet hit the open street, she did not know that this would be the last time she ever visited this market again.

CHAPTER 10

Arla always wanted to know what her own mother was like. Was she kind? Was she funny? Was she awkward? But those questions were never answered. No one spoke of her mother her entire life. She often wondered if it was because her mother was not memorable, but as she got older, she started to get a hunch it was because her father did not want to hear of her mother, so others had grown used to not speaking of her.

Regardless, if Arla had known her mother, she hoped she was a little like Leo's. Kind, warm, and open. Her name was Yolan Treterra and she had the same dark brown hair and sharp features as Leo, but that was where the similarities ended. Where Leo was centered and focused, Yolan was fidgety and reactive. She could neither sit still nor relax in the guest room that Arla had given her in the castle. She refused to bathe or eat, instead, she insisted on dusting the furniture and aligning them 'just right'. Whatever that meant.

Arla scrambled to help her, but Yolan avoided her. If Arla moved close, Yolan moved on to dusting the next thing away from her.

"Mom..." Leo reached out, but Yolan slipped by him too.

"I can do it," she insisted.

Leo retreated to Arla's side, giving up.

"She cleans when she is nervous," he explained. "She doesn't think it's right to stay as a guest in the Queen's castle."

"She thinks she should be a servant instead?" Arla watched Yolan rub away a streak on the mirror with fervor.

"Mom," Leo tried again. "Just get some rest. Arl–Her Majesty will get you some work to do so you don't drive yourself crazy, and I'll be here too."

It was sweet watching Leo with his mother. He purposefully hunched a little, making himself shorter so Yolan could look at him in the eye without straining her neck too much. His voice was low and gentle. He scrambled a little nervously too, even though he probably thought he didn't, as he continued to try to convince his mother to settle down. He readjusted the position of a nearby cup on a wooden table at least four times. As if there was a perfect position he could put it that would make his mother more comfortable and he just hadn't found it yet.

His mother's restlessness made him restless too.

Another hour went by before Yolan had finally exhausted herself enough to sit on the edge of the bed. And then after a few more minutes of struggle, Yolan finally gave in and let Leo tuck her into the bed, where she fell into a deep sleep, even though the afternoon had just begun.

They snuck quietly out of the room to give Yolan time to rest. The moment the door closed, Leo loosed a breath. The strain had finally gotten to him. She could see it in the dark circles that were forming under his eyes.

"Thank you for helping her."

"Of course," Arla replied. "She is your mother."

He paused. "And thank you for... stopping me. I wasn't myself."

"I know." Arla smiled sweetly to reassure him that everything was alright. He did not need to thank her or apologize, or feel guilty, if that was what he was feeling.

His expression darkened. "Sometimes I can't control myself when the people I care about get hurt... It's like I become someone else. I'm sorry if I scared you in any way."

Arla poked him playfully in his perfectly tight bicep. "You don't scare me. In fact, you're the only person I feel safe with. That's why I would do anything for you."

He looked at her with surprise.

Oops. Maybe I shouldn't have said that. How do I take it back though? It's too late.

A blush spread across her cheeks, and she hoped it wasn't too noticeable. Who was she kidding? She was a pale thing; the slightest embarrassment turned her into a tomato.

His surprise slowly faded until another emotion took over him entirely. "I…"

His hands closed into fists. He seemed to be battling himself before finally deciding to say nothing. His neck turned as if forced by an unknown entity so that he faced down the hall. "Should we walk together for a little while?"

Arla nodded, the blush fading from her face. "Let's."

For a while, they walked aimlessly with no destination, just enjoying each other's presence. It was peaceful. Arla wished they could do this for hours, because she was not ready to take on the rest of the day.

But the day came for them anyway.

"Arla!" From down the hall, Uro came frantically running. He skidded to a stop just in front of them, catching his breath. "I just heard. How is Yolan?"

"She will be fine. She's settling into one of the guest rooms now." Leo said.

"Good. Good." Uro flicked his eyes from Leo to Arla. "Um. I was hoping to have a moment alone with Arla, I mean–*Queen* Arla…"

Leo hesitated for a moment, but then granted his wish. "I will be just down the hall." He walked further down the hall and entered an empty room just to the side, far enough away that he could not hear them, but close enough to reach them if something happened.

Uro swiveled to Arla. "Leo is seeing someone, a young woman with red-hair."

"What?!" Arla unconsciously gripped her jet-black hair.

Uro leaned sideways to look down the hall. Leo did not reappear. Satisfied, Uro shook his head. "No. No. He isn't. I just wanted to make sure he couldn't hear us if we spoke at this volume."

Arla's heart took some time to regain its normal beat.

Wait. Why would Uro choose this thing to say to lure Leo out? Could that mean–

"I heard what happened with Yolan. Taking a Low-Born from a noble like that. It was really bold."

"Thank you." Arla was glad that Uro appreciated her efforts, unlike that red-haired Low-Born at the market today. She looked at her with such hatred that it still unnerved Arla now.

To be honest, she thought *that* was the red-head Uro was talking about earlier. That would have explained why that woman did not like her.

"It gave me hope."

"Hope?"

"I thought if you were willing to do that, then you must really care about us. You're making changes."

"I hope that I am. Slowly and surely..."

"So then I thought, if you could do that, then maybe you would be willing to help me."

"Of course I am. Anything."

"Arla..." Uro bit his lip in nervousness. "Will you... will you let me leave the army?"

Arla reeled back in shock. "L-leave the army?"

"I don't want to be a soldier anymore. I don't want to spend my entire life fighting. There has to be something else out there that is better, right? I'm really good at drawing. You saw it yourself. I was thinking I could apprentice somewhere. Maybe draw maps or other things like that. Think about it. Wouldn't it be wonderful if I could do that instead of swinging around a sword? I can use these hands to create instead of kill. Earn a living from something I'm proud of."

With a shaky breath, Arla replied, "Uro. You know that no Low-Born soldier is allowed to leave the army once they join. It's a life commitment. Anyone caught trying to leave is labeled a deserter and executed. It's been common law since the creation of Ulsana."

Even back when she was an isolated and naïve princess, she knew the rules. She could never forget the day she saw the old soldier beg for help as the lever pulled and the noose around his neck tightened. She remembered the horrible kicking his feet did before they fell limp, slowly turning in half-circles as the body swayed with the wind.

Uro's face dropped. "But Leo was labeled a traitor, and you were able to stop *that* execution. That's so much bigger than letting one soldier leave the army."

And it had cost her. She had lost the support of the High-Borns enough to have one of them hire an assassin. She wished Uro had asked for something else, anything, but this. Norendra was right. She was already losing the support of the nobles, any more antics and she could really lose her crown, her friends, her control. There would be no one to protect them.

"If I let you leave, then others might want to leave too. How can I justify you leaving but not allow the others? I can't afford to do it. Not right now. Not when the army is already dwindling and the throne is shaky."

Uro's mouth opened in disbelief. "Is that what you care about? Keeping your crown?"

"Uro, it's bigger than just me."

"Please," Uro begged. "I can't do this anymore. I'm not a soldier. I was never good at fighting. I hate waking up every morning, knowing that this is my life. That I have to train to be only mediocre at something. That I have to hurt people for a living."

Arla hated seeing Uro so desperate. Maybe there was something else she could give him. "When we replenish our funds I am going to give a higher wage and better living conditions for each soldier in the army and every new one that joins."

"It doesn't matter what new things you give. As long as I am trapped in this life it will always be torturous for me." Uro grabbed Arla's hands in his. "Please. Arla..."

Arla wanted to cry watching Uro beg for his freedom. "I... can't."

Uro shook his head, refusing to believe. "Yes, you can. You are Queen. You can do anything."

"I wish that were true, but it isn't."

The young boy let go of her hands.

"Please, Uro, you have to understand..."

"Why am I the one who has to understand?!" Uro shouted. "You High-Borns have everything. Land. Money. Power. Freedom. Why do Low-Borns always have to be the ones that bend?"

Arla pulled back as if she had been bitten. Never had Uro raised his voice at her like that.

She knew Uro was hurting. He was living a life he didn't want, but so were the rest of them, including herself. How could Uro think that Arla could just wave her hands and give him everything he wanted, when she couldn't even get what she wanted, or rather, *who* she wanted. They were all trapped in the world they were born in. And yet she knew what it sounded like to him. A High-Born with magic and power, refusing to help him, when she had called him a friend. Would she have felt the same way if their positions were reversed?

She didn't know, because that was not the reality they lived in. She was Queen, and she had to remain Queen or someone else would take her throne and threaten everyone she cared about.

"I'm sorry."

It was the only thing she could say.

Uro stepped away from her. "I thought you were different."

He turned on his heels and stormed down the hall.

CHAPTER 11

"Are you going to be sitting there the entire time?"

Arla stood rigid beside her bed, dressed in a formal day gown with its usual long sleeves and exposed collar. It was completely the wrong attire for one who was about to go to bed, but there was absolutely no way she was going to wear anything close to a nightgown tonight, not when Leo was planning to watch her sleep.

Leo pulled the red cushioned chair from under her vanity table to the corner of the room. Putting the chair against the wall, he faced it parallel to the bed so that he wouldn't be staring directly at her while she slept. Instead, he would be about six or seven feet beside her, looking at the entrance door.

"This is a good spot. I'll have vision on both the window and the door."

"Mmhm." She remained standing where she was, pulling at her sleeves.

She wasn't this nervous the first time they were alone in this bedroom only a few days ago, but that was because she was so worried he would be caught that she didn't think about it. But now...

Everyone knew Leo was in this bedchamber to protect her and Rose was stationed outside the room, guarding the halls. When Norendra heard about it, she threw a fit, saying it was improper to have a man alone with Arla at night, but when Arla asked if Norendra herself would then volunteer to guard her instead, she scoffed, saying such tasks were for Low-Born soldiers.

"Are you going to bed?" Unlike Arla, Leo showed no signs of being uncomfortable or nervous at all.

"I... um..." She gave a great sigh, no longer able to keep the tension in her shoulders. "This is too awkward, Leo."

Leo scratched the back of his head. "If you want Rose to come in instead–"

"No." She hopped into bed, heaving her large dress with her. She didn't fully trust that Rose wouldn't attack her in her sleep. She still had not spoken much to the soldier yet.

With a grunt, she pulled the covers over herself, which billowed like a mountain over her puffy dress, which made her look like a puffball.

Great. She could never look elegant in front of Leo, could she?

"I won't look at you or anything like that," Leo said, his eyes focused on the door and window. "So don't worry about being stared at while sleeping." His lips curved into a small smile. He was teasing her!

"I'm not worried you're going to stare," she lied. "Why? Do you want to?" She squeezed her eyes shut in regret. She wasn't supposed to say that last part out loud.

His eyes remained staring ahead, giving her a profile of his square jaw that tightened slightly at her question.

She changed the subject as fast as she could. "Have you spoken to Uro lately?"

Her last conversation with Uro had been weighing heavily on her. To have both Rose and Uro dislike her now was disheartening, to say the least. She had wanted them to be her guards to be closer to her, to protect them, but the closer they got, the more distance grew between them.

Leo shook his head. "No. I haven't seen him all day. He was supposed to train this morning, but he didn't show up. Something he's been doing more often now."

"I'm worried about him."

"Me too. He's been different lately. He's never been enthusiastic about training, but this level of disinterest is... concerning. The other day I caught him — never mind. He keeps saying he doesn't want to train. As if he has a choice."

"Uro asked me to pardon him from the army."

"He — what?" Leo swiveled in his chair, his eyes wide in surprise.

"I told him I couldn't and it's been weighing on me. I wanted to say yes, but–"

"You don't have to explain yourself. I imagine it was a hard choice." A heavy sigh escaped Leo's lips. "Uro is a dreamer. I wish he would just realize that there are some things you cannot change. The sooner he understands that, the better. We're Low-Born. We don't get to have dreams. He needs to grow up and understand that we can't have what we want." Leo laced his fingers together and pressed them into each other. His eyes fell to the floor in a moment of softness. "No matter how much we desire it."

Arla paused.

"Is there something you desire?"

He turned away from her and looked distantly out the window without giving her an answer.

Arla took in the moment: Leo bent slightly, his chest caving a bit, no longer straight-backed as before. His eyebrows knitted into a frown, shaded by a few renegade waves of hair that refused to be tamed.

To Arla, Leo was like a solid pillar, a structure meant to hold weight, and usually he did so with the resilience of a mountain, but today it seemed that weight was bending him in places she couldn't see.

"We may not get everything we want in the end," she said. "But we can still cherish what we have. I know I do. I guess that's all we can do."

Leo turned to meet her gaze with a forlorn expression. "Yes. That's all we can do."

A moment of quiet passed between them.

"Are you ever going to fall asleep?" he asked.

Arla looked up at the ceiling, getting hot from the dress and blanket. "I don't think so."

He gave her a small smile. "So should we just sit here in silence until you fall asleep? The boredom will eventually tire you."

"I don't think I could ever be bored with you. Even in silence."

Arla dropped her head between her knees. What did she just say?! What was wrong with her?! She couldn't keep her heart from using her tongue. Whispers! She was hopeless.

She didn't even bother to take the words back. Instead, she buried herself under the covers, unable to get herself to look at him. "Goodnight!"

CHAPTER 12

Sharpened tips of ashen black branches crept along the edges of the room. They extended and expanded until gray ash and obsidian trees covered the entire place.

All dead.

They were all dead.

Except one.

A figure outlined in shadow.

The Woman?

But the figure did not have the same feminine silhouette. Their back was to her, but she could see from the shivers of their shoulders that this figure was crying.

Don't be sad. She wanted to say. *Too many of us are sad already.*

But the figure did not hear her.

"Arla."

Sudden light and sound burst open as she woke from the dream. Her bare feet stood on the stone pavement under the night sky. She was suddenly facing Leo.

She uttered his name in disbelief as he held her by the shoulders, anchoring her to reality.

She had woken up earlier this time, not quite outside the city yet. Instead, they were in a small plaza of shops long closed for the night at the edge of the city walls just by the main gates.

"How did I get past you?" she asked breathlessly. Whatever momentum took her here had her body feeling wrecked in exhaustion.

"You didn't." Leo said softly. "You were sleeping and then suddenly you were gone. I wouldn't have even noticed if the snoring hadn't stopped."

"Sn-snoring?"

I snore? There was never anyone else in her bedchamber to tell her that. She flushed red in embarrassment. Of course Leo would be the first to discover this. "How bad was it?"

"You were gone only for a little while before I found you here."

"No. I mean. How bad was the snoring?"

Leo arched an eyebrow in confusion and then a speckle of amusement crossed his sharp features. "I think I suffered some hearing loss in my left ear."

Arla lightly pushed Leo away.

Leo chuckled. "It was like a song."

Heat rushed to her cheeks as she swatted at him some more. "Well, you're very lucky you got a front-row seat."

"I *am* lucky." He said it so genuinely, Arla couldn't help but hope he meant something else by that comment. Unable to hold his warm gaze, she swiveled her head in the direction she was going, out the city gates. What was pulling her here?

"I don't know why this is happening."

"We'll figure it out." Leo tried to reassure her.

A loud, high-pitched scream pierced through the stone walls from down the street.

They gave each other a quick look before they ran towards the sound.

A huddle of people was already there, circled around something in a dark alleyway. A middle-aged woman held her hand to her chest, breathing deeply. No doubt, she was the one who screamed.

Arla maneuvered through the group and to the center. The smell of sulfur and sweat assaulted her nostrils.

And then she saw it.

She covered her horrified gasp.

A dead man lay sprawled on the ground.

His face was a skeletal outline with thinned skin. His pale expression permanently frozen in horror.

She knew that face anywhere.

Lesandres.

His body was shriveled like dried leather, unnaturally gray and devoid of any liquid, no water, no blood. And his eyes... Arla had never seen eyes that had lost all its water. They looked like translucent raisins shrunken into the eye socket.

Why is his body like that?

No blade cut him. No object crushed him to death.

A grown man threw up beside her.

Arla did not look away. The scene should have unnerved her, but it didn't.

She had seen death in The Forest. She saw soldiers skewered by branches and disintegrate from the inside out. She had seen violence in so many different ways that it was becoming an acquaintance rather than a surprise visitor.

Leo stared down at Lesandres. There was something strange in his expression. It was so eerily cold and distant, not like the chuckling Leo she was speaking to just moments before. Instead, he was the emotionless soldier again, lost somewhere in his past.

"Leo!" Uro ran down the street toward them. "I heard the commotion. What is–" Uro froze seeing the body.

Arla suddenly felt awkward seeing Uro again.

"We just found him," she said to Uro, softly, like she was testing how cold the waters were between them.

Uro gave her a distant look, like he'd just noticed she was there, before turning to Leo. "We should–"

A high-pitched shriek rattled her skull, sending knives of pain behind her eyeballs.

Arla clutched her head, squeezing her eyes shut in agony.

"He is coming!"

The air bent and squeezed so tightly she thought it would crack every bone in her body.

Everything sucked into the alleyway and then back out, blowing her away into a nearby bush across the street. The broken edges of thorny branches dug into her rib cage and stole the breath from her lungs. Groaning, she rolled onto her stomach.

People screamed as they too were tossed into the air.

Staggered coughs came from her right. *Uro.* He was lying on his side, surprised, but not injured. Leo was nowhere to be seen.

The side of a nearby shop exploded away, leaving a gaping hole between the stones, and standing in that newly made chasm were three figures, cloaked in dark hoods.

"Stop him!"

A rush of adrenaline and something else, something deeper, surged through her body and out through her limbs, grabbing for control. The Woman seeped under Arla's skin, down her muscles and into her bones, forcing Arla's hands to press against the ground in an attempt to lift her up.

Arla railed against The Woman, kicking out with all the force her will could muster. Her vision blurred and pulled back, unable to focus on what was in front of her. In her struggle, she barely saw one of the figures move toward her.

A hand reached for her. To grab her. To harm her.

Uro pulled the hooded figure away from Arla. A knuckled fist bashed into the young boy's face with a resounding crack.

"Uro!" Arla shouted.

She shook her head, trying to clear her vision, but The Woman was fierce and kept her down, wrestling her body from her.

Uro's blurry body flipped and hit the floor so hard his head knocked back into the stone and bounced off it.

Gritting her teeth, Arla fought to regain control. She needed to help him. She needed to–.

Another blur. Someone sprinting. A crash.

A flash of beige cloth and tan skin streaked across the garden, and a sword slashed at the figure on top of Uro, immediately toppling the hooded enemy to the ground. Eyes as fierce as lions pivoted to her.

Leo.

He reached out for her but was immediately pulled off his feet and into the opposite wall by a force Arla could not see.

She heard a wrestling of bodies and metal and shouting. Everything was a blur, coming and retreating in fading light. And then she heard the thud of a body land harshly in front of her.

Leo's forearm pressed into one of the hooded figures, pinning the enemy against the wall. He pulled the hood off, revealing the man who had tried to kill her before.

Another hooded figure reached out his arm toward the man in a panic. "Rhyler!"

In one fast and sudden motion, the one called Rhyler struck Leo in the neck, stunning the captain long enough to pry himself away. And in that flash, Arla noticed a missing ring finger on the assassin's left hand.

The assassin lunged for Arla. Uro stepped between them and clashed with the man named Rhyler.

Her Whispers geysered up, ready to spill out of her mouth, and in that surge was The Woman, ready to take over. Arla bit her tongue to stop her.

Rhyler flung Uro off of him, but another body of armor blocked him. Braided black hair spun before settling across determined shoulders. *Rose!* Arla couldn't believe it. She had made it here.

Another blast opened up another wall, leading away from the street. Hearing the noise, more people rushed out of the buildings while others ran in. Rhyler took one look at the gaping hole and dashed through it.

"Stop!" Uro shouted.

"Uro! No!" Arla shouted.

But it was too late; Uro ran through the blasted wall after the assassin.

Stumbling, Arla sped after him. Two figures ran into the night ahead of her. She quickened her run, trying to catch up with them.

She saw the flash of the blade too late. The cold metal ran through her. And her eyes met a hateful glare. There was a hot burning sensation and then instant cold. She grasped her side, feeling warm liquid drip down between her fingers.

She opened her mouth, but no sound came out.

Someone was shouting. No. Screaming. Leo. Leo was screaming her name.

Metal cut flesh.

Another hooded figure crumpled to the ground.

She pulled her hand away from her side.

It was a mistake to look.

With every intake of breath, her ribs expanded, pushing more blood out of the hole in her side.

The blade wasn't there anymore. Where did it go?

Her heart pounded like a desperate thing in denial of what was happening.

Was she dying?

Cloth was ripped and then pulled tightly around her ribs.

She was lifted off her feet.

His sharp eyes were blazing now, full of terror.

"I'm okay," she tried to convince him. "I'm okay."

She repeated it over and over, each time her voice getting fainter, but he did not hear her. It didn't seem he heard anything at all. He just kept running.

CHAPTER 13

Leo kicked open the door, startling an old man who came rushing out of his bedroom in loose silken nightwear. What little hair he had left was ruffled in all different directions.

"What in the Whispers is–!"

The man silenced instantly, seeing Arla bleeding in Leo's arms.

Ceramic shattered on the ground. A table was cleared.

She was placed gently on the hard surface.

Leo was shouting as someone poured cold, bitter liquid into her mouth, making her choke.

And then the old man's calloused hands wrapped around hers. "This is going to hurt. *Hem-mem*."

The sting of something wet and harsh on the exposed insides of her wound flared. She screamed, whipping her arms out, but Leo held her down by the wrists.

Tears blotted her vision as she cried out for it to stop.

"It should take effect any moment now."

Whoever said that was lying.

"It'll only stop the internal bleeding. I still need to sew it shut," the man said.

She twisted herself to get away from the needle, but Leo's weight had her pinned.

And so she cried. Like a child she thought she had outgrown, unable to escape this pain, until, slowly, dizzying spots of light blinked into her world, making her feel like she was no longer there. Her body grew numb, and her eyelids heavy. Oh, so heavy.

And then there was nothing.

CHAPTER 14

She didn't know how long she had been asleep, but when she woke, it was quiet. The room she found herself in was simple, with a bed and a closet to the right and one window that was blocked by a thick curtain, making it hard to tell if it was morning or night.

Leo was leaning back on the only chair in the room that lay flush against the wall opposite her. His arms were crossed, and his eyes were closed with a deep frown wrinkling the space between his brows.

"I think sleeping like that is bad for your back."

His eyes snapped open. "Arla." He immediately rushed to her side. "How are you feeling?"

Sore. Itchy. Sensitive. Her side was only a little less painful than before. Whenever 'before' was.

"Fine."

His sidelong look told her he didn't believe her.

"Where are we?" she asked.

"We're at a physician's home in the city. It was the closest place I could take you to get you healed. He's out getting more supplies. I told him not to tell anyone we were here. I'd rather not make it easy for that assassin to find you."

"How long was I asleep?" she asked, still a little groggy.

"Two days."

"Two?!" She bolted upright, sending a sharp pain through her abdomen that elicited a loud gasp.

Leo sucked in a breath as if he was sharing that pain. He guided her back down to sit on the bed and propped up the pillow behind her so she could lean back.

The pain of the movement shoved her mind into place, finally remembering what had happened.

She grasped Leo's arm. "Where is Uro?"

Leo gave her a sad look. "Uro was taken."

Taken. Uro was taken. She had to repeat it to herself to believe it. And only when she did, did the dread come.

"They disappeared without leaving any clue behind them." Leo explained. "No footprints. Nothing."

Uro was taken. A horrible truth, but... he wasn't dead, right? Or else they would have found a body.

Leo shook his head. "I don't understand why they took him. It makes no sense."

"His accomplice called him Rhyler." A slip that angered Rhyler for sure.

Leo's eyebrows wrinkled again in thought. "So we have a name at least. That is something."

This was all her fault.

Uro would not have been taken if she had been able to use her magic. She should have done better. Norendra was right, she needed power. And the first part of that was to regain control of her body.

Tossing the blanket off of her, she scooted to the edge of the bed, every inch agony against her side. Clenching her teeth, she swung her legs off the edge.

"What are you doing?"

Arla held the bedpost for support to stand. "We need to go. We can't waste any more time here. We need to find Uro."

"You can't go anywhere. Not until the physician is done healing you."

"I'm fine."

"You're not fine!"

Arla dropped back down onto the bed, shocked.

Leo threw his palms to his forehead, pressing roughly against his skin. He took a deep breath to calm himself down. "I'm sorry I shouted. It's just... stop telling me you're fine when you're not. You keep rushing into things without thinking of your own safety. That's how you end up like this. You could have died."

He kneeled in front of her and grabbed her shoulders. Too gentle to be violent. Too firm to be loving. "You can't just keep throwing yourself into danger and leave me to watch. It's not fair." He looked at her with such a soft pleading, it made Arla's breath catch. "I–I can't keep watching you do that. Please stop making me watch you do that."

She didn't understand why he was pleading with her. Watching her do wha–and then it hit her.

In The Forest, Leo had watched her run into the deadly fog alone. He had watched the bricks divide them in the tunnels. Each time, believing it was the last time he would see her alive. All those times she had only wanted to save him from death, but she had never considered what it did to him.

How helpless he must have felt.

"I should be the one saying that to you." Arla bit back the stinging tears that threatened to fall. "I've had to watch you too."

I've had to watch you slowly die from poison. I've had to watch you burn. I've had to watch you scream and bleed out so much I didn't know if you had any more blood left in your body.

"I know," he whispered. "I..."

His words trailed away as he stared at her. Through her. Into her. Like he was looking for something. It was so intense, the rest of the world blurred away. He looked almost defeated, like he was buckling under an invisible pressure. And then something crossed his face. A decision. Or a complete collapse.

His eyes traveled down to her lips as he leaned forward at a slight tilt. Closer and closer. And with every inch that was removed between them, a tension tightened.

She didn't dare move.

Was Leo actually…

A part of her wanted to pull at the string between them, draw him closer to her, but the other part of her…

"I am a Queen…" Arla uttered, her throat dry. "And you are a soldier."

It was his words spoken back to him when he was in a healing bed and she was the one leaning. It had stopped her cold then, but for some reason, it was not stopping Leo now.

"I know," he said in a shaking breath. "But this soldier…can't keep away from you."

His hands glided from her shoulders, up her neck until his thumbs hooked in front of her ears and his fingers were in her hair.

Her heart raced against her chest like a thundering horse.

"I don't want to fight it anymore," he said, his eyes clouded in yearning. "I don't want to stay away. I want to be by your side for however long you allow me to be, even if that means living in the shadows."

She swore she was floating, with only his hands to anchor her to this world.

"Me too." Arla replied ever so softly.

It was the only answer he needed.

He leaned forward, she didn't know if it was fast or slow. Time was different now, entirely too long and far too short.

His soft lips met hers, gentle and absolute, and all her doubts scattered to the winds. She wrapped her arms around his neck, and he pressed himself closer to her. It was all encompassing. Intoxicating. The taste of his mouth.

The feel of his hands leaving her face and wrapping themselves around her waist.

She knew what he was doing. He was trying to anchor her, to keep her from moving too much, in case the wound opened up again. But there was no pain, only desire and joy.

Back then, their first kisses were fervent, unintentional, born from moments of heightened emotions. But *these* kisses... these kisses were different. They were focused and soft and full and slow. Ever so slow. There was no space between their lips that self-doubt or confusion could live.

And with these kisses, they sealed their fate.

CHAPTER 15

Arla stared out the window overlooking the street. It was a quiet and affluent neighborhood, judging by the excellent care given to the hedges along the edges of the homes. The physician must have been employed by the crown. No other person in medicine could afford a home like this one.

"Just rest." Leo had said just before he left. After their time together, Arla had fallen asleep, only to be woken up with Leo pulling his arm from under her head. "I need to find witnesses, maybe someone saw something about Uro that we didn't."

Being alone in the house gave Arla little distraction from the ballooning guilt within her.

You could have stopped Uro from running away. You could have summoned your beasts to block the path, shielding him from harm, but you didn't, because you have no control over yourself. You are afraid of your own magic. You are a coward.

Arla fisted the blanket covering her legs until her knuckles whitened.

No more. She would not let *her* win.

"Where are you?" Arla hissed into the empty air. "Show yourself!" Her side stung from the shout, but she didn't care. She searched for The Woman within herself. "You want me?! Come get me then! Come out!"

A shudder of wind brushed past her shoulder. Arla turned, looking wildly left to right. "Where are you?!"

No response.

And then she remembered once more, the dream of The Darkening. And a name. One she never heard, but it felt oh so familiar. And now she knew why.

"I know who you are."

The wind picked up around her, whipping her hair into her face in all directions. Like The Woman was challenging her. Well, Arla was not going to back down now. Half-blinded by a tangle of thick black strands, Arla shouted louder. "Stop it, *Wynera*!"

The wind froze.

Floating particles of dust floated in front of her, frozen in time.

And then the gust threw itself into her, sending Arla backward against the headboard.

"You know my name." A ghostly voice echoed in Arla's head.

"I know more than just your name," Arla replied, her back throbbing. "I know your memories."

Arla could feel Wynera moving through her mind.

"Where is Leo?" Wynera asked.

Arla stilled. "Why are you asking about him? And how do you know who he is?"

"I see what you see. I feel what you feel."

Arla suddenly felt exposed. "Can you hear what I'm thinking too?"

A lingering pause and then a reply. *"Even I have my limits. There are times when the connection is strong and other times when it is not, but when I can, I can experience the world through your eyes and your ears."*

"And my body." Arla clenched her teeth. "You took my body from me. You forced me to–to–" She stuttered, trying to breathe in the last words. "You forced me to kill my own father."

The wind skirted across Arla's back. *"But do you mourn him? Not once since his passing have I seen you light a candle to his name. Tell the truth, Arla, are you truly devastated that he is gone? Is anyone?"*

Arla thought of how a normal daughter would grieve for her dead father. The daughter would collapse in grief over her father's corpse. Her guttural cries would be the type of sound born from something that had lost part of its soul, but her tears that night were not really for him, were they?

There was an uncomfortable truth she didn't want to speak out loud.

"It is better that he is dead. Men like him only bring pain and terror to the world." Wynera curled around Arla, like a blanket made of thorns.

Arla wasn't sure if Wynera meant to comfort or hurt her.

"How is killing my father any different from Namkil killing your lover?" Arla challenged.

A sourly thorn slid across her chest. *"I did not kill your father out of spite. I did it to save Ulsana from another ruthless king."*

"Murder is still a murder."

"Then what do you think Leo does? You think he hasn't taken a life? Or Rose or Uro? You think they haven't spilled blood? The world is not so black and white, Queen Regent. You should know this by now."

Arla could not argue with Wynera on this. An uncomfortable truth was a truth nonetheless.

"We are running out of time. We must stop him."

Wynera's voice was getting more distant. Already Arla could feel the wind and shadow weakening around her. She didn't have much time left to make her point.

"How did you know he was going to try to kill me? How long have you known about him?"

"A long time. I gave you magic because of him."

So it was true then. The theory Arla had all along. Wynera has given her the Whispers she heard now. It was never an awakening, but a gift... or a curse. All for the purpose of stopping Rhyler?

Arla realized Rhyler was more than an assassin then. One so bad Wynera felt she had to interfere. What was going on?

"Why did you give *me* magic? If you need to stop this Rhyler so badly, why can't *you* do it?" Wynera did not answer. "You can't, can you? You need *me* to stop him, because you cannot summon magic yourself."

Wynera seemed to retract in anger, like a hissing cat. She was a spirit with no body. She could not interact with the world like Arla could.

She lit up. There was an opportunity here. "So, you rely on me then."

"You need my help."

She puffed herself up with determination. "If you try to take over again, I will take this body away from you. I will run headfirst into a wall, and there will be nothing left of me, and you will have no one else to control. Do you understand?"

Another chill came over her, but it traveled further down her spine.

"You cannot–"

Arla hauled herself to her feet. She knew she had told Leo she would be more careful, but...

Ignoring the pain in her side, she sprinted as fast as she could toward the stone wall.

"Stop."

Already Wynera's influence was spreading across her calves, trying to slow them down, but Arla pushed through.

"I said, stop!"

The wall was rushing to meet her, even as Wynera leadened her legs.

Just as she was about to slam headfirst into the wall, the expansion snapped back and Wynera retreated.

Arla pivoted at the last second, slamming her shoulder into the wall and skimming across it, tearing her sleeve. Small droplets of blood bubbled up from thinly peeled skin.

Arla hissed in pain. Admittedly, it *was* a dumb thing to do, but at least now Wynera knew she was serious.

Smug in her win, Arla continued. "So this is how we will interact from now on. I will try to help you, but in my own way, under my conditions. We will talk, but you will never try to take over my body again. Do we have a deal?"

There was no response. Maybe the connection had weakened too much.

Still, Arla did not move. Her hands gripped the edge of the nightstand as she waited, ready to slam her body against the wall again if Wynera tried to take over again, but that did not happen.

Instead, a faint ripple of a chuckle shimmied up her skin. *"I knew I chose you for a reason."*

"What do you mean?"

Wasn't she chosen because Arla was the closest body to possess?

But Wynera did not answer her.

Arla sighed in annoyance. "So tell me more about Rhyler. What is he after? Who hired him?"

Still no answer.

"Hello?" Arla reached out for Wynera in her mind, but there was nothing.

The wind had stalled.

Arla felt something wet on her shirt. Looking down, she realized she was bleeding again.

CHAPTER 16

"How could this have happened?!"

Her council buzzed with tension as they all paced the throne room in various directions, shouting and waving their hands in the air. Arla stood amongst them on the floor, leaving her throne empty.

She and Leo had only arrived back at the castle that morning after the physician imbued enough magic into her wound to seal it up for good. The area still stung, but there was no more risk of it bleeding again. Now the new issue was dealing with a frantic council.

Leo glared silently at the flailing adults like an annoyed parent amongst children throwing tantrums.

"This is a travesty! A High-Born murdered out in the open!" Docannon shouted. "Never in all my years has this ever happened!"

The others nodded, except Ametha, who loomed in the back. Arla had not invited the former Queen, and yet here she was.

Docannon swiveled toward Arla, his face bloated red. "Do you not understand the danger we are in? Not only has there been a murder, but it was out in the open in the middle of the city! It makes us look weak, and if word spreads to the other kingdoms that we might not be able to defend ourselves, they may see that as an opportunity."

Arla did not doubt that the other kingdoms would want Ulsana. They had a claim to the largest piece of the continent and held fertile land that grew almost anything.

"We must find out who this Rhyler is," Norendra said. "This noble must have a reason for killing Lesandres along with attempting to kill our Queen."

That was the puzzle. Why would Rhyler want her and Lesandres dead at the same time?

Docannon pressed his fingers to his forehead. "Why is this happening now?"

"I think we all know why." All eyes turned to Oberius, the oldest member of the council, who was staring straight at Arla. She remembered him well. He was the only one on the balcony that witnessed her being forced to watch Leo being whipped to death. He was just as stone-faced as her father was. "If King Mathus were still alive, no one would have dared to do this. Our enemies know we are vulnerable now. Your father ruled with an iron fist, unbending and merciless. His word was law, and no one dared to challenge him. Do you know why? Because people feared his strength. That is what kept us safe. That is what kept us prosperous." Oberius pointed at Leo. "And you spit on his grave for pardoning him."

They all looked awkwardly at each other in silence. No one spoke up to disagree.

'For now, Arla. You have the crown for now.'

"I understand how some may think that Ulsana is *weaker* now," Arla replied slowly, tasting the bitterness of that word again. "But they are wrong, and I will prove it. I will find this assassin and bring him here to be judged, and the world will know that no one can attack us so openly without punishment."

Oberius scoffed. "You can barely keep up with your Queenly duties now, what makes you think you can also find this killer on your own?" He didn't wait for an answer. "You can't. That is why we have come to a decision."

The council circled around them.

"What is this?" Norendra hissed. The shadows under her feet flickered aggressively.

"We were wrong to take your advice, Norendra," Oberius said. "She is not fit for this."

Arla was confused. *Norendra wanted me to be queen?*

Oberius closed in on Arla. "You will announce Ametha as Queen Regent, and you will leave this city. We will send you somewhere you can live out your days in peace. Think of how much easier that would be."

She shook her head. "No."

"Do not make it harder than it needs to be." Docannon joined.

She looked to Norendra for support, but her advisor just blinked, clearly surprised herself.

Simion stepped between them and gave Oberius a humorous smile. "Now hold on, let's talk about this."

"Stay out of this, *Yubal*," Oberius snapped. "You think you are smart, but really you're just another smiling buffoon who thinks that just because we like you it means you belong with us. Do not be fooled. You do not have what it takes to be a true councilman."

Simion's smile wiped off his face. And as much as that might have made Arla happy in any other situation, something in Oberius' words stung her deeply too.

"Leave him alone," Arla spat.

"Relinquish your title," Oberius demanded.

Leo gripped the hilt of his sword beside her. "Do not take another step."

The council members closed in on them. She could almost hear the Whispers on the tips of their tongues.

"There is no point in fighting us," Docannon said.

She couldn't let them toss her out. There was too much to do.

She had to be stronger. She had to be tougher. That's what it was going to take to save Uro. To protect everyone.

This kindness she had. It wasn't going to work. She was never going to win by asking nicely or trying to impress them.

Which left her with only one other choice.

If something would not be given, she would have to take it.

I am not going to lose.

"*Ceradas bival-ahala.*"

The stone floor shook and then burst, splaying pieces of heavy rock in every direction. Some hit council members so hard, they were knocked unconscious. And from the floor emerged the ten-foot nightmare that almost killed Arla in The Forest. Its scrawly legs smashed to the ground as it stood up to its full height.

A screech that could boil blood rang from its hideous mouth as it struck out one of its six knife-like legs into the side wall. Docannon screamed, diving to the floor like it would provide him some safety.

Another councilwoman shrunk, her entire body shortening until she stood only an inch high. Her magic was not going to give her an advantage here.

The monster roared and then spit a ring of yellow acid around the terrified council. Some specks of it caught on their arms and feet. They screamed as it gnawed away at their skin.

Oberius ran for the door. Arla willed the monster to block his path. The old man fell back onto his ancient rump and crawled away from the snap of the creature's serrated teeth.

"Get back!" Oberius cried out in sheer terror.

Arla loomed over Oberius, who stared up at her in fear, shaking in her shadow.

"These monsters... they were yours..." he breathed. It all made sense to him now. He now knew it was her who had helped Leo escape his execution.

She got down on one knee, hissing into his face. "You idolized my father, but if it were him standing above you now, would you still be breathing? I am not my father, and you are lucky for it. Do not mistake my kindness for weakness, Oberius." Arla turned to face the others. The council members were pale from fright, and that strangely thrilled her. "We are not going to waste any more time debating whether or not I should be queen. I've given you the answer."

Her monster crouched low as if it would jump at them.

"Y-yes, my Queen," Oberius stuttered.

Arla locked onto Ametha, who trembled against the wall.

Why did I ever let this haggard woman have so much power over me? I do not need her love.

"This was your idea, wasn't it?" Arla sneered. She didn't need an answer to know that it was. Her blood boiled. She had tried to be so kind and understanding to her step-mother and still she got not love from her. So what was the point in trying anymore? "From now on, Jun will stay in the room next to mine. You will not be allowed to see him anymore."

Ametha turned ashen. "He is my son! You cannot take him away from me!"

"I just did."

Ametha fell to her knees, her hands clasped like a beggar. "Please! I can't lose him too!"

"Then you shouldn't have moved against me!"

The sickly beast roared and swung its black legs. One crashed into the wall behind her stepmother, and the other came down right next to the throne chair, smashing into Arla's stone statue. It splintered into a hundred pieces, rumbling to the ground in a plume of rock dust.

Arla stared at the destruction. Her long-time companion, gone. Heat flared inside her veins.

Arla motioned for Leo to grab Ametha. "Take her to the dungeons."

Leo did not move.

He looked at her as if he did not know her.

"Captain," she said louder. "That is an order."

With great hesitancy, Leo grabbed Ametha by the upper arm and dragged her toward the door.

"No!" Ametha tried to twist out of Leo's grip. The monster growled and that quickly shut her up as Leo pulled her out of the room.

Norendra beamed at Arla with pride, her chest raised like a proud mother hen. Arla willed the creature to disappear, turning it into a flow of black ripples that evaporated into the air.

She glared at the council. "This meeting is over. Leave."

They all fled the room. Norendra paused just before leaving and bowed in reverence, barely containing the glint of pride in her eyes.

Finally alone, Arla lingered over the graveyard of the broken statue, its claw still open and waiting to receive, which was the only intact thing about it, while the rest of it was just chunks of unidentifiable stone scattered across the surrounding floor. Seeing her companion destroyed like this left her feeling... hollow and tired.

"Well, that was interesting." Simion appeared beside her in a haze of smoke. He watched her carefully pick up a piece of broken stone. "Was it your friend?" He barely contained his snicker.

"I thought I told all of you to leave."

"You must feel pretty good about yourself, my Queen. I know I do."

Arla gripped the stone harder in her hand, realizing it was going to be impossible to find the next one that would fit it. "I am not like you. I don't enjoy watching people suffer in front of me."

"That's not what I saw."

"That was different. They attacked me first. I had to defend myself."

"And you think I didn't have to defend myself?"

"What do you have to defend yourself against?" She snapped, finally turning to face him. "You loved making me feel small any chance you got. You chose to hurt me when I had done nothing to you, and I will never forget that."

"Ah. So, the sweet little girl was keeping score. I'm sure your father would have been proud if he were still *alive*."

That was it. This was the last straw.

Arla dropped the stone and pressed a finger hard against his chest. "From now on, you are not to bring up my father ever again. You will remain part of the council as my quiet and humble supporter, and I will not treat you with any special privileges. You are to devote your services to me as your Queen wholeheartedly." She glared at him, cold and intent. "Or I will kill you like I killed my father."

Simion's eyes widened in surprise, but then just as quickly a smile reappeared back on those lips. "I have to admit, my Queen, I like this side of you."

With a bow, he disappeared into thin air, leaving Arla alone in the disheveled throne room.

She stared down at the split stones of her statue feeling far away from herself and yet grounded at the same time. Slowly, she crouched to the ground and pulled the broken pieces to her, the powder of the stone turning the tips of her fingers white. She picked up a piece and placed it haphazardly on top of another, but they did not fit. Not anymore. They would never fit again.

A sense of loss spread over her as she tried to accept the truth. That nothing would ever be the same again.

CHAPTER 17

Arla was walking slower than she thought she would even though the room was cleared before she stepped in. It was as if her body was afraid of the outcome of this. The crib was on the other side of the room, yet it felt so much further.

All these months she had dreamed of this moment, and now that it was here, it was surreal, like a dream of someone else's life.

The sun had turned a sleepy orange across the sky, illuminating the walls with a soft glow.

She peered over the edge of the crib like a shy child.

Jun lay on his back, eyes closed. His plump little belly rose and fell in his slumber. And his tiny little fists were raised beside his head. He looked so peaceful. She envied how little he had to worry about anything.

She reached in and lifted Jun from his bed, careful to hold his head. Gently, Arla brought him up and put him against her chest. He leaned his head against her, not making a sound. A warmth she had never known glowed within her, and she blinked back tears.

He was so... soft. Like a cloud.

She dared to squeeze him a little more to close the gap between them. She had waited for this moment for so long. To be able to hold him without someone trying to stop her. And it felt... wonderful.

Jun woke slowly and rubbed his face into her chest before looking up at her.

She held her breath as she stared into his eyes, waiting for him to scream at the stranger holding him.

He blinked one slow, sleepy blink and then laid his head back down with a sigh, trying to get comfortable.

She loosed her breath, and the knot in her chest unraveled like ribbons and re-wrapped itself around Jun.

"This all started with you." Her voice trembled, trying to keep herself together. "I had to go through darkness and monsters and death, but I'd do it all over again. I hope you know that." She put her lips to his warm, bald head and closed her eyes, trying to hold this moment forever.

CHAPTER 18

Arla shoved the pillar of hay to the center of the ring.
Now!

The beast lashed out with its claw, shredding the bustle of hay, but its aim faltered too much towards its left and sliced Arla in the arm. Arla grabbed her bicep with a small shout. A warm trickle of blood filled her palm. The mud beast grumbled and took a step back, leaving muddy footprints on the impacted clay ground.

"At least it wasn't my head." Arla smiled at the creature. She still wasn't sure if it could understand her. If it did, then did that make these beasts real? If that was the case, where did they go when she dismissed them and their bodies scattered to the winds?

The beast shook, splashing the ground with mud.

Arla tore off a piece of her dress and wrapped her arm. Close combat was going to be the most difficult to manage. Her creatures could not protect her easily without risking injuring her too, no matter how precise she asked them to be. She had chosen the mud lizard because it was the most willing to obey, and an injury from it was not as devastating as the nightmare spider creature, whose legs could cut acid into its victims. There was little room for error with that one.

Something tugged at her ribs.

She shrugged off Wynera. *Don't interfere. I have to learn to get better on my own.*

So far, Wynera was keeping her end of the bargain and had not tried to possess her body again, which Arla appreciated. She was not eager to injure herself again to prove another point.

Arla hauled another five foot tall pillar of hay to the center of the arena. The goal was to pretend someone was trying to hurt her in close combat and she would have to figure out a way to shove them far enough that her creature could attack it without injuring herself while also keeping the creature in existence. Multi-tasking was difficult. So much so that Arla was sure it was not something humans were meant to do.

Arla punched the hay and ducked as if it had swung a returning blow. Crouched low, she shoved her shoulder into the pillar and pushed.

The creature roared and swung again, tossing the hay sideways straight back toward Arla's direction. The scratchy hay knocked her off her feet and flat onto her back. Her teeth shook from the impact.

She groaned in pain, her side stinging slightly.

"You alright?"

Leo's dark, intense eyes bore into hers as he stood above her, offering his hand. She was surprised to see him since she did not tell him where she would be.

Arla accepted his hand and jumped to her feet. "Never better."

Leo gave the beast a nod of acknowledgement, but the creature ignored him and laid on its stomach. "You're training by yourself?"

"I thought it would be good to focus on the creatures today, without endangering anyone."

He gave her a soft smile, like he was both proud and enamored by her. It was one of her favorite expressions on his handsome face. She still couldn't believe how much he wanted her. Given his looks, he could have had anyone, but he chose her.

Sometimes it was still hard to believe.

She touched his wrist lightly. "Did you want to train together?"

It was the only thing they could do in public, even though all she wanted was to feel those lips on hers again.

But it did not look like kissing was on Leo's agenda at the moment. His expression grew serious. "Actually, I am here because I wanted to talk about what happened with the council the other day… I'm worried about you."

"Worried?" Arla scoffed playfully and went to drag the hay pillar back to the center. "What is there to be worried about? I'm fine. More than fine, actually. I finally have the council under my control."

Leo quickly went to her side and picked up the hay. "Yes, but the way you did it was… forceful."

Arla frowned. The beast gave a snort of agitation as well. "Sometimes you need a firm hand. That's why soldiers learn to fight, isn't it? People don't respect someone who isn't strong."

Leo gave her a questioning look as he placed the hay upright. "Is that what strength is? Forcing someone to kneel out of fear? Taking away something they love?"

"I finally made them respect me."

"They don't respect you, Arla. They fear you."

"It's the same thing."

"No, it's not."

Heat flared across her chest. This was not the romantic moment she was hoping for. In fact, being judged like this by none other than the one person she thought was on her side was not anything she ever hoped for. "I'm not a child for you to reprimand, Leo."

"I'm not treating you like a child."

Arla snorted. "Oh? Then, why are you telling me how to act?"

"I just think the situation could have been handled better."

Whispers. He sounded like Norendra. "They were trying to dethrone me. Do you think I should have begged for mercy instead? Or asked in a nicer tone?"

The mud lizard stood on all fours, growing in size. Its shadow overcast them like a dark cloud.

"No, just –"

"Everyone thinks they know what's best for me. They tell me what I can do, and what I can't do. What to believe and not to believe. Maybe they would have easily controlled the old, weak me, but not anymore."

Norendra. Wynera. Simion. Mathus. Everyone who was ever close to her tried to fit her into their mold, unconcerned about what it did to her so long as they got what they wanted. If only she were someone else, they said. Someone smarter, faster, stronger, wiser.

And now Leo wanted her to be kinder. *Weaker.*

They want me to bend to their will. They want to hurt me. I won't let them.

She glared at Leo with venom on her tongue. "Are you going to be another person who tries to control me?"

Her beast took a step toward him, dipping its head, ready to spring.

"I am not trying to control you. I am just telling you my opinion, it has always been your choice to listen or not."

He's lying.

Unable to stop the rolling boil, she continued her attack. "You want me to change." Her beast growled, taking another step. Arla hardly noticed. "I wasted too many years of my life bending backwards to win the approval of people I shouldn't have even cared about. I won't do it again!"

The beast was inches from Leo now. Its breath blew Leo's hair away from his face, but Leo did not budge. He kept his eyes fixed on Arla.

"So then. What will you do?" he challenged. "Will you force me to kneel too?"

Arla stuttered back.

She looked up at the creature, realizing it was ready to shred Leo apart.

"I..."

What *was* she about to do?

What was happening? It all tumbled out so fast. The hurt. The fear. She felt like an animal backed into a corner.

The lizard sighed and misted away into nothingness, no longer blocking the sun.

She could only look at Leo with wide eyes. Unsure of herself. "I'm... sorry."

Leo pulled her into a warm embrace. "Arla, just because I disagree with something you do doesn't mean I'm trying to control you, or don't like who you are."

Her heart softened at his words.

He's not like them. He's not trying to hurt you. She tried to remind herself.

"I know that deep down you probably feel a little bad for what you did. You are a good, kind-hearted person, and that's not a weakness."

She pulled away from him. "I'm not so sure."

"What do you mean?"

"You keep saying I'm good, but... I'm not."

The weight of it was too much for her to bear any longer. If she was going to be with Leo and have him risk his life for it, he deserved to know who he was really committing to.

She meant what she said. She was done trying to win the approval of others.

And yet... imagining Leo's reaction... if he rejected her because of this...

"You should know." Her throat tightened, but she was determined to push the words out. "Leo...I-I killed my father."

The words sank in slowly. She could see him fighting the truth of them immediately.

He chose his next words carefully. "I understand that you feel responsible for his death in a way, but Arla, it's not your fault, it was an accident."

He was trying to make excuses for her. In the beginning, she did too. She blamed Wynera. That it was all her doing, but that wasn't the complete truth. And she knew that the truth was something she could no longer hide or run away from. Because it was weighing her down and she was ready to be set free. Just as calling the monsters on the council had somehow released something in her, so too, would this.

"No, Leo. I killed him. I burned him until there was nothing left of him."

At first, he was still fighting to make excuses. She could see it in his face, but then slowly he paled. "In the tunnel…"

Yes. He was understanding now.

"And the worst part is… I don't feel guilty about it. I know I should because it was wrong, but I don't. I don't miss him." She let out a breath. "The world is better off without him." Wynera was right, and strangely, it made her feel equally worse and better at the same time. "I cared more about being a murderer than having actually killed him. I was afraid of what that made *me*…" She stared at the ground. At anything but him. Arla could not watch the affection in Leo's eyes disappear in front of her. The price of her freedom.

She waited for the words that would divide them. Leo would surely reject her now that she was not the pillar of innocence and goodness he thought she was. He would join the long line of people who did not want her anymore. Who wished she was something else.

Arla tried to tell herself it was okay. That at least she told the truth. But part of her already wished she had continued to lie.

There were no more comforting words from Leo. Instead, the silence between them stretched out like a widening river.

There was nothing left to say.

"I found him!" Rose breathlessly rushed between them seemingly from nowhere, her long braid swinging behind her.

For a moment, they both acted like they did not hear Rose, that she was not there at all.

"I found Rhyler," Rose said. "Someone spotted a man with the same description."

Leo turned away from Arla. "Where?"

Rose's lips pressed into a firm grim line. "You're not going to like it."

"*Where*, Rose?" Leo repeated.

"The Underground."

Leo's face contorted as if he'd bitten into something rotten. Whatever this Underground was, it was not a place he liked.

"What's The Underground?" Arla asked.

"It's–" Rose choked. She placed a hand on her throat and frowned, like she was disappointed in forgetting something.

Strange...

Leo gave Rose a knowing look.

Rose forcibly cleared her throat. "It's nowhere a queen should be."

Arla looked toward the setting sun. "Whatever it is, we have to go soon if we want to make it by nightfall."

"*We* are not going anywhere together," Rose responded.

"I am going."

Rose scowled. "You will bring unwanted attention."

"I will disguise myself."

"You think people are so blind they won't see their Queen in front of them?"

"I'll wear a hood."

Rose snorted. "What a genius plan."

Arla reddened. "No one will notice me anyway. I am easily ignorable. They only see the crown when I am in public. Without it, no one will bat an eye at me."

The tension crackled between them as they glared at each other.

Leo stepped between them. "Rose is right. You should not come."

His voice was so distant, like he was talking to a stranger tagging along rather than the woman he claimed to have cared so much for only a day ago. Something in Arla retreated, placing a wall between her heart and the man before her.

"I'm going to look for Uro with or without you." Arla's eyes flicked to Rose and then back to Leo. "So we might as well do it together, for Uro's sake. We can find him faster that way."

Leo glowered. "I'm asking you to stay here."

Arla threw her chin up. "I won't."

With a coldness that sent chills down Arla's spine, he turned from her. "Fine." He waved Rose over to him. "We'll need horses immediately."

CHAPTER 19

The journey to The Underground was longer than Arla expected. Even on horseback, it felt far. They rode in complete silence, which Arla expected. Rose was not one to talk much, and Leo... well, Leo probably wanted nothing to do with her now. She tried not to think about it and focused entirely on finding Rhyler, who would lead them to Uro. That was her top priority.

They did not take the main road as most travelers did, instead, they took dirt paths along hills and through the woods until they arrived at an inconspicuous cave that looked like any other. Admittedly, she was disappointed at how ordinary it looked.

Rose and Leo sat on their horses, staring at the cave for longer than any normal person should. Maybe they were lost? But the way they looked at it made her think their hesitation was from resistance rather than confusion.

The pair begrudgingly got off their horses and Arla followed them into the pitch-dark mouth of the cave. The cave continued further down, stifling all the remaining moonlight, making her wonder how they were going to navigate their way around if they could not see anything. And just as she was about to ask this very question, a thin line of flame burst along the walls. Arla retreated, pulling her forearms to her chest. Her scars heated with memory.

The fire illuminated the entire cave, guiding them further along.

Whose Whispers are these?

Leo and Rose did not seem surprised by the fire, so Arla assumed this was expected and continued to follow them until, finally, they arrived at a door carved into the stone, etched with markings Arla did not understand, and standing in front of it was the largest man she had ever laid eyes on. He was taller than the door itself, with crossed arms covered in scars.

She swallowed hard. Were they going to fight this man to get through?

Arla was pretty sure one hit from his boulder-like fists would crush her without much effort.

"Hand," he commanded in a gruff voice to Leo.

Leo offered an open palm. The man Whispered, sending a pale blue light around Leo that traveled up his arm and into his throat. Leo let out a breath of blue smoke.

Arla leaned toward Rose, keeping her voice quiet. "What is this?"

Rose took a step away from her, frowning. "The keeper prevents us from speaking about what we see or do here. It's how this place has been kept a secret for so long."

"Is that why you choked yesterday talking about it?" Arla asked and then added rather smugly. "You forgot, didn't you?"

Rose threw her a glare, which Arla happily received. She used to be afraid of Rose, but now, all she wanted to do was provoke her. Maybe because she felt the same for Rose as she did Ametha. There was no point in trying to win over those that did not like her anymore.

"Leave your weapons," the keeper said.

Leo relinquished his sword and then the man allowed Leo to pass through the door behind him.

The keeper's focus shifted to Arla. "Hand."

She nervously gave him her open palm while clutching the hood that draped over her head. Was he going to force her to reveal her face?

Nope. The keeper paid no attention to her face at all. Maybe because she was not the first to want to hide her identity here.

"*Opula.*"

The magic was like a cool mint, tingling her skin until it reached her throat. Air rapidly filled it until Arla had no choice but to breathe out neon blue smoke.

Satisfied, the man let her pass.

The door cranked open, revealing more stairs chiseled into the ground where they descended into a long corridor.

The corridor was narrow enough that one could not get lost, but the darkness seemed to stretch forever. She slid her hand along the wall to help guide her through.

Soon, in the distance, the sound of drums beckoned them, getting louder and louder and louder. It was almost threatening, which made Arla a bit nervous.

And then, colors burst all around them.

The corridor opened up into the center of a large maze of stone streets in all directions. Each street boasted dizzying colors and shouting people and random animal screeches. It was like a hundred circuses smashed together, with no end in sight. It was hard for her to take it all in.

Everyone was wearing costumes that were unlike anything Arla had ever seen. They bustled in the streets with intention and unhinged desire in their eyes. Unlike the organized and neat, Ulsanan market, this place was a bottle of vigorously shaken colors and tangy smells.

A woman crossed in front of them, and Arla could not help but notice she had bright blue feathers glued to the edges of her cheekbones that trailed down her jaw and body. And then Arla realized that the feathers were all this woman was covered in. Blinding gold chains wrapped around the gripped fist of this woman, who stopped suddenly in her walk and yanked the chain, pulling a half-naked man on the other end by the neck.

Arla was immediately repulsed by such a sight, but then noticed the wide-eyed, crazed expression of ecstasy on the man's face. He was enjoying this? The scene made no sense to her.

A nearby man had an enormous diamond in his eye socket that glittered against the fire torches that lined the walls. Another man grabbed one of the empty carts strewn around the alley, wearing nothing but a shiny violet loincloth, and shouted gibberish to no one.

And skin...

There was more exposed skin here than the court of Ulsana would have ever allowed. Arla couldn't help but blush at seeing so much of it. The sounds of trumpets and harps and the whirl of movement completely overwhelmed Arla. It was as entrancing as it was confusing.

"What are all these people doing here?" she asked.

Leo's eyes narrowed, his entire body on edge. "People come here for only one of two things: pain or pleasure."

Pain or pleasure...

Arla turned to Leo, finally meeting his eyes. "You and Rose have been here before, right? Was it for pain or pleasure?"

Leo's face darkened, and he turned away from her.

A voice shouted from the crowd. "Come join the fun! Seven competitors. One winner always!"

Someone shoved past Arla, running up to a makeshift plank soapbox where a woman stood in front of the crowd. She had purple paint splashed everywhere on her face, with pursed blue-colored lips and gold glitter in her black hair. She raised a lone finger up in the air. "We need one more competitor!"

Standing in a line on a large platform were six people, looking hopefully into the crowd. The person who pushed Arla earlier clambered onto the platform.

"What are they doing?"

Leo did not reply. She was sure he knew. Was it embarrassment or shame that kept him quiet?

Arla noticed how many in the crowd were women with exposed bodies. Their thin clothing barely contained their curvy hips and large breasts. Arla swallowed nervously and glanced back at Leo, who was already searching for something (or someone) in the crowd.

She couldn't help but wonder, did Leo know any of these women?

Seeing the last volunteer scramble on to the platform, the purple-painted woman raised her hand in glee. "We have our competitors! Everyone, please turn your attention here as they attempt to stay on the platform. The last one standing wins it all!"

The crowd cheered as the competitors circled each other on the wooden platform which croaked and bent under their weight and didn't look like it could support them all. From the crowd, someone shouted, "*Eni-kia!*"

A gust of wind knocked one competitor off their feet. The others saw this weakness and banded together to push the poor soul off the platform. Just as they did, a blue-lipped woman gleefully shouted from the crowd, "*Je-en!*"

Another competitor screamed, waving his hands in front of his face. His eyes, which were once vivid, were now clouded gray. Arla gasped. The woman had just blinded him with her magic!

As the others scrambled to push this one off too, another High-Born in the crowd shouted, "*Dime-don!*"

The platform tilted, groaning as it moved back and forth, tumbling the competitors on top of each other. The crowd laughed, pointing and wiping their tears of glee off their eyes. Most of the people in the crowd wore fine silks and leathers, while those on the platform looked more malnourished with rags on their backs. That's when Arla realized what this was.

A game of humiliation.

The people on the platform were Low-Borns, and they were being subjected to the magical cruelty of nobles.

Arla's ears grew hot in outrage. "I don't understand. Why do they volunteer to do this?"

"For the money, obviously, at the cost of their pride," Rose said bitterly.

"Sometimes survival is more important than pride," Leo replied solemnly, his expression more empathetic than Rose's. "We have to keep moving."

"No, please!"

Arla swiveled her head to the distressed sound.

A young woman around the same age as her was crying profusely as a sweaty man dragged her toward the back of an alleyway.

Passersby watched without reaction, while others giggled and pointed.

The young woman reached out a hand to the passerbys. "Someone help me!"

But the people just continued to laugh, and walked past, ignoring her distress as the man grabbed a handful of her hair and yanked her into the shadows.

Arla didn't think, she just ran.

By the time she got there, the man was already on top of the girl, behind a line of barrels. His fist raised above her.

"Your father owes me a debt, girl, and you're going to pay it."

Red overlaid Arla's vision, blinding her in rage.

She shoved her shoulder into the man, sending them both rolling. Before he could stop tumbling, she lunged and grabbed him by the collar, reeled her head back and smashed her forehead into his.

Pain burst between her eyes.

She stumbled back, clutching her forehead.

"What in the darkening was that?!" The man shook his head to clear his vision and locked eyes with Arla. "You little–!"

"How dare you touch her!" Arla spat.

The man rubbed his bruised forehead. "I can do whatever I want with Low-Born filth. Especially those that owe me money." His nostrils flared. "Or those that attack me."

Whispers clamored in her head, ready to spill from the tip of her tongue, but she reeled them back. If she called them here, they would destroy the entire alleyway.

Arla stepped in front of the crying girl, her hood still covering most of her face. "Leave before you regret it."

He huffed in amusement and crouched ready to charge at her.

Leo hovered at the end of the alley, casting a shadow over all of them. "I would listen to her if I were you."

Seeing Leo, the man paled. "*You...y*ou're back."

Without another word, the man spun on his heel and ran in the opposite direction as fast as he could.

Arla went to chase him, but Rose stopped her. "We don't have time for that."

"But he–"

"I know," Rose said, teeth clenched. "I know."

The young woman curled into a ball against the wall. She kept crying and crying. Arla crouched on her knees to get to the woman's eye level. "It's okay. You're safe now." She had hoped to comfort her, but her attempts seemed to make it worse. The woman's sobs turned to full gasps of air.

It was hard to watch her tremble and not be able to stop it. Arla felt a bit useless in that moment, not knowing what to say to make her feel better. She reached out her hand to touch the young woman's shoulder, but then thought better of it. She didn't know if the young woman wanted to be touched. Arla wondered how long she lingered there, not able to decide what to do.

Leo knelt down beside her. "We need to get you home." He offered his hand. "Will you allow me to take you?"

Through her hiccups, the woman nodded.

Leo lifted the woman into his arms, and she immediately quieted down and buried her face into the crook of his neck, tears still streaming down her face.

"Did you come here with someone?" he asked her, his voice gentle.

She nodded and whispered directions in his ear.

It was so simple. *Why didn't I think of that?*

They walked in silence back to the entrance, where they found an older woman frantically searching the crowd. When the woman finally laid eyes on the girl in Leo's arms, she ran in relief toward them.

"Esme!" she cried out. Leo let Esme down, who ran to the woman, shouting, "Mother!"

Esme's mother stroked her daughter's hair. "Are you hurt?"

Esme shook her head. "I'm fine thanks to him." She pointed in Leo's direction.

"Thank y–" Esme's mother took in Leo and then ashened, just like the man in the alley before.

Which was strange because Leo had done nothing to warrant that kind of reaction. His expression remained neutral, and not once did he acknowledge her fear at all.

"I did not do anything, it was her that helped your daughter." Leo slightly pointed his chin to Arla without meeting her eye.

"Of course," the mother said shakily. "Thank you. We should go home now."

Esme nodded, but before they left, she came back and wrapped her arms around Leo's neck. "Thank you."

Leo gave Esme a small, soft smile. The one Arla thought he only gave to her. And it made Arla's stomach drop.

Maybe that's what he really wanted. An image of innocence, like Arla used to be, before The Forest and the magic and her father. A person she could never be again.

Leo lingered to make sure the pair made their way safely back to the entrance before turning back to them. "We have to go."

She followed them both back to the cobblestone alleyway in silence until they met the crowd once again. People constantly pushed and bumped into her. It was like walking up a stream of people, who were all trying to come down and push you back to your starting spot. Arla held onto the hood of her cloak to make sure her face remained hidden.

It was here, in this sweaty, hot river of people, that she learned to hate crowds. It didn't help that she was already in a sour mood. Leo's smile to Esme was etched into her mind like an annoying itchy thing that would not go away.

Finally, after much pushing and pulling, they wiggled themselves into what looked like a shop. A sharp bell clanged as the door shut behind them, informing its owner of their arrival. She shook her arms, trying to whip off all the sweat and gunk her clothes had just absorbed. She cringed at how damp her sleeves had become.

With enough space to finally stop and look around, Arla discovered she was in a store where all the walls were covered in crooked shelves of various jars of dried leaves, worms, fungus, and even... Arla pulled back in disgust. On her right, there was a jar of dried human toes with thick yellowish nails that cracked ever so slighting at the edges.

"Ah! Customers!" A short elderly woman hobbled in from the back and leaned on the glass showcase that separated her from them.

Arla would have smiled and greeted her if she wasn't instantly distracted by the top of her head. The shopkeeper's hair was at least two feet tall and so tangled it seemed to build on top of itself like a bird's nest. Strands of grayish-silver hair poked out from time to time, but most of it was curled into itself, creating a mound Arla had never seen in her life.

How was it standing on its own like that? And did it hurt the shopkeeper's neck to support it all?

"How may I help you?" The shopkeeper's smile revealed a full set of gold teeth, each decorated with silver swirls.

Leo stepped forward.

The elderly woman's smile dropped. "*You.*"

Hm. Another person who seems to know him.

"I need to speak with him," Leo said.

The shopkeeper rubbed her chin, which had one long silver hair growing on it. "Disappeared for two years and now suddenly back with demands, are we?"

Leo glared at the woman in rigid silence.

She gave a long, weathered sigh. "Fine." She pointed her chin (and one silver hair) at Arla and Rose. "They stay here."

He turned to Rose. "Thirty minutes."

Rose nodded knowingly. Arla wanted to walk after him, but it was clear the shopkeeper would not allow this. So she stayed back with Rose as Leo disappeared behind the counter into the back room.

CHAPTER 20

At first, Rose and Arla remained silent, staring at the door Leo and the shopkeeper went through. This was the first time they had been alone together and, undoubtedly, it was quite awkward, at least, it was for Arla. Rather than caving into the silence, Arla thought maybe this would be a wonderful opportunity to finally get closer to this woman who hated her.

Arla mused on what she could say to pique Rose's interest enough to have a proper conversation. After a few minutes, she finally landed on, "How have you been?"

Admittedly, it wasn't the most creative conversation starter, but she was genuinely curious how Rose was doing after everything that had happened. Surely, Rose was as worried and anxious about Uro as Arla was right?

Rose did not respond, as expected, so Arla continued. "A lot has happened, and I know it must be hard. You can talk to me if you want."

Rose's dark eyes flicked to Arla for a second before fixing on the back of the door. A small sign of hope that she was listening.

"When I get stressed, I like to snack on sweets. I'm not sure if you're like that, but if you want, I could get you some. I'm sure there are stands around here that sell them. Do you like–"?

Rose suddenly tossed something at Arla.

Surprised, Arla waved her hands around trying to catch it, but missed completely and the item dropped to the ground.

"What is this?" she asked as she quickly picked the object back up.

Pushing her thick braid off her shoulder, Rose pressed her lips together in an irritated fashion. "It's a blade."

"And you just tossed it to me?" That was incredibly dangerous.

"It's wrapped," Rose said bluntly, like Arla was stupid.

Arla tightened her grip on the old wrapped leather of the pommel, feeling the solidness of the sharpened steel in her hand. It was strange holding it. "Why are you giving me this?"

"Because I never attack an unarmed person."

"What do you mea-?"

And that was the last thing Arla said before Rose kicked her in the chest.

Arla crashed into the display case behind her, shattering the glass.

"What was that for?!" she shouted through ragged breath, trying to avoid pressing her hands on the glass. Her body shook with pain, still healing from the stabbing before.

Why was she always getting attacked?

Glass crunched a few times before Arla saw the flash of Rose's hand shoot toward her. Rose's fingers wrapped around her neck and squeezed. Immediately Arla went into a panic and grabbed Rose's wrist, trying to pull her off.

"Rose!" Arla shouted, her fear spiking. "Stop!"

Rose was so calm. There was no hatred or fear in her dark eyes. Only intent. Was Rose possessed by something? Or did she just completely lose her mind? Or... no... was she working for Rhyler?

Arla yanked at Rose's wrist again, but the soldier did not let go. "So you're trying to kill me too?"

"You cannot get out of a grip like this by pulling. It's a common mistake." Rose responded in a firm voice. "Raise your arm straight up."

Was she joking? No, Rose was always serious. Despite her instincts telling her not to let go of Rose's wrist, Arla released her grip and raised her arm.

Rose did not let up with the pressure against Arla's throat, but she did not squeeze tighter either. "Now twist your entire body, keeping your arm straight. The moment you twist, bend your arm ninety degrees and bring it straight down on my wrist, hard and fast."

Arla twisted and brought her arm down, hitting Rose's wrist, but Rose's arm did not budge.

"No," Rose reprimanded. "Put your entire momentum into it as fast and as intensely as you can."

"I don't understand what you mean." It was hard to talk with Rose's fingers around her throat.

Rose squeezed her throat harder. "Go."

Arla turned and slammed her elbow down like she was trying to break Rose's arm off. Rose's hand slipped from her neck and fell to the side. Not wasting any time, Arla rolled away from the soldier as far as possible.

Coughing, Arla straightened, her neck throbbing in pain. Why was everyone always trying to go for her throat?

"You're insane!" Arla shouted. "This isn't the place for a fight lesson!"

Rose snorted casually, like she hadn't just attacked her own Queen. "The more painful the lesson, the more memorable it is."

"That sounds like something my father would have said." Arla spat, glaring up at Rose. "Everyone hated my father."

"I've heard you've been emulating more of your father lately than I have," Rose retorted, straight-faced.

She was so sick of Rose's attitude. Her coldness. Her side glares. And now this. If Rose thought she could get away with this, she was wrong.

This time, it was Arla that charged. Rose shifted her weight and turned just as Arla swung, lurching her body weight up and over. Arla crashed into another display case, sending random objects of pearls and strange scented wood into the air.

Ignoring the new flare of pain in her ribs, Arla flipped herself around to find Rose standing over her.

"Were you trying to do something?" Rose asked.

The look of pure boredom on Rose's face made Arla fume. She grabbed a nearby jar of pickled human toes and tossed it at Rose. Rose knocked it away, shattering it against the wall. The smell of putrid flesh filled the room.

Arla gagged loudly.

Rose put a hand to her mouth, clearly distracted by the stench.

This gave her an idea.

She saw something rotting on the corner shelf above her. *Yes!* Arla swiped the slimy fungus and smashed it straight into Rose's nostrils.

Rose shouted, desperately trying to wipe the fungus out of her nose.

She went for Rose's midsection, but Rose dodged it.

Letting out a primal scream, Arla lunged again. "If you want to fight, let's fight!"

Arla kicked out at Rose's leg and knocked her off balance just enough to give Arla an opening. Rolling again, Arla scrambled to her feet on Rose's exposed side. She went for the hit. Elbow to the neck.

Rose stumbled to the side but regained her footing. Digging her toe to pivot, the soldier twisted, fist driving toward Arla's face.

This one is going to hurt.

Arla braced for the blow, but only a flutter of air tickled her cheek.

Rose's knuckles were an inch away from her jaw. A finishing blow incomplete.

Arla blinked in disbelief.

Rose bit her lip, holding herself back. It was like watching a lioness purposefully keeping its claws retracted.

"Finish the move." Arla challenged. "Hit me."

It was Rose's turn to be surprised.

"That's what you want, right? You want to hurt me. Well, I can take it." Arla spat on the ground a mere inch from Rose's feet.

Rose tightened her fist so hard her knuckles paled as it hovered a centimeter closer.

"You think a fist is the worst I've endured?" Arla splayed her arms wide to make her even more vulnerable. "This is nothing. I've been belittled, burned, and beaten all my life. What's another hit?"

Rose's eyes widened, but still she did not move.

"Do it!" Arla shouted.

But the blow did not come. Instead, after a long moment, Rose finally stepped back, dropping her hand to her side.

Exhausted, Arla leaned against the wall and slid to the floor, trying to catch her breath. The welts of the fight were starting to bruise and ache came in waves as the adrenaline slowed within her veins.

Rose too, leaned against the opposite wall and fell to a seated position across from her.

It was strange how... relieved she felt. She had been trying to endure Rose's animosity with kindness, all the while getting more and more frustrated, and for some reason releasing it like this felt... liberating. Her body felt light. So light that she inexplicably started laughing.

She laughed and laughed while Rose stared at her like she had gone mad. But she hadn't lost her mind, only her shackles. She felt free. Free to be chaotic and angry and vengeful.

After a while, all her laughter faded, leaving room for the question she had always wanted the answer to. "Why do you hate me so much, Rose?"

Rose narrowed her eyes. "Should I list the reasons out in alphabetical order or chronological order?"

Arla hesitated, not knowing if her ego could take whatever Rose was about to say.

I am a High-Born. One.

She hates people? Two?

Arla wasn't sure. What other reasons could there be to be a list's worth? Even so, the first on that list was reason enough. Leo hated her when they first met too, but Rose did not slander High-Borns the way Leo did, so was that really it?

Maybe it wasn't something, but someone...

Could it be?

Was Rose jealous of how much time Leo was spending with her?

Arla chose her next words carefully, so as not to hurt Rose's feelings. Revealing a heart's desire was no small thing.

"Is it because... of Leo?" she asked.

"Of course it's because of Leo," Rose snapped.

Arla sat up straighter, despite the ache in her shoulders. "Oh... I didn't know you felt that way about him..." She wasn't sure what to say. Despite Rose trying to beat her senseless only a few minutes ago, Arla couldn't help but still care about her feelings. She didn't want Rose to be hurt in any way (in the realm of emotions at least). "Rose, you are an important friend to Leo. He speaks about you so highly, and I know he values you."

Recognition crossed Rose's face, and then she snorted. "You think this is about romance? You are truly dense." Rose picked up a piece of glass and tossed it to the side. "Leo is my brother. He may not be blood, but he is family. As is Uro. And I love my family, Arla, I will do anything to protect them, but you threaten that."

Arla immediately became defensive. "How? I protect them, just as I try to protect you. I stopped your execution. I–"

"We were put on the execution block *because* of *you*."

Arla yanked at her cloak in frustration. "You were put there because Leo attacked the king."

"And why do you think he did that? Leo saw your father hit you. You think he would just stand there and do nothing? I see the way he looks at you. You are a fool if you don't see how much power you have over him. How far he would go for you. And putting him in a position where he has to be constantly near you... do you know how dangerous that is? Something is going on between the two of you. And whatever that is, it will get him killed."

Arla paused. There *was* something between them, but now that Leo knew the truth about her she wasn't sure if that something had turned sour.

Rose leaned back, hunching slightly as her face grew distant. "This is how it always goes. You'll hang on to the belief that maybe it can work out somehow. That it will be different for you two compared to all the others that came before you. Well, let me tell you now, there is no hope. There is only the execution block at the end of this road for him. This is how it always goes."

How it always goes?

Uro, who probably knew more about them than Rose did, did not mirror the same anguish that was fixed on Rose's face. No, this was the expression of someone who truly feared for her brother, a fear that came from something deeper.

"How do you know that?" Arla asked.

Rose stood up. "You don't need to know how."

Arla scrambled to her feet too. "Did something happen to someone you know?"

At first, Arla thought Rose might punch her again, but she looked like she might cry instead, a sight that frightened Arla even more. She had never seen that expression on Rose's face. Ever.

"I said you don't need to know."

"But I want to know. Rose." Rose made for the door, but Arla blocked her path. "Rose."

"Move."

It was a warning that she should have listened to, but Arla needed to know. Maybe there was a clue in this of what could happen to Leo in the future. Or some other danger she should know.

Arla raised her fists. "Are we fighting again? Because I will."

Rose pushed Arla to the side, but Arla grabbed Rose and pulled her back, not letting her through the door.

Rose was done with verbal warning. She threw a fist out, hitting Arla in the shoulder, sending a shock of sharp pain through her, but Arla did not let go.

"How do you know Rose?" Arla pressed.

Rose tried to break free, hitting Arla again in the arm, but Arla held on for dear life. She would not let Rose shake her off.

"Rose!" she shouted.

Rose shoved Arla to the ground. "Because I am a product of that type of union, Arla!" She drew in a sharp breath. "I am a Muren."

Arla gasped.

A Muren. Half-High-Born and half-Low-Born. Children of unions that were executed swiftly and quietly in the dark.

Ulsana had already lost magic through the generations, and it could not afford to lose any more, so it was unlawful to even pro-create with Low-Borns. Their blood could not hold magic the way High-Borns could.

Completely giving up, Rose put her hands to her forehead. "Would it surprise you to learn I used to have a sister? An older one. Just by one year. We lived with my mother in a town not too far from here. Growing up, our mother told us that our father was a very important man, so important that he was too busy to visit often. Only once a month, if that. I remember how excited she was to see him each time, and he seemed genuinely happy too. The few times we were all together, we were happy. It was perfect."

Rose's face relaxed and, for the first time since Arla had known her, she radiated... joy. But it disappeared as fast as it came, leaving a gloomy shadow over her face. "But secrets cannot be safe forever. One day my father came rushing in and told my mother to pack our bags. We had to leave, but it was too late. They came for us. We didn't have time to run. There was only time for one desperate decision. My mother threw me into a barrel and hid me in the basement. I thought she would do the same for my sister, but she didn't. Instead, she held her, sobbing, saying she was so sorry over and over. I didn't understand it then, but I do now. The guards came and took them."

She swallowed hard. "They hung them in the public square. And all the while, I was spared, because the king thought there was only one child. I had nowhere to go. No one knew of my existence. And so I found my way back to Ulsana and joined the army to avoid starvation. Ironic that I would sign up to fight for a ruler that killed my family, isn't it? But there is no place on this continent that wouldn't have done the same thing."

Arla could not believe what she was hearing. The horror of it all made her speechless.

Rose glared at her. "You wanted to know. Well, now you do."

"Rose... I–"

"Stop. I don't want your pity or whatever it is you're feeling."

It all made sense now. This was why Rose was so apathetic. She kept herself distant so as not to fill her emotional bucket up too much so it would not tip the scales too far one way or another. It was too painful for her to feel anything.

Rose's very existence was illegal and a threat to Ulsana. And she had just told the Queen of all High-Borns. Did that mean that, in some sense, Rose trusted her to keep this a secret? Of course Arla would, but it gave her hope that maybe Rose did not hate her fully after all.

Arla dared to hold Rose's hand in her own. It may earn her another punch, but it would have been worth it, because Rose needed to know that Arla cared about her.

"I'm not pitying you. I'm just hurting because you hurt. That's what friends do. They share pain." She squeezed Rose's hand. "And before you worry, I just want to let you know that your secret is safe with me."

Rose yanked her hand away, a blush of embarrassment on her cheeks. "I know. You care too much about us to endanger us on purpose. Even though you do it inadvertently all the time."

Arla couldn't help but be touched by this.

"I know what love can do to people, Arla," Rose warned. "It makes them believe in wild dreams, but it ends in tragedy."

Love?

"My store!"

The shopkeeper stood in the doorway, her fingers tangled in her nest-hair, her face beet red in rage. "What have you done to my store! How dare you! *Kiv-yel-e-om!*"

The earth shook beneath them, causing more jars to come crashing to the ground. The old woman's voice boomed like a force of nature. "You will pay for this!"

Rose and Arla exchanged one look that expressed only one word: *run*. The shopkeeper grabbed the edge of Arla's cloak. Without thinking, Arla threw it off of her and shoved herself out the door along with Rose into the overcrowded street.

"We need to wait for Leo!" Arla shouted, but when she turned, Rose was no longer beside her. An endless swarm of people surrounded her, pushing her left and right as they rushed to wherever they were going. Arla tried to maintain her spot, but the river of people was too powerful and pushed her down the street.

She felt this crowd would move her forever until she suddenly found an opening. An entrance door to a tall inn. She dove for it, landing on her stomach on a sticky wooden floor. For a moment, she was happy to have escaped the suffocating crowd, until she looked up and saw a handful of eyes peering at her.

"Is that–?"

Strangers' eyes widened in recognition. *Oh no...*

Her face was exposed. Arla quickly went to pull her hood over her head, but grasped nothing. Oh right. She lost that to the shopkeeper.

She ran further into the building. To where she did not know. She just needed to hide.

Turning, she sprinted up the nearest stairs.

She opened the farthest door on the topmost floor and ran inside, slamming the door shut behind her.

Arla pressed her ear against the door, listening for footsteps. Did they follow her up this far?

"Well. Well. Well. I cannot believe it."

Arla's skin prickled.

That voice...

She turned slowly, trying to deny her reality. Arla wished that the person she would face would not be–*Oh Whispers.*

There, on a lush velvet couch at the other end of the dimly lit room, sat Simion between two barely dressed women.

CHAPTER 21

Simion beamed with delight, completely at ease with each woman whose hands were placed lazily on his half-exposed chest. Even in the dimly lit room, Arla could see the surprising tightness of his muscles underneath.

Arla's mouth hung open, unable to speak or move.

In the center of the room, a well-worn bed separated her from the three. Arla had known prostitution existed, but had never seen it in person. Often, she heard the servants complain about their husbands visiting places like this, feeling powerless to stop them or leave them.

But it made sense for a man like Simion to be here. Even so, it was a little discombobulating to see Simion this way. He was usually in stiff council or scholarly-wear with the posture of a stick, but here, not only was his clothing loose, but his face seemed more relaxed as well.

He looked oddly...sensual. Something Arla never thought he could be.

Simion slowly got up and waved the women away. "Thank you for your time, ladies. Will you please excuse us?"

The women gave Arla a quizzical look, trying to figure out how they knew her face. She put a hand to her face to hide her eyes as they passed her and left the room.

Simion buttoned up his shirt as he walked over to her. "First the scene with the council and now you are visiting seedy places like this? I did not know you were that type of person, Your Highness."

"I'm not!" Arla barked. Her eyes caught the last of Simion's smooth skin being covered up. "But it seems you are."

Her heart beat harder in her chest from discomfort. She wasn't supposed to be in a room like this with a man like Simion.

"Are you a regular here?" She didn't know why she had asked. She didn't care for the answer.

"Yes," Simion purred. "But not for what you think. I'm here because I've heard rumors of the assassin visiting The Underground."

This snatched her attention. "How do you know that?"

Simion tapped his ear. "I always know what's happening in Ulsana, Your Highness, because I keep good company."

Of course. *The women.* In places like this, people were bound to spill secrets.

Arla looked to the door. "They trust you enough to tell you?"

"They trust my pockets are deep enough."

Arla was already exhausted from having such a long conversation with him. She really did not want to be in his presence any longer. Better to get to the point. "Why are you trying to find the assassin?"

"Despite what you may think of me, I don't like the idea of High-Borns dying needlessly in our kingdom. It's not the best reputation for us to have."

"So then, did you learn anything?"

A shade of disappointment crossed his face as he picked at a loose thread in his sleeve. "Unfortunately, those two were not much help."

"Maybe your pockets are not as deep as you thought."

Simion frowned. "Maybe I should have used more force to get the information instead. Like you did to the council."

Arla tightened. *How dare he!* "I had to do that."

"I understand completely."

Arla blinked, surprised. "You do?"

"Those uptight nobles only know how to respond to fear. You had no choice."

"I thought you wanted to be one of those uptight nobles."

"Only because they have power. I, more than anyone, understand that only power gets you safety. This world doesn't leave much room for anything else."

She could not believe that Simion was agreeing with her. And he seemed angry at the nobles too. What was this side of him she'd never seen before? Were these his true opinions, or was he just saying this to get on her good side so he could manipulate her in some way?

Before she could come to an answer, the door burst open.

Simion pushed her against the wall, blocking her with his body. He leaned forward, so close she could feel his warm breath on her face. His lips hovered just inches from hers.

"Is she in here?!" A gruff voice shouted from the door.

Simion turned his head toward the man. "I came here to enjoy what I paid for! Not to be bothered!"

"Apologies! I got carried away." The man bowed a few times as he shut the door.

From the other side, someone else shouted, "Maybe she left? Or went down to the basement! I swear I saw her!"

"You must have been imagining things!"

Feet stomped down the stairs.

Simion did not move, looming over Arla. She expected his eyes to be filled with smugness or dark enjoyment, but instead they were filled with something that looked like confusion.

She stared back with cold precision, her voice barely containing her loathing. "Please back away from me."

Her words snapped him out of whatever he was dwelling on, and his annoying smile returned. "That's the nicest tone you've ever used with me, Your Highness. Seems like getting out of here will be a little difficult without being recognized."

"You still have not backed away."

Simion leaned even closer, making Arla back up further against the wall. Anger shrilled through her. "Step back, Simion, *now*."

Simion grabbed something from around the corner of the wall beside her and then backed up, revealing a jet-black cloak in his hands. "I was just getting you this."

Before she could refuse it, Simion billowed it around her shoulders. "When it comes to stopping this assassin, I am on your side." He tied the cloak around her neck with a neat little bow. "I am always on your side, my Queen."

Despite her brain telling her this was a lie, Arla could not help but notice that Simion *did* look earnest...

His fingers lingered on the bow as he twisted it gently, enraptured by it.

And that's when the window shattered across the room.

Arla instinctively jumped away from the sound, accidentally leaning further into Simion's chest. Simion wrapped his arms around her as if he was trying to protect her, which was absolutely absurd. He didn't do that kind of thing.

Black boots came in first and landed on the floor, before revealing a tall figure with dark hair and sharp eyes that glared at Simion.

"Leo?!" Arla pushed Simion away from her.

Leo's eyes flicked from Arla's cloak to Simion and then back again at Arla. "Are you okay?"

Arla nodded just as Rose swung into the room after her captain.

Simion pouted, rubbing his chest where Arla had pushed him. "Kind of a dramatic entrance, no? Very loud. Loud enough to draw attention from the outside. The very thing we were trying to avoid... *Captain*."

Leo's silent glare was so intense Simion should have burst into flame right then and there.

"Why are you so mad?" Simion looked between him and Arla. "Oh." Simion walked over and patted Leo's shoulder. "Don't worry Captain, the Queen just wanted my company for a little while. Nothing to fret over."

Leo gave her a questioning glance, but Arla avoided his gaze, instead speaking to Rose. "Where did you go? I was looking for you in the streets."

"I got pushed around," Rose replied, a little distractedly. She was busy assessing Simion. "Leo found who he was looking for. We need to meet with them now."

"Then I shall join you." Simion replied.

"You will not." Leo growled.

Leo reached out his hand for Arla to take, a motion that completely surprised her, but not as much as what Arla said next. "I think he should come."

"What?" Leo gave her a confused look.

Arla fiddled with the bow on her cloak. Oh Whispers. What was she thinking? Well, she wasn't. She was trusting her intuition instead of her logic. "Simion could prove useful to the investigation. He is good at getting information. And he's interested in stopping the assassin just like we are. At least, that's what he says." Arla gave Simion a quick warning glance. "And if he is lying, he will be punished, but for now, I'm inclined to believe him."

Leo continued to look wary of her decision, but she did not want to give him too much time to refuse. Maybe she was wrong about Simion, but she knew that having more people on their side would increase their chances of finding Uro. So if it meant risking trusting Simion a little, then so be it. All that mattered was finding Uro.

Arla walked past Leo toward the open window. "Shall we go?"

CHAPTER 22

The private room they stood in now was even dingier than the seedy room she found Simion in. Located in the back of a basement bar with no windows, it was oddly humid and smelled of decaying wood. One lone lantern hung from the low ceiling, struggling to light the entirety of the place, which was actually a good thing in Arla's opinion. She did not want to know what other nasty things lived in the corners of such a drab establishment.

"You have a lot of nerve coming here, asking for my help."

The man speaking was named Hae-il. He was in his mid-forties and looked weathered from working mostly outside with too much sun and not enough food. Still, he wore nobility clothing with gold sewn into the borders of his collar. It was a strange combination for Arla to see, but the most noticeable thing about this man was the black patch covering his right eye.

Earlier she had asked what was so special about this Hae-il, in which Rose replied, "Because his Whispers can track down magic signatures. You give him a scent of magic, and he can follow it to its original owner."

Arla was awed. Someone with such abilities could easily lead them straight to Rhyler and then, surely, to Uro. What a find.

When she first met Hae-il, she thought he would be like Leo and Rose, loyal and driven to do good. Because those were the types of people they associated with, right?

But seeing this man in front of her now. She wasn't so sure.

Leo was incredibly stiff. Clearly, he would rather be anywhere but here. "You're the only person who can help us."

Hae-il slammed his mug of beer onto the sticky wooden table where he sat. "And why would I help you? After what you did to me?"

Leo did not respond.

Arla wondered if Rose would say anything, but the soldier stood quietly by her brother's side. She inwardly sighed. It would have to be her. "Sir. Whatever issues you have with Leo, I'm sure we can work something out. A deal perhaps?"

Hae-il looked at her for the first time since she had walked into the room. He ducked low to peer at her face.

Arla tugged at her hood, just to make sure it was covering her enough, although she doubted the man could recognize her under such poor lighting.

He clutched hard onto the handle of his mug. "You make it sound like what this boy did is forgivable. Which means you don't know anything about this do you?" He grinned. "Shall I catch you up little girl?"

Little? She was sixteen. Why was he talking to her like she was ten?

"We don't need to rehash the past," Leo interjected.

"Oh? Is that right?" Hae-il mused. "Little girl, did you know that Leo and I used to work together? You see, here in The Underground, many nobles get into tremendous debt. It's easy to overspend, over-promise. And those generous givers wanted their debts repaid. So, back in the day, I would track down those wanted High-Borns and Leo here would bring them in, usually beaten and bleeding. He was relatively young, but oh so skilled at hurting people. It was astonishing to see so much anger in such a young soul."

What was this guy talking about? Leo was a soldier. A man of principle and morals. He wasn't some thug that just hurt people for money.

She shook her head. "You're lying."

Hae-il leaned back in his chair, smug. "Am I?"

Arla looked at Leo, who looked away in shame.

Oh.

This explained the looks in the street. Why Leo was met with fear and shock here. He was a debt collector. A violent one.

Arla couldn't believe it. She always thought Leo was a pillar of honor and always made the right choices, but turned out, he was a thug as much as he was a soldier. And he had the audacity to tell her *she* was out of line with the council?

She let out a bitter chuckle.

"What is so funny?" Hae-il asked.

"The hypocrisy," she answered. "Fine. Don't make a deal with Leo, make a deal with me. I can pay whatever amount you name."

"And how can you pay me?" He waved her off. "You look like you can't even afford my regular prices."

Arla removed her hood. "Because I am your Queen."

Hae-il gaped, staring for quite some time, before bursting into laughter. "Oh! What a fun thing you've caught, my boy!" He wiped a few tears from his eye. "There are some things money can't buy, Your Highness. And one of them is an eye." He tapped the side of his temple where the eyepatch was. "When Leo here left our last job incomplete, he left me to do it myself. And as you can see. I'm no fighter. So, I failed. And for my failure, they took my eye as payment. You have to love High-Borns. They really know how to punish a guy. So now... I think it's only fair that Captain Treterra here pays the same price."

Arla paused. "You want his eye?"

He grinned menacingly. "I do."

"There has to be something else."

This was not a deal she could make.

He pondered this for a moment and then leaned back in his chair with his arms crossed. "Alright, Your Highness. Make me your consort. The title, the riches, the land. And that includes all the benefits of that role." He leaned forward, close enough that Arla could smell his foul breath. "I can teach you many things, young Queen."

Leo's sword rang as it was pulled from its sheath. Its sharpened tip pressed against Hae-il's throat.

"How dare you speak to her like that," he growled.

And this isn't using power to force someone to kneel?

Arla bit back another laugh. The line of when it was 'appropriate' to use force was not as clear as Leo made it seem.

Simion burst into deep laughter from behind them. "You really shot for the stars, didn't you, one-eye? I commend your gaw, sir, but unfortunately, my Queen's loyalty cannot be bought with favors or blackmail. At least not for long." Simion gave her a teasing wink. "So, I think we can agree on the first exchange."

Silver glinted from Simion's palm.

"No!" Arla yelled.

She thrust her hand out.

Metal pierced through ligaments and muscle.

Blood splattered on Leo's forehead.

Simion's blade stuck clean through her palm, its tip only a centimeter from Leo's eyeball.

Simion gasped, letting the blade go.

Arla grabbed her wrist and brought her hand to her chest, shaking in pain, but she did not scream. This wasn't the time for that.

"Arla!" Leo grabbed her wrist to see the damage, but she pulled away from him. Hurt crossed his face before he redirected it to Simion. Leo grabbed him by the shirt. "You idiot!"

"Stop!" The wound throbbed around the blade that remained embedded in her hand. It was better left in, to prevent further blood loss.

She looked to the one-eyed man, her breathing tight. "As you can see, I'm surrounded by violent people, who will take your head at any moment, so I would be very careful with your next decision. You *will* help us in exchange for more than fair payment and your life."

Unfettered, Hae-il scoffed. "You assume I value my life."

Arla yanked the blade out of her palm, letting out a sharp gasp, and then rammed it straight through Hae-il's hand, pinning him to the table. He screamed and tried to remove the blade, but she held it there, not letting it go no matter how much he scratched and pulled. Her blood oozed down the metal into his own gaping wound.

"Do you value your life?" she hissed.

She could feel the other's eyes on her. They were shocked just like the council was. She could imagine what they were thinking. The previously helpless princess, now a blood-thirsty tyrant, sticking a knife into a poor man's hand.

Hae-il gripped his wrist, trembling. "You're insane."

"Do you?"

He conceded, tears brimming in his eyes from the pain. "I do."

"Then we have a deal?"

"Yes! Yes!"

Arla yanked the blade up, releasing him. Hae-il whimpered as he cradled his bleeding hand. The blade clattered to the floor. Her left hand grew colder as blood dripped to the floor.

Simion stared, paling more with every drop of blood that left her.

Rose pulled the man up from his seat and dragged him toward the bathroom. "Let's get you cleaned up and ready to go."

"We need to close that wound." Leo ripped the edge of his shirt and pulled Arla into the adjoining room, leaving Simion alone in the main one, who remained staring at the floor, unmoving.

CHAPTER 23

Arla noticed little about the unfamiliar room as she marched in with a huff as Leo trailed behind her like a worried handmaiden. Holding the cloth, he grasped her hand to wrap it quickly.

"What did I say about jumping into dangerous situations?" he grumbled.

Arla yanked her hand away, splattering more blood onto the wooden floor. "I don't need another lecture from a hypocrite."

Oh, that reprimanding tone. She hated it. She didn't want to hear it ever again. Who was he to tell her what to do?

Leo grabbed her wrist, more forcefully this time, and started wrapping it again. "We have to stop the bleeding."

She pushed him away, letting the cloth drop to the floor. "Admit it, you're a hypocrite! You had the audacity to tell me I went too far with the council and Ametha, but all this time you were hiding the fact that you beat High-Borns for money?!"

Leo picked up the cloth from the ground. "I needed the money for my mother."

"Don't lie!"

"Arla, you need to wrap that up." Leo tried to grab her hand again, but Arla kept dodging him, splattering more blood everywhere, even on her face.

"There are other ways to make extra money!"

"Arla–"

"You did it because you hate High-Borns and you wanted to hurt them!"

"Arla–!"

"Admit it!" She was an unstoppable carriage, unwilling to stop even if it was heading towards a cliff. "I've seen it in your eyes. When you fought Wilkins. When you were beating Lesandres. You enjoyed hurting them!"

"You're right!" Leo shouted. Exasperated beyond his wits, his beautiful face twisted in anger. "Is that what you want to hear?! It wasn't just for the money. I wanted to inflict real pain. I wanted all High-Borns to pay for how they treated us. You're right. I was in no position to tell you that you were wrong to do what you did, because I've done it too. I still do it now!"

His nostrils flared as his chest heaved up and down in rhythm with Arla's own raging heart.

"Then why did you tell me I was wrong?!" she shouted.

"Because I was afraid!"

Arla startled. This wasn't the answer she was expecting.

Leo looked to the ground, sullen. "I was... I was afraid of losing you."

"Losing me? Losing me to what?"

"To the darkness."

The darkness...?

"I don't understand."

All the anger from before misted away and Leo became soft again. He reached out for her hand again. "Please. Let me wrap that wound before you bleed out, and I will explain."

Arla's hand was feeling more and more numb, but she refused to pay attention to it. How much blood had she lost already? The lights in the room were getting brighter, and beginning to feel a bit woozy. Maybe she should stop the bleeding.

This time, she let him take her hand, and he carefully started to tighten the cloth around her wound. "I was afraid you'd become like me. Angry and resentful. Choosing violence to get your way."

She thought of the smile he gave the young woman, brimming with innocence. "Because you wouldn't want to be with someone who is like that, right? You want me to be a ray of light, positive and innocent all the time."

Leo tied the cloth into a knot, finally stopping the bleeding. Then he looked at her with intense directness. "I *want* you to be happy. And I know too well that when one keeps making decisions from anger and bitterness, it only leads them to misery."

"What do you mean?"

He gave a long sigh and leaned back. "When I joined the army, it was a few days after my father's death and I was... *different* from who I am now. My father. He was a kind man. He loved us deeply and worked hard. Too hard.

"I watched him wither away, his cheeks sunk into his hollowed face like a skeleton. He coughed constantly with permanent dark circles under his eyes. I didn't realize how much it chipped away at me too, seeing him deteriorate like that before my eyes. And when the exhaustion overcame him and he accidentally slept in for too long, he missed the number of crops he was supposed to pick that day.

"Lesandres beat him until his face was no longer recognizable. It was the last straw on his weathered body and within a few days he was gone. I wanted to kill Lesandres for what he did to my father. I wanted to break every finger on the hand that struck him. But I couldn't. Because if I killed him, and was executed. There would be no one to help my mother.

"And so I found another outlet for the rage.

"The moment I stepped foot through the army gates, I was eager to fight. I got into trouble every chance there was. Over anything. Even when it meant I broke my hand or bloodied my nose every week. It was an exhausting way to live, but something in me kept screaming to get out.

"And when we were sent out to fight, I did it with glee. But it still wasn't enough. I wanted to punish nobles. I wanted to see them bleed. And so I took up Hae-il's offer and thought it would satisfy the thirst, but it didn't.

"Every new High-Born I pummeled and brought back to be 'dealt with' made me feel emptier and emptier.

"I couldn't figure out why until the day I met Rose.

"That day, I goaded another soldier into tackling me to the ground. I saw Rose standing on the side with that unreadable expression she always has, you know the one. And I hated it. I hated how she could be so calm when I felt so *much*.

"I tossed her plate to the ground, shattering it to pieces. I shouted at her to hit me. I wanted her to hurt me. Break my teeth in. I wanted to see my blood flow on the ground, but she didn't budge. Instead, she looked right at me and asked, 'Did it make it go away?' That one simple question caused something to ripple through me, and I realized it didn't."

Arla thought of Rose then and the secret that she was a Muren. All that pain she went through losing her parents and her sister caused her to shut her feelings away from the world. She, more than anyone, would have understood Leo's pain in a way Arla never truly could. That made her both grateful and sad at the same time.

Leo held her wrists so as not to touch her injured hand. "I know you've been hurt. And you're angry. And you want to feel powerful. I wanted that too. That's why I joined the army. To learn how to hurt others. Why I took the bounty job." Leo gently took her chin and lifted her face to meet his eyes. "I don't care that you murdered your father. I've killed people too, and I didn't feel remorse for it either. I didn't care that Lesandres was dead. A small part of me even enjoyed it. But another part also knew it was wrong.

And that's the part of me I want to keep. And I think that's the part of you I was afraid to lose when I saw you in the Great Hall."

Leo sighed. "I'm sorry I made you feel like you were a child or a bad person. I was just scared. Arla…I'm… I'm angry… all the time. I'm afraid it will consume me. And in that room, I saw it in you too. I wasn't afraid of your anger. I was afraid of what it would do to you. Of how unhappy it would make you, like it does me. And if it gets a hold of you too tightly, I'm afraid you'll turn to it more than you turn to me."

Arla couldn't believe it. Never in her life had someone said such words to her. She shook with the overwhelming feeling of it all. And more importantly, he was baring himself to her in a way that she was sure he had never done to anyone else. She felt so lucky to have him trust her enough to do so.

"Leo, you're not going to lose me. I'm here."

It finally made sense to her now. Leo was only trying to help her the way she helped him. That's what they did for each other. They kept each other from going too deep into the dark.

Leo kissed the inside of her wrist. "I can't lose you, Arla."

All the hair on her arms stood up. "Oh."

He raised his head. "Oh?"

"I–I'm just still surprised. I thought that after I told you the truth about everything, you wouldn't want to be with me anymore."

Leo smirked. "You think killing a king and forcing an entire room of nobles to do your bidding is going to stop me from caring about you?"

"…Yes?"

Leo lightly brushed his lips against the inside of her wrist again. "I'm too stubborn to be scared off by that."

Were they deranged, speaking of death and affection like this? Maybe spending so long in The Forest did that to its survivors.

He touched the end of her sleeve. "May I?"

Arla swallowed hard before nodding. Even though she did not want Leo to look at her scars, she wanted his touch more.

"Arla... do you know how much you affect me?"

He slowly pulled her sleeve up until the first scar appeared. He kissed it with such gentleness, Arla wanted to cry, because for the first time, it did not hurt. In fact, it sent jolts of longing through her.

"I want to heal everything that hurt you," he mumbled against her skin.

He kept pulling up her sleeve, inch by inch, and with each newly exposed scar, Leo kissed them oh-so-gently.

"I want to make you smile."

His lips moved onto her neck, where his tongue found her collarbone. Arla let out a small sigh.

"I want to argue with you."

He looked almost dangerous when the shadows cut across his sharp features as he lowered her gently to the floor, but Arla was not afraid. In fact, her heart fluttered.

He kissed her jaw, then her ear.

"I want to make up with you."

He hovered over her, his breath heavy. "I want to pleasure you."

Arla stared up at him, her midnight hair sprawled everywhere on the floor. Her heart beat wildly in her chest as heat spread across her cheeks. Whispers, he looked so... lost in her. Like she was the only thing that existed in this world.

Just an hour or so ago, she really thought Leo would no longer want to be with her. That it might have been the end for them, but now... the way he looked at her... she felt almost foolish thinking that. Rose was right, Leo was completely enraptured by her and it was a truth she had a hard time accepting. For so long the thought that anyone could care for her so much this way felt like an idiot's dream. But now, here was this man, strong and grounded, wanting her. And there was nothing more she wanted than him.

She hooked her good hand around his neck and pulled him down to her. His lips met hers with such intensity it sent shivers down her entire body. His hands moved underneath her shirt, exploring the untouched skin beneath.

The more he explored, the more the fire within her grew until it was screaming to be released from a place she had let no one go before. And in the throws of passion, she grabbed Leo's hand and led him to the waistband of her pants.

He gripped the band, twisting it in his fist, like he was trying to stop himself from going further. "We shouldn't, you're hurt."

She lifted her hips against him, eliciting a hiss through his teeth. "I want to."

"Are you sure?"

She kissed him hard before breathlessly replying, "Yes."

He smiled and bent down to her ear. "Hold on to me."

Before she could respond, his hand slid down below.

Arla gasped when his fingers found her. She tightened around him, and he let out a groan. "Arla..."

And then he moved, achingly slow, which sent Arla's head back and, for the first time in her life, she let out a moan. She slapped her hand over her own mouth, half-embarrassed, half-surprised. Leo gently pulled her hand from her mouth. "Don't." He quickened his fingers, which sent another wave of pleasure through her. "I want to hear you."

"But the others..." she barely breathed out.

Leo seemed to have forgotten they were only a room away from their companions. Leo lowered his ear to her mouth. "Then just loud enough for me."

Arla did not know how long they remained on the floor, entwined in each other. She only knew it was after Leo had to kiss her to muffle her last moan before they relaxed into a cuddle on the floor. She wanted to go further, but Leo stopped her, afraid it would exacerbate her injury.

"There will be other times," he assured her.

Which made her flush crimson again. A part of her couldn't believe what they had done in this random room. Leo was the first person to ever touch her this way and it felt amazing and yet so vulnerable at the same time.

"We really should go see a physician now," he said a bit worriedly.

She buried her face where Leo's broad chest met his shoulder. "Just a few more minutes." Feeling the motion of her head going up and down to his every breath felt so peaceful. How wonderful it was to be in his arms again. She wanted it to last forever.

And then came a voice from the doorway, strained with disgust.

"What. Is. This."

CHAPTER 24

Norendra's tall figure loomed in front of the closed door, the final wisps of her shadows disappearing into the wooden floor.

Arla's blood ran cold as they both scrambled to their feet. "Norendra!"

Leo instinctively pulled Arla behind him.

Seeing him so close to Arla, Norendra looked like she might spit at his feet. "So this is the real reason you pardoned them. Deep down, I knew you cared for them, but *this*. This is disgusting. To be involved with someone so *low*."

Arla stepped out from behind Leo. "There is nothing disgusting about it."

Norendra stalked forward, her teeth bared. "What did he do? Did he trick you? It must be. You could not willingly taint yourself with such filth."

"I wasn't tricked," Arla said. "I chose this."

"You know the punishment for this." Norendra hissed.

"And are you going to be the one to punish me?" Arla challenged. "Are you going to exile me?"

Norendra hesitated. Her lips pressed firm into a line. "My loyalty is to Ulsana. I exist to serve it. To make sure it remains powerful." Norendra paused, like she was thinking about what to do. And then, she shook her head. "We cannot afford to lose a queen now. This was just a mistake of a foolish young girl. It's going to be alright, Arla. I can fix this." Shadows crept from the corners of the room and pooled at Norendra's feet. "Do not worry. I will steer you back onto the right path."

Whips of darkness wrapped around Leo's wrists and legs and anchored him to the ground.

"*Benai.*"

A shadow spear pierced up from the floor and shot straight at Leo's head.

"No!" Arla screamed.

Whispers flew out of her mouth, unleashing her creature of wind and water. The room immediately burst apart, the creature too big for the small space. It destroyed the surrounding walls, leaving them exposed to the streets.

Her monster ripped through the shadow whips with its teeth, snapping them into oblivion. People screamed at seeing the creature openly in the decimated room.

So much for being discreet.

Simion raced in, face ashen.

"You!" Arla screamed at Simion. "You brought her here, didn't you?!"

Simion teleported, dodging a spear of shadow before reappearing beside her. "I swear to you, I didn't!"

Norendra swung her hand to focus her shadows on Leo, who was already fighting several shadow tentacles that whipped at him in every direction.

"Stay away from him!" Arla yelled.

"I cannot let you ruin your life!" Norendra threw out her hand, throwing another spear of shadow, but Arla's creature stood in its way once again and curled around Norendra, blocking her vision of Leo.

Arla laughed mockingly. "*Now*, you care about my life? Where were you the last couple of years?"

Norendra's face twisted, like she did not understand what Arla meant.

"You stood by while my father harmed me all my life. You watched me cry out for help, and you did nothing!"

"It was not my place to meddle in his personal affairs."

Of course. In her typical fashion, Norendra showed no remorse or guilt, which only incensed Arla more. Her heart tightened as she strained to ask the words that made her feel like she could unravel at any moment. "Did you ever care about me at all?"

Norendra paused, as if Arla had hit a tender point. "How can you ask me that?"

A sudden burst of black lightning struck the ground between them, sending them flying in opposite directions. Coughing, Arla rolled to her side, but hissed in pain when her injured hand tried to push her upright again. She couldn't see where Norendra or Leo were. Were they alright?

Footsteps approached her. "I heard you have been looking for me."

Norendra screamed from somewhere in the chaos.

Shadows enveloped Arla, shielding her.

And then a deafening crash took over the room. Before she could react, something hard hit her behind the head and darkness took over.

CHAPTER 25

Arla's vision came back slowly, her head still throbbing from the blow. She reached to touch it, but her hands did not move. She tried again, but nothing. Snapping fully awake, Arla realized she was in a small room, bound to a chair, and her hands were tied roughly behind her. She shouted, but a leather muffle silenced her screams.

In an instant, her memory transported her back to the arena, bound to a chair, forced to watch Leo whipped to unconsciousness. Was this a nightmare?

The pain from her wounded hand jolted her back to reality. No, this wasn't a memory. Once again, she was restrained.

"Good, you're finally awake."

Arla's eyes snapped up to see Rhyler leaning against a wooden table across the room, watching her with curiosity. Without the hood or the darkness to shroud his face, he looked much younger than she originally thought. The dark circles under his eyes aged him, but he looked closer to thirty than forty.

After all this searching, she was finally facing the assassin out to kill her. She quickly scanned the room and realized she was alone with him.

Where are the others?

As if reading her mind, Rhyler spoke. "They aren't here, but you'll see them soon. I wanted to ask you a few questions alone." Rhyler pushed himself off the table. "My people told me you and some Ulsanan soldiers ventured into the center of The Forest and survived its wrath." He knelt in front of her, grabbing her chin. "Not only that, but you came back with magic." She tried to rip her chin out of his grasp, but it only made him hold on tighter. "It's very strange..." he said, forcing her to look into his eyes. "Very strange indeed."

Arla yanked her face away, trying to kick and pull at her restraints, but the ropes wouldn't budge. She shouted the words that would summon the worst of her creatures, ones dripping with acid and mud, but the muffle kept her mute.

He cocked his head to the side. "You're different. I can't take from you what I can take from others."

Arla glared at him to show him she wasn't afraid of whatever he was planning to do to her. Sighing again, Rhyler motioned for his guards to surround her as he untied the binds around her feet.

Fool.

The moment the rope loosened, Arla kicked up at Rhyler's face, but he caught it with ease and forced it back down.

"Behave," he commanded. "Or I will bind your feet back together with something worse than a rope."

The warning brought ice to her veins. The guards lifted her up and pulled her toward the door.

"Come. There is something I want you to see."

CHAPTER 26

The guards dragged Arla across the floor. They were still in the Underground, in some basement that looked more like a cave. How many dingy dark rooms were there here? The place was filled to the brim with people with sunken eyes and scraggly clothing. *Low-Borns.* A few she recognized from that cruel platform game, bruised and mangled from the ordeal and clumsily patched up with cloth and splints.

And in the center of the room was a small raised platform, large enough for a handful of people to stand on.

They pushed her along the edge of the crowd, keeping a hood over her head to hide her face, and then stopped just in sight of the platform, but far enough away that she was not part of the crowd.

This confused her. Why was he making her an observer?

Rhyler walked onto the platform and looked out into the crowd. Judging from their confused faces, it was clear they did not know him. Rhyler raised his hands in the air to quiet the crowd. "Thank you for waiting, good people of Ulsana."

From across the way, Arla spotted Leo, Rose, and Simion, restrained and gagged just like her. Much to her relief, they looked uninjured. Leo was scanning the crowd, looking for her. She wanted to shout for him, but she was still muffled.

Rhyler continued to speak to the crowd. "I'm sure you're all wondering why you've been gathered here. Well, it is because something needs to be said. A truth that has been hidden for too long." Rhyler looked at the crowd, his expression growing serious. "I was like all of you once, a simple cook from Yeler, forced to live out my days performing backbreaking labor as the High-Borns profited from my pain. They used to laugh as they beat me for sport, saying I deserved it because I had no magic, or at least, that's what I was told. But I am here to tell you all that is not true."

The crowd murmured to each other in confusion. What was this strange man saying?

Rhyler looked slightly behind him and gave a slight nod. A cloaked figure hiding in the crowd came up to the stage, and when they reached the center, the figure pulled back their hood.

Arla gasped behind her muffle.

There stood a young boy, his eyes sunken from lack of sleep, his dark hair disheveled from lack of washing.

Uro.

He was right there! Uninjured and alive. Relief washed over her as well as a sudden burst of adrenaline. Arla struggled against her guards, trying to get to the young boy, but they yanked her back.

"Do you recognize this boy?" Rhyler asked the crowd, looking for confirmation. "He's one of your own. Born in a poor Low-Born village, like many of you. Tossed away by his parents, he was forced to become a soldier against his wishes, or else he would have starved. This is a common story in our ranks." He raised a finger for dramatic flair. "But it's not a story we have to continue anymore."

He motioned for someone else to come forward and, in a few moments, a burly man dragged a woman onto the stage.

Arla paled. It was Norendra. Her nose was broken and bloodied and her usual pulled back hair was yanked out and disheveled, draping over her shoulders. They had gagged her, just like Arla. She couldn't believe they were able to capture Norendra at all. She was a formidable Whisperer and not easily defeated.

The brutality of Norendra's injuries did not seem to faze Rhyler. In fact, he looked at her like she was not even human. "Today I will show you the truth you deserve to hear. This is Norendra Renden. The Queen's primary advisor and the former King's as well, famous for her unique shadow magic. For years she has helped those in power keep us Low-Borns on our knees, begging for a respectful life."

Us *Low-Borns?*

The sentence buzzed in Arla's ears.

Norendra uttered something incomprehensible behind her muzzle, her eyes still sharp in defiance.

Rhyler ignored her. "She sees herself as a protector. Responsible for keeping Ulsana safe." Rhyler turned to Norendra with hate in his eyes. "But you have only protected *your* Ulsana. The kingdom you believed it should be. The same one that forces us to live in suffering. If that is your purpose, then you are no longer needed because there is a new Ulsana coming, and you do not belong in it."

Rhyler gripped Norendra's throat. His mouth uttered words Arla couldn't hear. Her head pounded from sudden pressure.

Black veins crawled underneath Norendra's face, pulling something from her and into Rhyler's hand. It moved up his arm and into his head. Norendra struggled helplessly against him, her eyes wide as her muffled screams unleashed from her throat.

Arla couldn't breathe as she watched her advisor, who never showed fear, seize up in terror.

Within seconds, Norendra's skin shriveled and turned a sickly gray until the light drained from her eyes. Finally, he pulled his hand away, sending Norendra's limp body to the ground like she was trash.

Arla screamed, lunging for Norendra, but the guards pulled her back. She railed against them, but there were too many holding her down.

Uro stared down at Norendra's shriveled corpse, horrified.

Rhyler motioned for Uro to come to him, but the young man did not budge. A pulse of irritation crossed Rhyler's face before his pleasant smile quickly replaced it. Rhyler glided across the stage to him with open arms. "I know it is scary, but everything will be alright. Trust me."

But Uro remained frozen.

Rhyler bent close to Uro's ear. "She hung a Low-Born once, for spilling hot soup on her lap."

Still unsure, Uro looked at Norendra's corpse and then back at Rhyler. "She was cruel to us."

He said it like he was trying to convince himself. Why did he do that?

Nodding, Rhyler placed both hands on either side of Uro's ears. "Yes. She was. They all are. And now, it is time we take back our power." Closing his eyes, his forehead furrowed in concentration. "*Kere-ishim nalan.*"

White veins glowing with gold crawled down Rhyler's neck, into his arms and through his hands into Uro's ears. Uro cried out in pain and clutched onto Rhyler's shoulders to stop his knees from buckling beneath him.

Rhyler continued to Whisper. "*Hul jowa.*"

Tears fell from Uro's eyes as he strained to keep his pain contained, and just as he opened his mouth to scream, Rhyler let go. Uro dropped to his knees in a cold sweat, struggling to maintain his breath.

Without giving Uro time to collect himself, Rhyler crouched down, speaking sweetly to the boy. "Can you hear them?"

Uro remained in a fetal position, covering his ears.

"Uro." Rhyler repeated, his tone firm. "Do you hear them?"

Uro stared wide-eyed at Rhyler. "I hear... something."

Rhyler stepped back, letting Uro take center stage. "Then, by all means, let it out."

Uro shook his head. "It's too... painful."

Rhyler frowned and grabbed Uro by the back of his collar. "Life is pain. We have to learn to push past it. Now," he yanked Uro up. "Speak what you hear."

Uro continued to shake.

"Uro," Rhyler hissed.

With trembling hands, Uro reached out toward the floor. "*Benai.*"

Slowly and awkwardly, small slivers of shadow squiggled up from the floor like wispy grass.

The crowd gasped.

Arla stopped breathing. *No, it can't be.*

Those were Norendra's shadows.

"How can this be possible?" someone asked from the crowd.

"You are a Low-Born!" another shouted.

Uro choked. In an instant, the shadow retreated into the floor, disappearing, leaving Uro stunned to silence again.

Rhyler put a reassuring hand on Uro's shoulder. "It will take practice, but you will get it." Pleased, he turned back to the crowd. "We have been taught our entire lives that magic belongs only to the High-Borns because they were 'chosen' by The Forest, but that is a lie! Magic does not just belong to them. It belongs to all of us. It is a natural force that flows through everything. We just need to be taught how to harness it. My followers have already learned how."

One by one, figures in black hoods along the edge of the crowd released their magic. A woman blew ice from her breath. Another levitated a few feet off the ground. While another conjured water in the palm of his hand.

The earth underneath Arla spun. Her world was crashing around her as she tried to grapple with what she was witnessing. It was incomprehensible.

A Low-Born just wielded magic in front of her. Something history had told her was not possible.

"There are no chosen ones!" Rhyler shouted. "The nobles created these boundaries and kept magic from us to keep them in power and oppress us! They have burned their own history books to keep us from knowing the truth!"

"He's right!" someone shouted.

"They're liars!" another yelled.

Seeing the crowd turn in his favor, Rhyler grew wilder in his gestures, taking on a more menacing look. "I have been beaten and humiliated all my life just because I was a Low-Born. You all have! Well, no more! You all deserve better! And the nobles need to pay for the suffering they've caused! Follow me, and I will give you the magic you are owed! I will lead you into a new world, and the nobles will burn at our feet!"

The crowd roared. "Burn them! Burn the High-Borns!"

Their chants shook the cavernous room with the stench of violent desire until it was all Arla could hear.

CHAPTER 27

Time seemed to move without her as Arla was led back to the dingy room they started in. Rhyler's followers forcibly tied her back to her chair, her mouth still gagged. She could barely comprehend what was going on when a group of people entered and started chanting. A golden dome encompassed her, caging her within. To her surprise, Rhyler stepped into the dome with her.

His eyes filled with wonder at the beauty of the golden dome. How could he speak so joyfully? A swirl of hate and fury raged in her blood. How could he act this way when he had just murdered her advisor in cold blood? She glared up at Rhyler, wishing he would keel over and die right there.

Unbothered by her murderous glare, Rhyler unclasped the bind around Arla's mouth.

She wasted no time. "*J'en-ath gurth-u dal!*" She waited for her creature, but it did not come.

"It's extraordinary, isn't it?" Rhyler motioned to the surrounding dome. "Magic that can repress other magic. Of course, it takes a large number of Whispers for it to work. Luckily, I have followers who can hear those Whispers."

"*J'en-ath gurth-u dal!*" Arla shouted again.

Rhyler gave her a bored look. "I told you, your magic does not work in the dome."

She wanted to try again, over and over until her throat was hoarse, but she knew Rhyler was right. She was just as powerless now as she was before The Forest and she hated it.

"Is it all true?" she asked.

"Nothing can be truer than what you see with your own eyes. And if the scholars of the past hadn't burned the evidence, you would have seen it in your own history books."

"But why did you kill all those High-Borns? For revenge? To take their magic?" Rage filled her, remembering everything this monster had done. "You killed Norendra."

"If it were the other way around, do you think she would have lost any sleep killing a Low-Born like me? How many Low-Borns lives have ended by her hand?"

The memory of the hanged thieves flashed across her mind. Arla remembered how Norendra looked at their writhing bodies with no sympathy.

"It doesn't make you any less of a cold-blooded killer," she spat.

Rhyler chuckled to himself. "You think you're a victim, don't you? An innocent who has been wronged. Did you not hear a word I said? *You* are the problem, not us. We are always suffering under the thumb of you nobles." Rhyler pulled up his left hand with a missing ring finger. "Your kind cut off my finger just for looking at one of you in contempt once. And these scars." He pulled up his sleeves to reveal the hundreds of healed cuts on his arms and Arla could not help but think of her own burns on her own arms. "Each one for being late, for serving the soup too hot, for being too quiet, too loud, and some were just for fun, but the worst one is the one that gave me my magic. Do you want to know how I got the Whispers?" Rhyler leaned closer to Arla, hatred in his eyes. "The noble family I worked for decided they wanted to play a fun little game. It was called, 'How long can Rhyler run for his life?'

"They said if I wanted to keep my life I would have to outrun their horses. The entire time they rode behind me they threw rocks at my back, shouting at me to run faster. Cackling. They chased me like the animal they believed I was. And just as I reached The Forest's edge, they decided they were bored and finally, one of them shot me in the back. But I did not die.

"I crawled my way through The Forest, asking why my life was meant to be this way. Why did I suffer for no reason? And that's when I saw him. A man with red eyes. And then I collapsed. When I finally awoke I was fully healed as if nothing had happened, but I knew something was different. That day, I heard the Whispers and learned what I could do. All I need is to grab someone's throat and I can take the magic from them. I can hear the Whispers they heard and use them and give them away."

Arla could only stare at Rhyler. No one deserved what he had faced. It was the type of cruelty that scarred a person so deeply it made them into a killer, but this knowledge didn't quell the rage she felt toward him.

"You don't have to kill the High-Borns for what you want."

Rhyler let out a bitter laugh. "I disagree. It's the only thing that seems to work. When we asked for equality peacefully, they hung us."

The memory of swinging feet stung across the back of Arla's mind. She remembered how justified Norendra looked that day.

"If you ask me," Rhyler sneered. "You all deserve to die."

Arla stuck her chin up, challenging him. "Then do it already. You want to kill me, I can see it in your eyes, so why haven't you done it already? Why did you keep me alive to watch your speech on the platform? Wouldn't killing the Queen be a bigger statement than an advisor?"

Rhyler pulled back, his face darkening. "If only I could. I cannot take your Whispers, Queen Regent. At first I didn't understand it, but now, being near you, I can feel it. You were blessed by The Forest. Just like me."

The air grew heavy as Arla felt a wave of intense magic shroud them, growing the longer they remained close to each other. Whatever magic The Forest gave him was reacting to what was swirling within her.

Rhyler's expression softened. "You feel it too, don't you? What powers me, powers you. When you were in The Forest, did you see him?"

Him?

Arla said nothing.

He sighed, suddenly looking very tired. "I don't understand why you were gifted the language like I was. It does not make sense, but it doesn't matter. I will fix it in time."

"In time? You plan to keep me here alive?"

"For as long as I need until I learn how to take your power."

"Why do you want my power so badly?"

"The Forest knows it made a mistake giving power to the greedy all those years ago and it chose me to fix it. You are the last piece. With your abilities I will become unstoppable and then finally…" Rhyler broke into a smile. "All High-Borns will die."

CHAPTER 28
Simion

How extremely unfortunate.

Simion stared directly into Leo Treterra's eyes. They were so dark it reminded him of the unknown abyss hidden in the deepest cracks of the ocean. It was the ugliest sight Simion had ever seen. Leo's frown deepened the longer Simion stared, no doubt wanting to tell him off, but alas neither could, because they were both bound and gagged to chairs facing each other in Whispers knew where.

The other soldier. What was her name again? Rosette? Roselyn? She was tied to a chair directly behind Simion out of his view.

He sighed inwardly, wishing it was her he was facing instead of the grumpy captain. Women were always easier to look at.

Their room had neither windows nor furniture that made it stand out. Only a wooden door and a slow drip of water coming from the ceiling that was starting to irritate him. Perhaps they were below a bath, or... Simion gagged, a sewage line.

If only he had Whispered himself away in time, he wouldn't have been caught by that Rhyler fellow and he wouldn't have been forced to see that boy take Norendra's magic.

He had truly never been so shocked in his life, which was an uncommon state for him. He had spent so many nights burning an exorbitant amount of candles in the library, reading everything about Ulsana's history and never had they mentioned that The Forest had gifted magic to *everyone*. He really did not like not knowing something.

Simion pulled against the ropes that held his hands behind his back. If only he could get this gag off somehow before Rhyler's lackeys came in here and killed them off. Or worse, torture them for fun before ending it all.

Was that what Rhyler was doing to Arla right now?

Something sharp blocked his throat at the thought of that. If he could take Norendra's powers so easily, he could surely drain Arla until she too was nothing but a wrinkled bag of skin. He suddenly felt nauseous and panicked at the same time, which surprised him.

Was he worried about Arla?

How silly. Of course he was, but not because he cared about her well-being, but because she was his ticket to gaining power of his own. She was merely a ladder to step on to elevate himself to a position where no one could touch him.

This thought rendered an image of himself physically stepping on Arla's hand as he rose to the top, the very hand he had accidentally stabbed while trying to gouge out Leo's eye, and it brought up that uncomfortable feeling again.

He was a man of logic. Of self-service. Of political ambition. His only goal in life was to climb so high that no one could look down on him ever again. And the only way to get what he wanted was to give that mercenary what he wanted.

An eye for a literal eye seemed the most fitting at the time, but when that knife drove into Arla's hand instead, he found himself horrified.

He could not believe she would go that far to protect the captain. What was it like to have someone care so much about you, that they were willing to be stabbed for you? Simion did not know. The only people who populated his life were those who would toss him under carriage wheels without flinching, just to get ahead. And he was fine with that.

In his life, he had learned that smiles were for getting someone to put their guard down; they weren't for expression of joy. Yet, disgustingly, he found himself grinning against his will with *her*, for no purpose other than to share a bright moment.

Rosette/Rosanna/Ronnie/whatever her name's head knocked into the back of his skull hard. He let out an aggravated yelp. What was that woman trying to do? She knocked her head against his again. He returned the action, letting her know he was not one to be trifled with. She stopped and started wriggling in her chair. He felt fingers tug at his rope.

And then it all made sense. She was trying to get to his rope. He stretched his wrists toward her as much as he could without feeling like his arms were going to snap off. It seemed she could reach them, even though he could not reach hers. It was probably the height difference.

He felt her fingers tug hard at his wrists. Finally, after what felt like hours, the rope loosened. Simion yanked his arm as hard as he could, freeing his own hand. In one swoop, he pulled the gag from his mouth.

"Wow, that took long enough," he joked, although he was sure Rosetta was not smiling from behind him. Leo grunted, directing his eyes to Rosyln/Roma's restraints. He was expecting Simion to free her too.

He looked down at Leo. What had this Low-Born done to make Arla care about him? And... could Arla care about Simion just the same way?

He shuddered. What was he thinking? He needed to go. Save himself first. That was the way of this world. He would return and tell the good people of Ulsana that the Queen was dead, leaving room for Ametha to become Queen Regent. That old crow would be easy to manipulate, and soon she would make Simion her First Advisor. A spot that conveniently opened up recently.

"Oh, no thank you. I'm fine." Simion said to Leo, rubbing his wrists. "I think I'll take my leave now." He mockingly saluted Leo. "Good luck, Captain."

Simion didn't stick around to hear Leo's muffled shouting. It wasn't worth his time. He felt the ground move beneath him as his body disappeared, pulling him along an invisible plane as it always did when he teleported until he would inevitably land in the main castle courtyard where he would—

He lurched unexpectedly, as if he had tripped over something, and fell face first into hard dirt. He coughed, holding his bruised nose.

This was new.

He sat up, realizing he was in another windowless, dark room built of grey stone. Impossible. How was he here? He could only teleport to places he had already been, and this was not a place he'd visited before. What was this?

Wood rattled behind him.

Simion turned, and his mouth dropped open.

Arla was tied to a chair, her back to him, struggling against the ropes that bound her. She screamed beneath her gag, turning her wrists red with effort. At this rate she was going to chafe her wrists right off. Unless... that was her plan.

Judging from her efforts, it seemed like it was.

What an idiot. Hurting herself just to get free. Probably for some trivial reason like wanting to rescue them. Who did that?

So, so... stupid... He watched her struggle without helping. She was clearly getting tired, and yet she persisted. Simion should have pitied her idiocy, but instead he found himself... admiring her effort. No. Admiring her stupidity. No. Pitying her stupidity. Yes. That was what he was doing.

He turned to leave. He had to ensure his own safety. He had to –

His body moved without his permission, and before he knew it, he was standing in front of Arla.

She blinked up at him, eyes wide in shock. Made sense. He stared down at her with the same expression, just as shocked. He expected the usual look of disgust to form on her face next, but her eyes softened, and she looked... relieved.

Simion froze.

What was this tingling feeling?

Simion slowly unbound her mouth, still numb to his own body. Was he possessed?

She half-coughed, half-spit out the words, "Simion! You're alive!" Her voice quivered with ecstatic relief, which made the tingling in his limbs become worse. Was he suffering from frostbite? Or perhaps an unfortunate degenerative disease that decided to appear at this very moment.

"Unfortunately for some, yes, I am alive," he said as he untied her arms, freeing her from the chair.

His eyes went to her wrapped hand. The cloth was dyed entirely red.

He reached for it.

She shot up immediately, unaware of his hand. "We need to find the others!"

He silently cursed. She wasn't going to leave this place without the soldiers, was she? He could have lied, told her they escaped so they could leave.

But then he found himself worrying, *what will happen if she finds out the truth?*

So what if she did? Why would that matter?

He didn't know exactly why, but he realized it *would* matter to him.

So, he reluctantly replied, "I know where they are."

Simion kept low behind a group of barrels, motioning for Arla to crawl to him. Making their way back to the room he had just escaped from was a pain in the ass. His original suggestion of teleporting alone was denied immediately. Arla insisted they stick together. Which was why they were now crawling across dirt. He really hated getting his clothes dirty.

"Which one is it?" Arla asked, peeking her head just barely above the barrels.

"How can I know?" he replied curtly. "I've only seen the inside."

This was going to take forever. They would have to check every room. And then get past more than a handful of Rhyler's followers lurking in the dingy underground hall. How were they going to get through all of them?

Simion was annoyed for letting himself get dragged into this situation. This was the opposite of survival. This was so stupid and illogical and–

A man burst out of a room into the hall. "They're gone!" He pointed at the nearby guards. "You three go north, you two to the south. You four come with me! We'll search the grounds!"

Simion couldn't believe his luck. He gave Arla a shrug. "Well, looks like they escaped safe and sound, so we can go."

Arla pulled him by the sleeve away from the hall. "We need to find them before they do."

He pouted. "And put ourselves in more unnecessary danger? They escaped. They are probably headed for the castle. We can meet them there."

"I need to know they are safe."

"Aughhhh." Simion slapped a hand to his face. "Fine!"

They crouched low, ready to crawl away when a foot stepped right in their path. They both looked up to see an older man staring down at them. "They're here!"

Simion pulled her from behind the barrel. "Time to run."

They rushed down the hall and up a flight of stairs as another man joined the first behind them.

"Stop!" the two men shouted.

Arla opened her mouth and then thought better of it. The hall was way too small to hold one of her conjured creatures. They popped back onto the crowded street of The Underground. Good. The more people, the harder it would be for them to be found.

"Run into the crowd!" Simion shouted just before he disappeared.

Simion reappeared just behind the man closest to Arla and landed right on top of him. Arla kept running further into the crowd, who cursed her as she shoved past a flurry of color-clad passerby.

One down. One more to–

A fist knocked him backward. Simion fell onto his back. A passerby screamed, dispersing the crowd.

Not good.

The second man held a rock above his head, ready to crush Simion's skull with it, but then he was suddenly no longer on top of him. The rock tumbled beside him as none other than Arla tackled the man to the ground. She grabbed Simion's hand and yanked him up.

His skin prickled with a strange sensation at her touch.

"Hurry!" she shouted.

Sweaty and out of breath, they ran deeper into the crowd, up through the entrance and burst out the front, where the guard of silence stumbled back in surprise.

"Don't mind us," Simion patted the brawny guard's large bicep. "We're just so excited to have–" His throat closed up, the silencing magic doing its work. He coughed. "Well, you know."

"Come on!" Arla shouted, running past him.

"Always a good time," Simion grinned at the guard one last time before taking off behind Arla.

They kept running until they were out of the cave entrance and off the road, hiding in a pocket of darkness in a nearby wood. Only when Arla made sure no one had followed them did she allow herself to relax a little, bending over and trying to catch her breath.

Her face was flushed pink from running, her little button nose flaring with each new intake of breath. He found himself absorbed as he watched every part of her expand and shrink.

"We have to go back for them." Arla took a step back toward where they had come.

He grabbed her arm, exhausted by her insistence.

"Are you dumb?!" he hissed. "Do you have any sense of self-preservation at all? We barely got out ourselves!"

She snatched her arm away, equally irritated. "Unlike you, *Simion*, I protect the people I care about. They are worth risking my life for, and I would do it over and over again."

"You are such a self-righteous, stubborn—aughhh." Simion lost the words. She was so frustrating. Never in his life had a woman gotten under his skin deep enough for him to lose his words like this. He wanted to shake the senses back into her, and he almost did, when his eyes fell on her bandaged hand. "You're bleeding again."

Arla gave her hand a cursory glance. "It doesn't matter."

She was right, it didn't matter. It shouldn't have mattered. But all the irritation left him then, and he suddenly felt the urge to tend to her wound. What was this?

"You're not going to give up are you?" he asked, fisting his hands so he wouldn't reach for her again.

"No."

Simion gave a big, theatrical sigh. "We won't be able to go undetected. Not like this." He groaned inside for what he was about to suggest. "Let me teleport around and find them first, and then I can lead them back here."

She squinted at him, no doubt suspicious. As she should be. "We'll go together."

"Do not worry," he purred. "I will not abandon you."

"I'm not worried about that. If you were going to abandon me, you would have done so by now."

"Then why do you insist on coming with me?"

"So I can make sure *you* don't get hurt."

Simion let out a laugh. He didn't know how else to react. No one had ever said this to him before. Surely, she was joking. Who said things like this, especially with such earnestness in their eyes?

"Pfft, *you* want to make sure *I* don't get hurt?"

Her face remained serious. Oh, Whispers. She wasn't joking, was she?

"Yes," she said. "I don't want to see you get hurt. Is that so bad?"

Simion just stared at her, dumbfounded. Probably looking like a fool with his mouth ajar.

And then her expression changed. Her eyes brightened like the stars, and oh, how she radiated.

She moved towards him, her arms reaching for him.

His heart stopped beating.

Was she going to hug him?

Her mouth opened into a dazzling smile.

She *was* going to hug him, wasn't she? *Oh, Whispers.* He instinctively opened his arms. It wouldn't be so bad, would it? No, it wouldn't. It would actually be... nice. It would be–

Her hair brushed his cheek as she ran right past him.

"Leo!" she exclaimed.

Simion turned around to see the captain, covered in dirt and sweat, which unfortunately made him look even more ruggedly handsome. Why was he always wearing light-colored tunics too tight around his chest? It was disgusting the way he showed off.

Arla threw her arms around the brute.

Arla inspected the captain's face and arms. "Are you okay?!"

Leo nodded in silence, his eyes full of relief, tracking Arla's every movement. His gaze grew dark when he noticed the blood on her lip and the bruises around her wrists. He lightly placed a finger on her jaw.

Arla blushed at his touch and put her bleeding hand behind her back. "I'm fine."

Pangs of *something* traveled up Simion's chest. The way the captain's gaze bore into Arla's, Simion knew this relationship had gone beyond a passing affection.

"Good," replied Rosanne/Rosette/Romaine, who appeared just behind Leo.

Great. The captain's righthand survived as well. Just great.

Leo noticed Arla hiding her hand and carefully pulled it back into view. His eyebrows furrowed. "It's bleeding again." He gripped the end of his shirt, about to rip off the edge.

"Ah, ah, ah." Simion stepped between the two and pulled out a handkerchief from his pocket. "I got it, Captain, thank you kindly."

Arla gaped at Simion as he quickly undressed her wound. When he saw the pierced skin and muscle, he winced. "It must have hurt." He didn't mean to say the words, but they came out anyway. "I didn't mean for it to happen that way."

Leo gripped Simion's shoulder, squeezing it painfully. "You bastard."

Simion jutted out his chin at him. "Why are you so angry, Captain? Are you the only one allowed to help her Majesty? Awfully eager to be close to her, are you?"

He knew fully well that wasn't what Leo was angry about, and yet he wanted to tease him anyway. Or rather punish him, but for what, he wasn't quite clear yet.

Arla jumped in. "It's okay, I can do it." She grabbed the handkerchief from Simion and awkwardly fumbled to tie it with one hand. Simion and Leo both reached for her.

A frustrated grumble. And then suddenly, the female soldier was between him and Arla, tying the last knot around Arla's wound a little too tightly and too fast, which made Arla yelp slightly.

Simion pushed Romainia. "That was too tight, imbecile!"

In hindsight, he shouldn't have done that. Because it finally pushed the captain over the edge.

CHAPTER 29

Arla was so relieved that Leo and Rose were safe. Unfortunately, that relief was short-lived.

Leo shoved Simion against a tree and pinned him underneath his forearm. "You conniving little man," he growled. "You dare to act this way after what you did? I knew you would abandon us the moment you were free!"

Arla tugged at his shoulder. "Leo! Stop!"

"You High-Borns think you can treat us this way?!" Leo shouted, baring his teeth. "You took everything from us. Our lives. Our freedom. Our magic! You conspired to shove us under your feet!"

Simion disappeared from under Leo's arm and reappeared behind him. "Unfortunately, Captain," Simion brushed off imagined dirt from his collar. "I wasn't there when the decision was made to keep magic from you Low-Borns, so your displaced rage is pointless."

Leo lunged for Simion again, only for the latter to disappear and reappear again several feet away. But that didn't stop Leo from chasing after him.

"Leo!" Arla shouted again. "It's not his fault! He didn't know. Neither of us did. And he didn't abandon us, he helped me escape, and look for you."

Leo glared at Simion. "Did he tell you that he—"

"What's really important is that we're together again," Simion said. "AND that we leave now before they catch up to us."

Leo and Arla spoke at the same time. "Not without Uro."

Simion grimaced. "Oh, that boy that got Norendra's magic?" He scoffed. "I don't know if you've noticed, but he seemed pretty fine with his new friend Rhyler."

"He's clearly being manipulated," Arla rebuked. "We need to get him out of Rhyler's grasp."

Simion squinted mockingly. "But is right now the best time to get him? I don't think Rhyler is going to hurt his poster boy, and we're not exactly in the right position to get him back. If he even *wants* to come back."

"Of course he wants to come back," Leo spat.

Yes, Arla thought, *of course he wants to come back.*

"Look," Simion said. "A powerful Whisperer just announced he is going to try to kill all High-Borns, not one little boy Low-Born he just gave magic to. If we give chase to find this Uro now it could take us a while and there will be no one to warn or help the nobles."

"Why don't you just go warn them then, High-Born?" Leo snapped.

"I don't think that kind of message should come from me," Simion retorted.

Arla thought over what Simion said and, unfortunately, it made sense. They were in no position to find Uro right now and Rhyler was out to kill more nobles. "Maybe Simion is right."

Leo looked at her with disbelief.

"We will find Uro, but right now, we need to regroup and create a plan. I don't believe Rhyler would hurt Uro now that he has… Norendra's magic." She swallowed back her emotion. "He can defend himself better now. Her shadows were very powerful."

For a moment, it looked like Leo might have argued with her, but eventually his shoulders slackened. "You're right, we need a plan."

"Actually," Simion stuck a finger up in the air. "I think you mean *I'm* right. I said it first."

Leo moved to grab Simion's collar again, but the scholar disappeared out of his reach.

"There is something else we need to discuss," Rose interjected, flashing the boys an annoyed look. "We've just learned something that could rewrite Ulsanan history forever, and we need to decide what to do with this new knowledge."

"We need to tell the Low-Borns," Leo said.

"Oh," Simion reappeared beside Arla. "Do we now?"

If Norendra were here, she would have refused to tell the truth. Keeping power was the most important thing to all nobles, but it wasn't the right thing to do. Arla had always felt that the way they forced Low-Borns to live was cruel and thought that she was changing Ulsana in her own way, but now those small changes felt like nothing at all. They were not enough to create the world they deserved.

A world where Leo had no reason to resent the upper class. Where his father would have lived. A world where Uro didn't resort to siding with a killer to be free of his shackles. A world where Rose did not have to hide her true identity.

"Yes," Arla replied. "Everyone deserves to know the truth. Everyone deserves an equal chance at magic and a good life."

Leo looked at her with relief. "We should tell them immediately. We need to hurry back to the castle and–"

Arla gently touched his arm. "We can't tell them now."

"What do you mean?"

"You've seen the tension between our people. Telling them now without a plan could cause more harm than good. We need to choose the right time."

Simion nodded in agreement. "Wise. Very wise, my Queen."

Leo's eyes widened. "The *right* time? And when will that be? Days? Months? Years? How much longer do Low-Borns have to suffer?"

"And how many will die if we tell them now?" she countered. "There will be a rebellion. Fights in the streets. People will die on both sides. I want to keep everyone alive."

"You want to keep us in our place!" Leo snapped.

It was like he had slapped her. The sting of his words held her silent, and Leo immediately recognized the hurt he dealt.

He looked away from her. "I'm sorry. I know it's not... you."

The fact that he was not completely convinced of his own words, worried Arla. He must have noticed because he quickly defaulted to glaring at Simion like he was the one at fault for their problems.

Simion mockingly raised his hands in the air. "Are you going to attack me again, Captain?"

Leo marched toward the fool with his fists clenched, ready for another round, but Arla stepped between them, sick of their fighting. "We can't distract ourselves with this."

"She's right," Rose said.

Arla almost choked on her own saliva. Did Rose just agree with her?

With both hands on her hips, Rose gave out a long, laggard sigh. "We cannot recklessly rush into something as big as this."

Leo frowned. "The more space we put between *knowing* the truth and *telling* the truth, the more time the High-Borns will have to stop the truth from coming out."

Simion perked up. "You know what I think, Captain? I think you are afraid." Simion closed in on Leo. "But I am not. Do you know why? Because I trust our Queen will get the truth out, but I don't believe you do."

Arla looked at Leo. Was Simion right? Did Leo not trust her to do the right thing? Or did he not trust her to be capable of it?

Emotion drained from Leo's face, leaving behind a neutral mask. He spoke in a strained, even tone. "It's not that I don't trust her. I just don't trust the other High-Borns." He turned to her. "They will try to stop you."

Arla tried to ignore that he had put on his mask, hoping it wasn't because of her, but because of Simion. "I won't let them. I promise."

To her relief, he finally softened. "Okay. I trust you."

CHAPTER 30

There was no body to bury. Arla did not know where Norendra's remains ended up after that horrid night in The Underground. She preferred not to think too much about how Rhyler disposed of her advisor. No doubt it was unceremonious.

Arla stood alone on that bitter dewy morning at the edge of a lake, holding onto a golden wreath with her mostly healed hand and a torch in the other. She stared out into the fog that hung low above the water and let the dreary silence seep into her bones.

Yesterday, when Arla had returned from the Underground, she immediately announced Norendra's death to the council. She was disappointed to see that no one mourned the loss. Instead, they were only concerned that Rhyler had been able to kill Norendra so easily. They huddled together, fearing for their own safety, and demanded Arla double the guards allotted them. They also vetoed a grand funeral because they feared Rhyler would find his way into the crowd and attack. Begrudgingly, Arla agreed. Rhyler wanted them all dead, and what better way to gather them in one place than a funeral?

Which was why Arla stood alone now, on a gloomy morning, staring at a lake, cradling a modest wreath of ivy and gold in her hands.

She had purposefully not told the council that Rhyler and his band of followers were all Low-Borns, in fear that the council would retaliate against the Low-Borns in the city. Instead, she let them continue to believe he was just a noble out for more power, a lie that was easily believed.

Arla placed the wreath at the edge of the water, hoping the golden blooms were bright enough to light Norendra's soul back to The End, where all life returned.

Dry grass crunched behind her. Arla swiveled to see Rose marching toward her.

"Rose?" Arla looked for signs of distress from the soldier. "Is something wrong? Did something happen?"

Rose looked around as if she were expecting more people there. When she was sure it was just the two of them, she crinkled her nose like she smelt something foul. "Makes sense." She stood beside Arla. "Where is Leo?"

Of course, Rose was looking for Leo. That's why she was here.

"I didn't tell him about this," Arla replied. She thought it would be too mean to ask Leo to honor Norendra, when she had tried to kill him.

"Mmhmm." Rose crossed her arms and stared out into the water.

Arla waited for Rose to leave.

"Why are you staring at me?" Rose asked.

"I just told you where Leo is, so shouldn't you be leaving now? You got what you wanted."

"I wasn't looking for Leo." Rose waved her hand forward to usher Arla to continue the funeral. "Get on with it."

Arla stared at her, dumbfounded. She did not understand what was going on, but she did as she was told and crouched low with the torch and lit the wreath. Using the wooden end of the torch, she pushed the wreath toward the center of the lake before dipping the flame into the water to smother it out.

Typically, this was when someone would say words of admiration for the deceased, but in this moment, Arla had none. There was a time when Arla would have tried to say something kind, just to make others feel at ease and show there was a brightness in everything, but she wasn't that person anymore. Instead of wanting to ease others, Arla found herself desiring truth instead. And the truth was bitter.

"No matter what I did, I could never please her, just like my father."

Rose crossed her arms, her brow wrinkled in thought. "Maybe she thought that tough love would have strengthened you."

Arla gritted her teeth as the anger nipped at her heels. "It wasn't love. It was shame. She thought I was weak."

"Or maybe she just wanted you to survive this shitty world."

Arla dropped the now smothered torch onto the grass. "You don't have to say something nice about her just because she is gone. She always hated the fact that Low-Borns were allowed to look her in the eye. If she had it her way, she would have had you all crawling on the ground beneath her feet."

Rose grunted in acknowledgment. "She was not my favorite."

"Then, why are you here?" Arla asked curtly. If Rose was going to keep defending Norendra, Arla would much rather be alone with her anger.

Rose kept her eyes on the burning wreath, bobbing its way further down the lake. "I'm not here for her."

"Then why are you—"

Oh...

Arla realized what Rose truly meant.

She is here for me.

Arla's eyes stung a little from the bubbling emotion in her chest. She held it back, afraid that any sign of tears would send Rose heading for the hills.

Arla sucked in a breath. She wished she could understand this enigma of a woman. Did Rose hate her or care for her? Maybe it was both.

Even though Rose's tone was distant and cold, her words were kind. Maybe Rose wanted Arla to see Norendra in a more favorable light, not for her advisor's sake, but for Arla's. It was always more comforting to believe that someone loved you, even if it was in a cruel way.

"Even if she was mean and cruel and never had anything nice to say to me…I—" Arla's voice cracked. "I hope she was trying. I hope that she did care. Because I cared about her." She let out a bitter laugh. "Does that make me stupid?"

"I think it makes you human."

Arla huffed out another laugh. And another, until she was laughing out of her belly. She didn't know why she was cackling like a madwoman. It was like her body needed a way to expel the sadness in her soul, and this was the only way it could do it.

Norendra was gone. Arla would never hear another lecture from her again.

And that last thought turned her laughter to tears.

Rose did not say anything to try to cheer her up or stop her crying, instead, she remained silent and unmoving. To anyone else, it would have appeared cold, but Arla knew that Rose wasn't trying to be cruel, in fact, it was the opposite.

She was acting like an anchor in the sea, unmoving and solid, to keep Arla from getting lost in the waves of her sorrow.

And so Arla held onto that anchor and let herself weep, for the advisor she despised, the woman she admired, and all that could have been if they were only given more time.

CHAPTER 31

Losing Norendra affected Arla more than she thought it would. It left her a little lost. Norendra usually accompanied her to every meeting and guided her when she did not know something, but she was no longer there to do those things. And so Arla was left to face the council and enact judgement on the woes of nobles alone. The various papers she had to read and sign made little sense to her now that Norendra wasn't explaining things.

It left her exhausted. And on this particular day, as she struggled to go over large stacks of policy and laws she did not quite understand, she felt was just about to explode from overwhelm, when a small note slipped under her door. Curious, Arla picked it up.

6pm. Kitchen.

Based on the handwriting, she already knew it was from Leo. Even the way he wrote was direct, just like him. Arla couldn't help but snicker a little at it.

The day moved incredibly slow until, finally, the clocks turned six. She couldn't get to the kitchen fast enough, and when she pushed open the doors she was shocked at what she found.

Leo was incredibly focused, standing by a large pot of boiling liquid. His brows furrowed in concentration as he tasted some mysterious spice from a jar with his finger. Satisfied with the flavor, he sprinkled it into the pot.

His shirt was half unbuttoned due to the heat of the stove, revealing a lot more of his chest than usual. He turned to her with a smile that made her knees weak. "Right on time."

"What are you doing?" she asked innocently.

Leo stepped back from the stove and dusted the leftover powder from his hands. "I thought I would cook for you."

She pointed at herself sheepishly. "For me?"

Leo nodded and pulled out a chair for Arla to come sit at the table beside him. Arla practically skipped there. "I hope you're hungry."

"I'm always hungry."

He grabbed a ladle and dipped it into the pot. "It's not something you would find in a recipe book." He turned around with the ladle in his hand, blowing gently to cool the thick liquid. "Try this."

She drank the broth and almost fell off her seat. It was so good. Rich in beefy flavor. Just salty enough with a hint of sweetness from the carrots. "Wow."

"You like it?"

"It's amazing. How long did it take you to make?"

Leo poured her a bowl and placed it in front of her. "The broth takes at least an entire night to simmer for the best flavor, and the rest of it another three." He was about to sit down when he noticed something. "Oh. The spoon." He got up and retrieved the spoon before placing it beside her bowl. "My mother used to make this soup for me whenever I got sick, and it has comforted me through tough times. I was hoping it would do the same for you."

Arla looked down and fiddled with her fingers.

"What's wrong? Does your stomach hurt?"

"I'm just so lucky, that's all." She touched the outside of the bowl, like the precious thing it was. "Thank you for this. Things have been... really hard lately. For both of us."

Leo reached over and put his hand over hers. "It has."

His touch comforted her, and she squeezed his hand back. "Remember when I cooked that soup for you and Uro in the meadow? It wasn't good, was it?"

"It was... an experience."

Arla laughed. Oh, Leo. Always trying to make her feel better.

"I hope he is okay."

Leo's expression became solemn.

"I don't mean to bring down the mood," she continued. "But I can't help worrying."

"I'm worried about him too. That's why the longer we wait, the longer we risk something bad happening to him."

Arla nodded. "We need to get him back. Once I figure out how to tell everyone the truth."

"It doesn't have to be complicated," he said. "Just tell them."

"I told you, it needs to be in a way where no one will get hurt."

"I don't think you understand, Arla. There is no outcome where no one gets hurt. This kind of lie... people are going to get angry."

Arla scratched at the edge of the bowl. "Then what do you suggest I do? You think it's easy, being the one to decide?"

"Of course it's not easy, and you're not alone in the decision. I will be there when you tell them. They will see a Low-Born soldier supporting you. That's a good thing."

"I just don't think that's the right thing to do."

Leo pulled away. "I see."

The entire mood changed and she felt the distance he put between them.

"There's got to be some other answer." She pushed. "Something better. Where no one has to suffer."

"You keep saying that."

"Because it's true," she urged. She wanted him to believe her. That she was delaying for a reason, but the warmth in his eyes had left already.

"Right." Leo eyed the soup. "You should eat. It's getting cold."

He got up and stirred the pot more with his back to her. They did not talk much after that.

CHAPTER 32

Arla paced the empty throne room late into the night. Her dinner with Leo made her feel so unsure of herself. What was she going to do? She stared out through the glass at the ghostly moon, full and bright amongst a starless sky. The white hue reminded her of Wynera when she first met her in The Forest.

"Did you know the truth too?" she asked.

A familiar breeze encircled her, looping through her hair and fingers before forming into an opaque shape of the princess lost to history, sitting on the windowsill.

Wynera looked almost inhuman in her ethereal beauty, and her voice was like a cool ocean breeze, chilling her bones. *"I knew."*

Arla stepped closer, trying to see more details of the spirit that had changed her life. Wynera looked so melancholic, which was heartbreaking because Arla knew what Wynera looked like when she was happy in her memories.

"Who are you really?" Arla asked. "How did you become this way?"

Wynera looked forlornly at the moon. Its rays cut through her ghostly form, making her eerily glow. *"In the beginning, The Forest gave magic freely to all those it deemed worthy. It loved humankind. So much so that it birthed its own creature that resembled one of them. A gift."*

A gift. The words sounded familiar... Arla sucked in a breath. "It was you, wasn't it? *You* were the gift."

Wynera nodded. "I was found and raised by a noble family. They were kind, albeit willingly ignorant of what was going on around them. When I was born, the shift was already happening. Those blessed with magic became greedy for power. They wanted the Whispers for themselves, so they made a pact to spread lies about who could wield magic and created the separation between Low and High-Borns. They sent their armies to The Forest to prevent anyone from entering and killed off those that disagreed with their plan. By the time I came of age, the classes had already formed and I was engaged to the king, but I loved another man."

Arla couldn't help but feel bad for Wynera whenever she mentioned her love. She couldn't imagine having to watch the man she loved killed in front of her. Well... she almost did, didn't she? Images of Leo's bleeding back as he was whipped in the arena made her cringe.

"What was his name?" she asked.

Wynera smiled sadly. *"Dehen."* She looked at Arla. *"I begged The Forest to help us. To show us a way to be together and it told me the truth. That I could help my love gain magic and together we could make a new life."*

Arla was surprised to hear this part of the story. Her brief flashes of Wynera's memory did not show her this. She couldn't help but grow hopeful. "So you know how to transfer magic, just like you did to me? Just like Rhyler can? How? How did you give magic to Dehen?"

Wynera grew sorrowful, looking at her feet. *"I did not give him magic. I knew that if I told him the truth, he would want justice, which would surely have gotten him killed. I could not let that happen."*

Arla leaned back in disbelief. "So you kept the secret."

Wynera nodded. *"It was a mistake to lie to him."*

Arla realized how complex Wynera truly was. She had killed Arla's father but also saved Arla from dying in The Forest. She was a being that lied to her love but also wanted to save the world from a murderer like Rhyler. It was hard to tell what she would do next.

"Then help me not make the same mistake." Arla urged. "How can I give people magic?"

"You cannot give magic. Only The Forest can do that."

"But you gave me magic."

"I transferred my magic to you, and it formed into something entirely different within you. It was... unexpected."

"Rhyler can transfer magic too. He can take it from others and give it away."

"But he cannot create new Whispers. That's the difference."

Arla was growing frustrated. So only The Forest could give someone new Whispers, whilst Rhyler could transfer them at the cost of the original wielder's life. "I don't understand. Rhyler said he went to The Forest, and it gave him this magic. It must have known what he would do with it, right? Then why—wait... does The Forest *want* Rhyler to kill all the High-Borns? Is that why it gave him this magic?"

Wynera opened her mouth, but no sound came out. Her form faded instantly, like she was yanked back to where she came.

"Wynera!" Arla reached for her, but it was too late. She was gone.

The morning light crept along the floor. What time was it? Had she really been awake all night long?

A frantic knock sounded from the door, and then Rose entered the room.

"Arla." Her tone was quick and short. A bad sign. "Leo's mother is missing."

CHAPTER 33

"Leo!" Arla barged into Leo's room. "Your mother, she's—"

"She's not missing." Leo calmly folded a black tunic on his bed.

"What do you mean? She isn't in her room." Arla looked around, hoping to see Yolan there. Maybe she was hiding behind the door.

"It's because I've moved her," he said. "There is a village a few days south of here I've gone to before. They are kind people, and they've agreed to house her."

"Why would you do that? She's safer here, in the castle."

"Is she?" Leo folded another shirt carefully into a small square.

And that's when Arla noticed what Leo was wearing. Thick boots. Shirt and jacket made for travel. His sword was strapped to his side. And then there was the open bag on the bed, already half-way full of clothes and food rations.

"Are you going somewhere?"

"I'm going to find Uro. Make sure he's safe." He still did not look at her.

"Rhyler won't hurt him."

"We don't know that for sure. It's been weeks, Arla. Things change."

"Then, I will come with you. Let me just pack my bags."

"I don't think you should."

She stopped short. "Why?"

There was a long silence. Leo's fingers lingered on top of his bag. "Because I don't know if I'm coming back."

"I don't understand."

"Arla..." He said her name in such a soft whisper it made her ache. "I can't stay here any longer knowing what I know."

What was he saying? She didn't understand. "We're going to find an answer. We're going to solve this."

"Are we? I've given you options on what we could do. I've waited and tried to help, but you still haven't told the truth or decided on a plan."

"I told you–"

Leo threw a shirt into his bag in frustration. "You're making excuses, and you know it."

His anger flared her own. "So you're going to find Uro and just disappear? You're not going to stay and help?"

"Help do what? Help High-Borns keep their magic? Or help Low-Borns finally get what they deserve?"

Arla stepped back from him. "What they deserve? You sound like Rhyler."

Leo tied his bag closed. "Maybe Rhyler isn't completely wrong." He closed his eyes and took a breath. "This place has only ever brought me pain, and I'm tired of suffering. I'm tired of feeling like I'm fighting on the wrong side."

"You realize that Rhyler's side involves killing High-Borns. People like me."

He gave her such a look of such despair, it made Arla rethink what she just said to him. "No, Arla, never you. I would never hurt you. Look, I don't know what I'm going to do, I just know that I need to find Uro."

He picked up his bag.

She jolted in panic. She was going to lose him. If he left now, he would never return.

She gripped the doorframe, physically blocking his only exit. "Don't go, Leo. What happened to not losing yourself to your darkness?"

Leo pressed his palm into his forehead. "I don't know. I don't know anything anymore. I just know I can't be here right now."

No. No. No. He couldn't go. He couldn't just leave her. After everything they've been through together, this was how it was going to end? She would not allow it. Urgency and panic jostled her, reeling up a beating heart soaked in desperation. A heart that beat to one truth.

"I love you," she blurted out.

It was something she knew deep down but was holding back for the right time. And now that she was going to lose him, she needed him to hear it. To know the real consequences of his actions and who he was leaving behind.

Leo breathed in deeply, shaken by the confession. "Arla..."

"Please don't abandon me here to face this by myself," she begged.

Don't leave me.

He stared at her for a moment, taking her in and then slowly placed his bag back on the bed.

The world lightened again. It was working. He was going to stay.

But she could not ignore the shade of resignation on his face. He wanted to leave, but his heart held him in place, and she knew it was because he loved her too, but there was no joy in his eyes in this truth, only a grim defeat.

And then Arla did something she rarely did before; she thought of the future.

She foresaw Leo staying for her, all the while his soul festering from continuing to defend a side he did not believe in. And then one day he would realize she was not his love, but his prison, and he would see her tears and love confessions as chains. And he would hate her for it.

She was not experienced in love, let alone romantic love, but she was sure that it wasn't supposed to be used to control someone.

And even though she was terrified of what would change if Leo walked out that door, it was not her decision to make.

She forced herself to pry her fingernails from the doorframe and unblock the way. "I'm sorry. You have every right to be angry. And you have every right to choose." She picked up the bag and gently placed it in Leo's hands, careful not to brush her fingers against his. It would have been harder if they had touched. "I hope you find what you're looking for."

And I hope you come back.

Leo tightened his grip on the bag, his eyes speckled with sorrow. "I'm sorry."

He brushed past her and through the door so fast she was sure it was because if he didn't, he would have stayed. Arla's eyes lingered on the door, waiting. Because even though she knew she had made the right decision, she still wished he had turned around and come back for her, but he never did.

CHAPTER 34

The first time she met darkness, she was shoved into it.

She was only ten when she saw the group of boys hovering around a newly formed hole in the wall in the southwest tower. The castle had been slowly falling apart, and stones had been cracking and collapsing everywhere, but her father made sure to fix most of the damages, except for this side of the castle. And this time, the crumbling of the structural arch in a small hall had left behind a rather large hole that caught the curiosity of the High-Born children.

Arla twisted the fabric of her sleeves in excited nervousness. She had been wandering alone for so long, she was desperate for company. Maybe these boys could become her new friends.

One boy with dark skin and even darker eyes, began to climb inside. "Let's see what's in there."

Another yanked him back. "Are you stupid? It's unstable. It could collapse on us."

"What are you doing?" she asked shyly as she approached the hole.

The cautious boy swung around, at first curious, but when he saw her, his face immediately twisted in disgust. It was an expression she would grow used to over and over again from the young Simion. "Nothing involving you, Princess."

"Maybe I can help," she squeaked.

"Maybe you can just go away." Simion waved her off, his eyes still on the mysterious dark of the gaping hole.

Arla threw her chin up. "I am your princess, you can't treat me this way."

Simion cackled, his white teeth glinting. "No one considers you Ulsana's princess. You don't even have magic! No one cares about you."

"Yes, they do!" Arla argued, even though she knew Simion was right.

A cruel amusement flashed across his pupils. "Should we test this out then?" He rubbed his chin. "Yes, let's test it. Let's see if anyone cares about you, Arla."

He shoved her hard. It was too fast for her to even shout. Her heel caught on the jagged edge of a broken stone, and she tumbled backward into the darkness.

Laughter echoed above her as she fell until stone met her again a few seconds later.

She let out a cry of pain.

"You should get used to it in there!" Simion yelled from above. "Because no one is going to come for you! No one will even notice you're gone!"

The laughter on the other side faded far away until only silence was left.

The ache in her back held her in place for a while until it stopped throbbing enough for her to get up. It was so dark wherever she was that she could not see a foot ahead of her. Arla curled up into a ball, her tears soaking her feet.

This was the first time she had experienced Simion's cruelty. And it was also the first time she had discovered the hidden tunnels that looped and dipped behind the walls of the castle.

She had waited in those tunnels for an entire day hoping someone would come for her, but no one did, just like Simion said. So she wandered for another day and a half, until the tunnel led her to an opening in the kitchen, where she climbed out, starving and weak.

·

She used to hate the tunnels. It reminded her of how alone she really was, but now, six years later, as Arla stepped barefoot onto the cold stone, the darkness felt like home. A place she belonged.

A small breeze went through her unwashed hair. It was as if the tunnels were once again greeting her.

Five days had gone by since Leo had left, and the only thing that brought her comfort was this place. And so she found herself often sitting against the wall in the dark, going over the problems that needed to be addressed. What she should do. What she *needed* to do.

What if I make the wrong choice? Can I live with the consequences? Can Ulsana?

Will I ever see Leo again?

She wasn't the only one Leo had abandoned. Rose, too, was left behind, or rather, she chose to stay. Rose had told Arla that Leo had come to her and asked her to join him, but she refused.

As much as she wanted to connect with Rose over the shared loss of Leo, all she could think about was the fact that Leo had asked Rose to join him, whilst he did not give the same offer to Arla. He wasn't even planning on telling her he was leaving.

Did she mean so little to him? Was she so easily cast aside?

'No one cares about you at all.'

Simion's words once again pierced her.

She sat in the cool dark for hours, oscillating between deep thought and emptiness until soon emptiness started to win out. This type of dark was a dangerous place for a mind to wallow. A depth she was afraid she was wading too deeply into, and yet she could not pull herself out.

Maybe she could hide here forever. Maybe this time, she would not try to leave the tunnels.

A puff of shadowed smoke suddenly burst beside her. Wobbling arms and legs struggled to find balance before falling backward onto Arla's feet. Arla shouted, pushing the figure from her.

"Ouch!" The figure coughed, pulling himself up.

"Simion?" She blinked in disbelief, trying to see Simion's face, but it was barely visible in the dark. "What are you–how did you–"

"Ugh. It happened again."

She could tell from his tone that he was confused and, strangely, concerned.

"I thought you could only teleport where you've been," she accused. "You lied."

"I didn't lie." Simion replied, clearly offended. "My magic has been... changing lately. I've been hearing more Whispers."

"You have?" This piqued her curiosity. This had never happened before. Usually, once a High-Born got their Whisper during puberty, that was it. No new Whispers appeared after that. "You can teleport anywhere now? Even places you've never seen?"

"Seems that way. But sometimes it sends me places I wasn't even intending to go. It's like it's drawn to–" He paused.

"Drawn to what?" she asked.

"Nothing." Simion rose and dusted himself off. "What is this place?"

Reluctantly, Arla answered, "A tunnel behind the castle wall. They loop around the castle."

Simion scraped his finger across the stone. "Oooo, secret tunnels. So this is where you've been hiding. How did you find this place?"

"When you shoved me into a hole six years ago."

Simion remained silent in the dark.

Arla did not try to fill the silence. She wanted it to linger. She wanted him to remember what he had done.

"I think you've been here long enough. Let us go, shall we?" He reached out his hand, which was close enough for Arla to see. There was something crusted around his fingertips.

"What is on your hands?"

He quickly pulled his hand away from her. "Are you coming or not?"

His curt tone sent her onto the defensive. "No, I'm not."

He paused for a second, like he might say something sincere for once, but the moment flittered past and instead he scoffed. "Suit yourself."

He made to shove past her, pushing his shoulder into hers, but the moment they touched, the entire tunnel sucked into itself.

CHAPTER 35

"*Tre'lehen... ah-naq.*"

Arla gasped as she fell forward into a well-manicured garden, lined with torches. Simion stumbled beside her.

"Did you just teleport us?" she asked, irritation biting at her heels. "You have no right to—"

Simion straightened his jacket. "I didn't do it on purpose."

Arla thought of the Whispers she heard Simion say. "I thought your Whisper was *Tre'lehen*."

"It... was."

"But you said something else after that. *Ah-naq*. Did you... did you hear a new Whisper?"

"Not new... just extended. It just came to me just now."

"But that's impossible."

"I thought so too."

High-Borns only heard their Whispers when they hit puberty and did not hear new ones for the rest of their lives. And what little Whisper they did hear was usually just one word.

Simion stared down at his hands in disbelief. It was then that she finally noticed that they were covered in white powder. The edges of his nail beds were bleeding from dry, cracked skin. What could possibly cause those—.

Her back pressed against something cold, too cold to be human. She turned and gasped. Not two inches from her face was an all too familiar outstretched claw, palm faced up toward the sky.

"My statue..." she breathed out in disbelief.

Its three snake heads curved at awkward angles. Pieces of its etched scales were missing, while the rightmost head was gone altogether. Its lion-body was battered with holes, barely standing on its three partially re-glued legs. Its one reaching arm lacked the slenderness it had before, instead, it was cracked in every direction with random stones jammed into it.

Arla touched the middle snake head fondly, her mouth still open from shock. There were stone pieces that were so small that it was a miracle they were found at all. One could tell it was a painstaking process to do. "You put it back together?"

Simion scoffed, folding his arms. "Barely. Fun fact, fractured stone is almost impossible to patch perfectly, but you seemed stupidly attached to it when it broke, so I thought I would give it a try."

She turned to him then, swept up in emotion. "Why did you do this?"

"*Why* were you in the dark for so long?" he retorted.

Arla was about to snap back, annoyed by his rude tone and insensitive words, but his expression stopped her. Despite the fact that he was grimacing like he was disappointed in her, his eyes looked... concerned.

He pointed his chin at the statue. "Your ugly statue is back now, so stay out here with it instead of in those dreary tunnels, shut away from everybody."

It didn't make sense. This was his chance to take control of the council. In her absence, he could have gathered more support, manipulated others to follow his orders, but instead he spent his precious time meticulously collecting broken stone and putting this statue back together piece by piece for so long that his fingers bled?

"Are you ill?" She wasn't sure why she asked.

"I don't know." He said it so genuinely, like even he could not understand his own actions.

"You've been saying that a lot lately."

Simion rolled his eyes. "That fact has not escaped me." Avoiding her analytical gaze, he picked up another stone from a pile on the ground and pretended to look for its spot in the statue. "So are you going to stay out of those tunnels now?"

Arla sighed as she picked up a small stone of her own and busied herself in finding its rightful home. She was about to place it in a crack where she thought it might fit, but then she suddenly worried that if it was too small, it could get stuck and they would not be able to get it out and then it would never find its rightful place, ruining the entire statue. She hovered over the placement, neither putting the piece in nor taking it away. That was the problem, wasn't it? This indecisiveness of hers.

Her overthinking was cluttering her mind, blocking her. And she needed to let it out, or else it would explode.

"I don't know what to do about the truth... Ever since I got this crown, every decision I've had to make has felt so heavy. There are consequences to my actions that affect everyone. And everyone has wanted me to make them so differently. Norendra wanted me to be ruthless, like my father, and for a moment I tried to be like that, and it was disappointingly effective. Leo wanted me to be kinder. And I wanted to not make a mistake." She drew the stone back to her chest. "I don't know what the best decision is. I don't want people to get hurt. I don't want to be the reason everything falls apart."

Simion shoved his rock into a crevice where it clearly did not fit. Instead of pulling it away, he took a chisel and a hammer and started chipping away at its edges so that it would mold into the place he wanted it to go. "My parents expected the best from me. To be the most charming, intelligent, powerful person in the room. There was not a sentence I spoke that wasn't corrected. No action that wasn't scrutinized. I had to be the best, there was no room for error. They wanted me to be a scholar for the sole purpose that one day I would be First Advisor, so I could sit in the second most powerful seat in all of Ulsana." He hammered the chisel harder into the stone. "If I wasn't that, I would be nothing. And so every day I studied." He hammered harder. "I acted." Another strike. "I played the part. Nothing was allowed to go wrong." He gave the chisel a final hit, and the stone cracked in two, both pieces falling to the floor. He dropped the tools on the ground and looked at her. "I know what it's like to feel like you can't make a mistake."

Arla wondered how much of himself Simion had to chisel away to fit his parents' expectations of him. How many pieces of himself did he abandon on the floor while he climbed for power for someone else's sake?

"It's a terrible feeling," he said.

"Yes. It is."

Simion picked up another stone and went back to chiseling it into the perfect shape.

She held onto the small stone in her hand. "I thought you were going to give me advice, or a solution."

"Like a wise old sage?"

"Like a First Advisor would."

Simion snorted. "Is that a job offer?"

"No."

"I do not work for free, Your Highness."

"But you do still work for me."

Simion laughed. "That is true, my Queen." He pressed the stone against the statue to squeeze it in. "What do you know for sure, *Arla*?"

The way he said her name made her nervous, but she chose to ignore his tone. "What do you mean?"

"What are your truths? The things you don't have doubts about?"

She took a moment to think about her answer. "I know I care about my friends. I know I want to be a good leader. And I know I want to tell the Low-Borns the truth, but I don't want anyone to get hurt. I also know I don't want to be like my father, but I also know that every tactic he used wasn't entirely horrible. No one is completely evil or completely good, there is an in-between we all live in. Even Norendra had a point about needing allies…That's it!" she exclaimed, turning to Simion. "We need allies! On both sides, to support our cause and calm each side without inciting a rebellion."

Simion thought about it for a moment and Arla was sure it was to criticize or reject her idea, but instead he widened in equal enthusiasm. "We can start with a small group, make sure they are trustworthy and then once we get enough, we can have a public announcement. I know who would be more willing to help than others among the nobles."

"Because you know everything that happens around here?"

"Exactly. You see? What you once found annoying about me is proving to be incredibly useful now, isn't it?"

"We need to start right away." Arla practically ran to the door in utter excitement.

Simion followed her with equal fervor. "Right behind you."

Arla paused, her hand on the knob, and turned around. "Simion. Do you really want Low-Borns to know the truth?"

"At this rate, that is the future we are heading towards, seeing as how you are a Low-Born sympathizer. And I just go with the tide."

"As long as you are on the winning side."

Simion clicked his tongue as he nodded in feigned-wisdom. "You know me so well, Your Highness."

A small smile crept up her face. "I guess I should be flattered that you believe the winning side will be mine."

He smiled back and, shockingly, it wasn't laced with sarcasm or cruelty, just humorous delight.

"I didn't know you could smile like that."

He playfully smiled and touched his cheek. "Should I tuck it away?"

She laughed. "No, it suits you."

He suddenly grew serious and he held her gaze, like he was genuinely touched by what she said. And then he shrugged it off, like he was uncomfortable with such real emotion. "Let's go find some Low-Born sympathizing nobles."

CHAPTER 36

For the first time in what felt like a long time, Arla felt emboldened by her decision, and it was all thanks to Simion. It was peculiar that it was him of all people that ended up helping her in her time of need, but she was quite thankful for it even though she still held some resentment toward him too.

She had to keep reminding herself that Simion was still that cruel boy somewhere deep down, because lately he was doing so much to prove otherwise and it worried her that it made her vulnerable to whatever trick he may pull in the future. Still, it was getting harder and harder to convince herself that Simion was still a snake.

In their last meeting, Simion had mentioned that he had found a few possible candidates to approach, but wanted to make sure their interests aligned with theirs and that they were the type that could keep secrets, which Arla thought was the right decision.

Arla held the squirming Jun in her arms as she tried to rock him to sleep in his nursery. Already he was heavier than the week before and more active. He was itching to learn how to use the strange appendages attached to him. He grabbed her hair out of curiosity, which had Arla hoping he had not learned how to yank things yet.

A knock came from the door before swinging open with dramatic flair. Arla turned expectantly, knowing who it would be. Ametha strolled into the room, her golden hair tied up in a well-groomed bun, every inch of her once again refined. She was looking quite well for someone who, less than two months ago, was curled up in a corner cell.

She reached out her arms, not looking Arla in the eye. "It is my turn now."

Arla willingly gave Jun to her stepmother.

She had released Ametha soon after coming back from Rhyler's grasp, and over the weeks they had come to a tense understanding. Arla could visit Jun, but Ametha would still have the majority say of how he was raised. It was an extension of goodwill that Arla hoped would blossom into a tolerable relationship, where Ametha would at least stop looking at her with such disdain.

Jun wiggled as Ametha tried to release his grip from Arla's hair until finally Arla gently unclasped his fist.

"He's been fussy this morning." Arla pulled at a rolled-up sleeve around Jun's pudgy arm.

"Of course he was. He was without his mother."

A young servant girl with hair the color of fire, slipped into the room, her head bowed low. Ametha snapped her fingers and pointed at the crib by the window. "Get it ready."

The girl hurried over and began preparing the crib, neatly folding the blanket and rearranging the sheets.

"I'll be back to visit tomorrow morning," Arla said, but it incited no reply from Ametha. Accepting that she was no longer wanted, Arla turned to go, making it to the door when she heard a loud gasp.

Did Ametha see something on Jun? A rash?

Arla turned.

The scene before her did not make sense.

Ametha was slightly bent.

And a knife was jutting from her stomach.

The servant girl stood rigidly straight, her shoulders back in pride. Her dress was stained with Ametha's blood, and hooked in her arms was Jun.

Jun.

The girl grabbed Jun and thrust open the window, letting in the afternoon wind.

No!

Arla dashed across the room. The girl saw her coming and pulled another knife from behind her skirt.

"*I'et lamel al'para-tet!*" Arla screamed.

Vines pushed through the stone cracks and whipped at the girl's face. The knife clattered to the ground as Arla reached. Her hands met soft roundness. She pulled Jun free from the servant's grasp and brought him to her chest as a vine yanked the girl to the ground.

She willed the vines to multiply and wrap themselves over and over around the girl until she was completely subdued.

Arla's heart pounded against her chest as Jun cried. She turned to her stepmother, whose wild eyes stared up at her.

"Ametha!" Arla fell to her knees, trying to rip off part of her shirt to wrap the wound with her free hand. An impossible task.

Ametha took another strangled breath before grabbing Arla by the collar. Her mouth opened and shut, but no words came out. And then in a blink, the light faded from her eyes, and she was gone. Arla stared down at her stepmother.

This wasn't real. How could it be? It was too fast. Too sudden.

She shook Ametha. "Ametha! Ametha, wake up!"

The girl cackled behind her. "Serves you right!" she spat. "You all deserve to die!"

Jun's cries grew louder in Arla's ears.

"Who are you?!" she shouted.

The servant grinned sinisterly. "I am revolution. I am your reckoning, High-Born."

And then Arla remembered. Those hatred-filled eyes. That bright red hair. This was the girl that glared at her in the market when she took Leo's mother away.

From the corridor came a sound that made Arla's blood turn to ice.

The bell.

The bell was ringing.

Ulsana was under attack.

The girl closed her eyes, as if listening to a beautiful symphony. "He is here."

CHAPTER 37

Clashing swords rang down the hall, growing closer by the second. Arla left the servant bound to the vines and ran into the hall before the attackers found them. They needed to get out of the castle. Jun let out a loud wail. Arla's skin spiked in panic. She couldn't let the invaders hear them. She pivoted and ran into her room, locking the door behind her. She would be safe here temporarily, until she could figure out a way to–

A creak alerted her to the figure behind her.

He stood like a statue in the shadows of her room.

Rhyler.

The armoire was open, and in his hand was the tattered journal. The one that saved them from the worst of The Forest's horrors.

How did he get in here?

His tall frame and dark walnut hair made him look even more threatening in the shadows of her room and yet he seemed so relaxed. In fact, he seemed unaware that she even entered the room at all.

Arla clutched the still-crying Jun closer to her, trying to hide him in her arms as she backed toward the door. She was in no position to fight Rhyler right now with an infant in her arms.

Rhyler gently flipped to another page with a nostalgic expression. "Uro told me all about the journal that saved your lives. The moment he told me, I knew it was mine."

Arla froze.

His?

Her mind tried to wrap itself around what he had just said. *The journal is Rhylers? No, he's lying.*

"I don't know why, but something compelled me to write about my journey. I wanted to warn other Low-Borns who were forced into that nightmarish place like me." He slapped the journal closed with a grimace. "It wasn't meant for you noble scum."

The pieces slowly came together. He told her earlier he had survived The Forest, the only one to have done so in a hundred years, didn't he? So, her survival was thanks to him?

Arla continued back toward the door, she was almost there.

"I found it in the library. Why was it there?" she asked, hoping to buy more time as she inched her way back toward the door.

Again, Rhyler got lost in his memories, allowing himself to reminisce. "I worked here for a little while to gain allies, so that they could one day help me take over the castle. It was frighteningly easy. When you nobles believe we are harmless idiots, it breeds opportunity for us." He tossed the journal back into the armoire like it was tainted. "Ironic that it was me that saved your life in The Forest, isn't it? Or was it all some sort of plan in which we are both just pawns? Maybe you are my final test. The last thing standing in my way and I must prove that I am strong enough to overcome it." Rhyler looked at her, his eyes full of calm, violent intention. "I've learned that I cannot take your magic, Princess. So there is now only one other option."

She grabbed the doorknob behind her.

"*Dem'an'al'i un seol.*"

Black lightning cracked alive from Rhyler's fingertips and shot out at her.

Arla ducked just in time as the lightning destroyed the door, sending wood splinters everywhere.

Before she could speak, the heat of crackling sky shot at her again. Dread filled her. She would not be able to dodge it this time. She braced for the searing pain.

A gust of wind encircled her as a familiar feeling went through her.

Wynera?

Rhyler shouted in pain and when she looked, he was holding his chest like he was having a heart attack. Wynera's spirit floated above them.

Black ooze floated off of Rhyler's body and into the air.

Another man's voice, much deeper and much more agonized, screamed. "*No. No. No. She must die!*"

Arla blocked Jun's ears from the boom of this crazed voice.

Rhyler clutched his skull. "Shut up!"

Now was her chance. She darted out of the room and peeled down the hall. She needed to get to the tunnels.

She ran down a flight of stairs, but her mad dash caused her to step too short. She flew forward, losing grip of Jun. For a moment, he was levitating out of her arms and then gravity brought him down, head first toward the stone.

She screamed, reaching for him in desperation.

And then the air distorted. Someone grabbed her arm and pulled her back.

"*Tre'lehen ah-naq.*"

Everything blurred around her and then the world snapped back into place, placing her somewhere else entirely.

Simion held her wailing brother in his arms in front of her.

"Jun!" Teary eyed she lifted Jun from Simion's arms and hugged him a little too tightly.

Simion was ashen. "That was too close."

Overcome with gratitude, she pulled Simion into a tight hug. "Thank you."

His body eased against hers and he wrapped his arms around her. He gave out a small contented sigh, but it only lasted a moment, before he pulled away. "We need to go."

"No. we can't just leave everyone. Rhyler is here to kill as many High-Borns as he can."

"No time for that." Simion wrapped his arm around her waist. "*Tre'lehen ah-naq.*"

The air pulled tighter around her, her form already shifting. "No!"

Something lurched them forward and then pulled them back as if stopped abruptly. Her body was thrown forward again before she luckily found her feet stable against the ground once more. The jolt silenced Jun, too shocked to even make a sound. He stared wide-eyed at the chaos that they stumbled into.

They were in the courtyard, right in the middle of a chaotic battle. Soldiers fought Low-Born servants who were suddenly wielding magic. Bursts of air flew out of one of their hands while another turned entirely into rock, crushing a soldier underneath them. Screams of pain assaulted her ears.

"What did you do?!" Simion shouted through the onslaught.

Is he seriously blaming me for landing here?

A glint of metal swung by her side. Arla jumped back, the weapon barely missing her. She didn't even bother to face the attacker, instead she ran, grabbing Simion along with her. She caught a glimpse of a familiar figure in the distance. Dark hair and even darker eyes.

Leo.

Amongst the chaos of the battle, time slowed down around Leo, who stood tall and determined, his dark wavy hair flowing beautifully in the wind.

His sword was raised over someone in golden silk. A noble. She could only see the top back of the noble's head as the rest of the rubble covered her view. Leo was shouting at the High-Born who raised his hand against him. And then Leo's sword swung down.

Dread and sorrow struck her so intensely her feet stopped.

Was she seeing things? It was her imagination, right? It was too far away. There was no way that was Leo.

But she would have recognized that face anywhere.

The noble's hand was no longer raised. His entire body was blocked from her view, but no doubt... he was dead. Murdered by the former captain.

Her chest bottomed out. How could Leo do this?

Simion pulled her close to him. "*Tre'l–*"

She slapped her hand over his mouth. She shook away her thoughts of Leo. Now wasn't the time. She needed to focus. "I can't leave! I have to save them. Rhyler is here to kill all the High-Borns."

Leo is here to kill all High-Borns.

Simion yanked her hand away. "Absolutely not! It's too dangerous!"

She grabbed his wrist so tight her fingers turned white. "Simion! Listen to me! I am the Queen. I cannot abandon them."

She held his focus with pleading eyes until Simion shouted in frustrated defeat. "Fine! What is your plan, *your Highness*?"

Arla pushed Jun into his arms. "Take him and put him somewhere safe. And then come back here so we can keep teleporting the others away."

"You trust me to hide the next heir of Ulsana?"

"I do."

Simion softened for a fleeting moment and then he gave her a stern look. "Fine. Just stay alive while I'm gone then, will you?"

She nodded. "I'll try."

CHAPTER 38

There were so many High-Borns, she wasn't sure how she would get to them all, and yet she needed to try. Some nobles went willingly, while others fought her, hanging onto heavy possessions that slowed them down. Simion had to nearly knock them unconscious to get them to part with their treasures.

"There are more in the gardens." Arla shoved two noblewomen into Simion's arms. He was already looking haggard from his multiple trips. "How many more times can you teleport?"

Simion wiped sweat from his brow, which earned a disgusted look from himself. He really did not like getting dirty. "Maybe two."

Her heart sank. There were so many more left to take.

A shout beyond made her turn and run towards the noise. Someone needed her help. "I'll be right back!" she shouted at Simion.

She rounded the corner and skidded to a stop.

Shadows pinned Docannon and three other council members against the wall of the garden. Those were Norendra's shadows.

Which meant–

Arla turned.

Uro stood on the other side, the shadows attached to the bottoms of his feet.

At first, Arla felt immense relief to see her friend alive and well, but that quickly morphed into fear.

"Uro! Stop!" she panted, out of breath from the running.

Uro looked at her wide-eyed. "Arla?"

What was he doing here? Wasn't he just a symbol of Rhyler's revolution? She didn't think he would be forced to fight.

"I'm so glad you're okay. We were looking for you everywhere."

Uro frowned. "Leo told me you all looked for me."

So it *was* Leo she saw. They had found each other.

"He's the only one who actually came for me," Uro said, accusingly.

"It's not what you think. We thought you were safe and we needed a better plan to get you."

"So what was the plan?"

Arla blinked, unable to answer.

Uro closed his hands into fists. "That's what I thought. You were never going to come for me."

"That's not true!"

"It's okay." Shadows flickered underneath him. "I'm where I belong now anyway."

She took a step closer. "Uro. Listen to me. Everything is going to be okay. Whatever Rhyler is forcing you to do, you don't have to do it. You can come back with me."

"Come back with you?" His face darkened. "What will happen if I do? I'll tell you. I will be forced into being a soldier again. Live under the rule of High-Borns. No." The shadows shivered. "This is the only way to be free."

Who was this boy in front of her? Arla hardly recognized him. Uro used to always smile and bounce on his heels, now his eyes rimmed with red and hatred etched in his skin, making him look much older. And whose fault was that? Rhyler's? Or hers?

"It doesn't have to be this way. I can change things. I *will* change things."

Uro snorted. "No, you won't. I asked you to free me and you didn't. You cared more about keeping the 'peace' than helping me."

In this moment, words could not express how much she regretted not returning for Uro when they were in The Underground. She never thought of the possibility that Uro would turn to Rhyler's side. She had believed he was just playing along to stay alive.

How naive she was.

"I'm sorry, Uro. I was afraid. I made the wrong choice, but I can fix this." Arla reached out her hand to him. "Come with me."

Uro stared at her with conflict in his eyes.

"Please," Arla said. "Give me the chance to help you."

Slowly, he raised his hand toward hers. Hope filled her chest. It wasn't too late. Uro could be happy again. They could all be happy again.

An inch. That's how far his hand was from hers.

And then, suddenly, he retracted it back. "You say this now, but I... I can't trust you. You're a High-Born, why would you want to help Low-Borns when you have all the power?" She could almost hear Rhyler's voice through him, his influence rooted too deeply now.

He raised his hand, and sharp shadows pulled up from the ground. "We have to kill all our oppressors."

She stepped between him and the councilmen. "Please don't do this."

Uro did not pull back the shadows. As she stared at the growing shadow swords, she wondered if Uro would cross the line and pierce through her to get what he wanted.

"Uro," she begged.

A tear slipped down Uro's face. "I'm sorry."

The shadows shot forward.

"Stop!"

The shadows dissolved into the air.

Arla blinked in disbelief.

Leo stood between them, drenched in sweat and blood, his sword raised in a blocking position. "Not her."

Uro stepped back, hurt drawn all over his face, like a brother betrayed.

Leo reached out his hand, torn over his own decision. "Uro–"

Blood splattered onto Leo's face.

Uro screamed and went to clutch his chest only to touch the tip of a sword piercing through it. Leo paled as Uro collapsed to the ground, revealing a standing Docannon behind the young boy, free from his shadowed chains.

Arla screamed, running toward her friend. She got to him just as Leo did, who scooped Uro into his arms.

Uro wheezed, his lungs collapsing with every breath. He looked so afraid as he wrung his hand in Leo's shirt, spreading blood all over it. "All I wanted was to live. Is that too much to ask?"

"You will live," Leo said with a shaky voice. "You're going to be okay."

Tears streamed down from Uro's bloodied eyes. "We can never be free."

"Uro!" Arla shouted.

Uro took in a last desperate breath, and then his hand loosened, falling to the ground.

Arla stared into Uro's lifeless eyes.

This wasn't real.

This was a dream.

A nightmare.

Something that happened to others, but not to Uro. He was too innocent. Too young. Too much of a dreamer. She couldn't speak. Couldn't utter a sound.

She reached out and touched the young boy's face.

A teardrop fell on her hand, and then another and another, but they were not hers.

Leo clung to Uro's limp body, his entire body shaking. And then he let out a cry so devastating, she swore the sky might have ripped open right there.

She wished Wynera had given her the magic of time instead. Then she could go back and mend all her mistakes. She would have saved Uro. If only she hadn't rejected his dreams out right. If only, she could have found another way to help him. If only–

"What are you doing?" Rose appeared from the battle, blood soaking her shirt. "We have to–" Her eyes widened seeing Uro. She slowly crouched over him, her voice so soft that it hardly sounded like her at all. "Uro, this is no time to rest, we have to go."

When her brother did not answer, Rose shook him. "Get up!"

But Uro's eyes still stared at the sky, empty of life and hope. Rose kept shaking him, unable to accept her brother was now gone. Her worst fears, realized.

Docannon spat on the ground. "Low-Born rat."

Rage filled Arla. Wynera's words came rushing back to her.

'*It is better that he is dead. Men like him only bring pain and terror to the world.*'

Yes. It would be better if he was dead.

Arla shot up, her hand outstretched. "*Mo'tek en –*"

Are you letting in the dark?

Arla froze mid-word.

What kind of leader will you be?

She lowered her hand.

An arrow whizzed by Arla's cheek, barely missing her as it embedded itself straight into Docannon's chest. Docannon gasped before crumpling to the ground. Before Arla knew it, they were surrounded by Rhyler's fighters.

Leo remained on his knees, staring at nothing as he held onto his dear brother. Rose snarled at Rhyler's fighters, thirsty for blood.

Arla was relieved that now there were others to direct her anger at.

Arla threw her Whispers out first, pulling her mud monster to protect them from the onslaught of attack as Rose swung her sword. They came at them in waves that felt unending, and still Leo did not move, like a shell devoid of will.

This could not last. Where was Simion? Could he find her in this chaos? Or was he injured himself trying to get to her? The thought made her panic. She couldn't handle another death.

Rose shouted in pain beside her, clutching her arm, which now bled profusely.

They weren't going to make it. She was going to have to watch Rose die too, and Leo.

I can't let them die. I can't let anyone else die.

I refuse!

A pulse ran through her entire body and into the ground with a magnitude she had never felt before. It was like the entire world shook for a moment. And then the pulse returned back and hit her with an onslaught of noise.

Whispers loud and quiet, fast and slow, berated her ears. They screeched at her. Clawed at her. Bellowed their demands. She covered her ears, but that did not stop the sounds.

The Whispers pulled her forward. Her feet moved without conscious effort until she felt herself bump up against something. She looked up. Her statue stared back at her, disfigured and incomplete, its claw open. For her.

It was here the entire time. This was the garden she and Simion were at only a few days ago, so damaged and broken from the fighting, she didn't recognize it.

And now the statue seemed to beckon her.

She reached out and placed her hand in the statue's claw, and it was like a jolt of the entire universe went through her. Whispers in tones she had never heard rushed through her blood. The statue itself was talking to her in an ancient language and it kept repeating the same phrase over and over. Imploring her to repeat after it.

More of Rhyler's fighters streamed into the garden.

Over and over it repeated itself until her mouth opened and she let the Whispers take over.

"*Ithrid gu-lia bukami chrek-ek noon-tha. Ther-gul eil dan huy-uq-tha. Loren vuy-i-al-san chryu.*"

The stone darkened to black like it was burning from the inside and then crumbled into pieces as crimson flesh burst out from stone. Three heads of hissing snakes twisted toward the sky followed by a giant lion body.

Arla gasped. Her stone statue... had come alive.

The creature arched its back in a wild cry as large wings burst from its back. Everyone in its vicinity was thrown backward. Rose gaped at the monster while clutching the wall to keep herself steady. Leo hardly noticed at all.

This was it. Now was their chance at escape.

Arla pulled at Leo. "Rose! Help me!"

Rose heaved Leo to his feet, practically dragging him along with them toward the creature. Arla scrambled up the creature's back first and then heaved a comatose Leo up, nearly throwing out her back in the process. Then she reached out for Rose, but just as she went to pull her up, Rose was violently yanked back.

"Rose!"

Three Low-Born rebels dragged Rose back to the ground. Arla willed the creature to attack. Spears pierced its arms and legs. The creature screeched and flapped its wings, taking flight.

"No!" Arla screamed as they launched into the air. "Go back! Go back!"

But the creature ignored her and soared higher and higher.

The last thing she saw as they touched the sky was Rose being swallowed up by the crowd next to Uro's lifeless form.

CHAPTER 39

The beast made no sound as it flew across the sky and neither did Arla and Leo. The shock of losing Uro and Rose had her numb and empty. It was all she could do to hold onto Leo and the creature as it descended back to the ground. Somehow it knew where to take them even when she did not command it directly.

The creature landed in a dense forest where Simion had teleported the other survivors. She couldn't remember clearly, but somehow she managed to slide off her statue-beast with Leo and someone had come and taken Leo away. She wasn't sure who.

The only she knew for sure was that moment she landed on the ground, she collapsed to her knees overcome with emotion, but she had barely let out a guttural gasp before noble men and women rushed to her, asking where their children were. Had she saved their parents? Their friends? There were so many injured and bleeding, and no one knew what to do.

Her beast let out a sharp screech and then turned to dust, covering everyone around it with a layer of grey. And she knew, deep in her bones, that she would never see it again. She closed her eyes, thanking the statue in silence for helping her one last time.

But she had no time to dwell on more loss. Her people needed her.

So with a strength she herself did not know she had, she shoved her feelings down and got to work.

There were fewer than she had hoped. Only a hundred or so Low and High-Borns made it back with them to a secluded wood leagues from the city. Here, they set up a modest camp with bare essentials that Simion managed to teleport back from nearby towns. He made sure they were far enough away that no one would be able to follow him or guess where he was going. After that, he had exerted himself so much that he had fallen into a deep sleep for days afterwards.

Oh, Simion. Arla could not help but feel bad about how exhausted he had become.

She called for all able physicians to tend to anyone who needed healing and created an area for them to prioritize who received immediate care and who could wait. She also assigned a few High and Low-Borns to gather all the supplies and distribute them evenly, but their prejudices immediately had them sharing only to their own classes. Arla had to stand there for hours making sure they were fair. A task that drained her immensely.

She had barely slept the next few days, only managing to do what was needed, all the while eager to see Leo, who shut himself in a small tent and had not come out since. Finally, when the third day was over, she dragged herself to Leo's tent, even when her body screamed at her to sleep.

"Are you sure that's wise?" Simion had asked her. "Wasn't he killing High-Borns for Rhyler, oh, just a few days ago?"

She couldn't deny that fact, but she knew she would not imprison him. Instead, she just had a few guards watch over his tent, in case something were to happen.

She groaned as she bent down to enter the tent Leo was being held in. The stench of sweat and stagnant air hit her so hard, she was shocked awake.

"Leo?" she coughed out, waving the surrounding air.

Hunched in the corner, Leo remained in his bloodied clothes, staring at the ground. Heat burned behind her eyes. Whispers. He had not even changed his clothes... Gone was the put-together man she knew, and in his place was an empty husk. Had no one come to see him or help him bathe? Did she not assign someone to do so? Shame pierced her. She swore she had told someone to look after him, but clearly they neglected him. She should have checked on him earlier.

"Leo?" She reached over to touch his shoulder.

"I said leave me alone!" he shouted, throwing out his arm.

Arla dodged his swipe and backed away. Maybe someone had tried to look after him, but gave up. Judging from his reaction, it made sense.

"Leo," she called out to him again, gently. "It's me. Arla."

He did not act like her name made a difference. He just continued to stare at the ground.

"Come on. Let's clean you up."

She dared to reach for him again, and this time, he let her hold his shoulders. Relieved, she tucked her hands under his armpits to pull him up, but the weight of him was too much for her and he did not budge. "Leo. I need you to help me. Can you get up?"

No response.

She called his name again, but he still did not stand. She was really worrying now.

"Please get up. We have to get up. We have to get ourselves together so we can rescue Rose."

His hollow eyes remained fixed on the tent cloth in front of him. "Rose is dead."

"No, she's not." She kneeled in front of him, so he was forced to look at her. "She's imprisoned by Rhyler. We need to get her before something bad happens to her."

She was sure Rose was alive. She had to be.

Tears formed in his tired eyes. "They're all dead because I was too weak." He looked her straight in the eye, devoid of hope. "I failed."

She wondered what he thought he had failed at. Killing all High-Borns, or protecting the people he cared about? Maybe both.

"Leo, what happened when you went to find Uro?"

He turned away from her.

For some reason, that was the last straw.

She wanted to swing him around and shake him.

Stop ignoring me! You think you're the only one in pain? You killed nobles I was supposed to protect! You abandoned me when I needed you!

She wanted to scream in his face. *We don't have time to mourn, we have to save Rose! We have to save who is left! I need you! Don't abandon me again, you selfish bastard!*

Was it fair to be so angry at him? He was suffering too. But she couldn't help but want him to absorb her pain, so that she could break and do nothing. She wanted to hide in a cave too and not come out, just like he was. There was just so much pain and nowhere for it to go.

She wanted to comfort him and hurt him at the same time. She also didn't know if she could trust him. Would he kill other nobles in the camp when she wasn't looking? Or would he self-implode like he was doing now?

Yet, despite her anger and distrust, she still loved him. It was all so confusing.

She wanted to shout and cry and be held and soothed. But... she was a Queen. And Queens had duties.

She pulled herself up. "We don't have to bathe today. We can try again tomorrow. I'll come by then, okay?"

He did not answer her. He did not seem to care whether she was there at all.

A hundred and twelve steps.

That's how many steps she endured in getting back to her own tent. It was how many steps she took holding her breath, keeping herself stitched together by sheer will. And only when the tent cloth behind her draped closed did she shatter.

She met the ground in a heap of tears and covered her mouth to muffle her wails. She wanted to throw up her pain, let it leave her tired bones and forget all that had happened.

Why did all this happen?

Uro. Norendra. Ametha.

They were all dead.

Their faces flashed in her memory, one after the other — each in their final moments. In tears. In blood. In fear.

It was all too much.

She bit her hand trying to stop the tears, but they came like a flood that threatened to drown her.

She couldn't breathe. She couldn't think. She was–

A wisp of black smoke appeared. She felt him before she saw him. A presence that was becoming more and more comforting.

His arms wrapped around her awkwardly, like he had never held anyone before.

He was always just appearing when she needed someone, wasn't he?

"Why are you here?" she hiccuped.

"I was called," Simion said simply. "I'm no good with tears, but if you want to keep crying, you can."

Something strange happens when someone touches you when you are fragile. It makes you break even more. Except you don't shatter in the cold by yourself, you crack in a warm hearth. A place you can break and someone will keep you warm.

And so she broke, pouring her sorrow over him, and he held still, gathering up her edges so she could find them again when the pain had left and the tears had dried.

CHAPTER 40

Simion did not stay. He helped her to her cot, staying uncharacteristically quiet, and covered her in a blanket, telling her to get some rest, before disappearing in a whiff of smoke. She slept for what must have been hours because she woke to the high afternoon sun beaming through the rips in the tent cloth above her.

Her throat was dry from crying so much the night before. A part of her didn't want to face the day, but Ulsana needed her, and so she sat up. To her surprise, her foot knocked over a glass of water on the ground. The earth immediately soaked up the water because it was just as parched as her throat. Another glass lay a few inches next to the knocked over one and another a few inches to the right of that. She turned her head to see another three in a row, each exactly a few inches apart, the same width as her foot.

She bent down and picked up a note wedged underneath the second glass: *To replenish what you have lost, your Clumsiness.*

She couldn't help but smile.

She drank at least three full glasses, and when she was finally quenched, she took a deep breath. Okay. It was time to get her answers.

"Wynera," she called out.

The Forest-Born princess did not emerge in physical form, instead, she stirred within Arla. *"I am here."*

"When I was fighting Rhyler, something else was there with him. He was screaming. Do you know who that was?"

There was a long pause before Wynera woefully replied, *"Yes."*

It was the tone of her voice that told Arla everything she needed to know.

"It's him, isn't it?" Arla said. "Dehen. The man you loved. The one that died in The Forest."

Wynera curled into a ball deep within Arla's chest. *"Yes."*

"Did you know he possessed Rhyler, like you possessed me?"

"Yes," Wynera said again.

It all made sense now. Wynera had known all along that her love had possessed Rhyler for revenge. That's how she knew he was coming to Ulsana.

Arla felt bad for Wynera. Her former lover was now bent on destroying all those who took his life from him. He wanted revenge more than being reunited with Wynera. He even went so far as to push Rhyler to attack her, the vessel that Wynera lived in.

"I'm really sorry. This must be hard for you."

A light curl of wind fluttered through her hair as if Wynera appreciated her empathy.

Shouting burst from just outside her tent. Arla sighed. Another thing to take care of. She put on her shoes. "I guess it's time to face the day. We can talk more later."

Arla walked out of her tent only to be met immediately by a crowd surrounding a small group of people who were trying to kill each other, of course.

"You all deserve to die for how you've treated us!" A Low-Born shouted as his fist cracked into a nobleman's face.

"Traitors!" another High-Born screamed, throwing a bucket into the back of a Low-Born.

No doubt the truth had gotten out.

"Stop it!" Arla shoved herself between them, but they kept fighting.

A part of her itched to call her creatures, to make them all bend to her will, just like she did with the council. It would have been so easy.

But that was not the leader she wanted to be, nor was it the leader Ulsana needed.

Uro died because he didn't believe in her leadership. He didn't trust that she would help him. That was the problem, wasn't it? Fear and violence could not create trust. It would not motivate people to follow you forever. She needed to earn their trust. And one built trust through action, something she had avoided for a long time. In trying to find the perfect answer where no one would get hurt, she had done nothing, giving ample time for Rhyler to attack and leave them like this.

She would not allow that to happen ever again.

Arla shoved the fighting Ulsanans hard, knocking one off their feet and into the arms of the crowd.

"Enough!" She glared at the crowd. "Haven't we had enough pain? Haven't we lost enough? Why are we fighting? Because one of us has magic and the other doesn't? Is that really a reason to separate us?" The crowd went silent, shocked that their short and weak Queen was yelling at them, something Arla had never done before. "The Ulsana we know is gone, it will always be gone, and good riddance! That is not the home we should have striven for. It is not the home we deserved. Don't you want to stop suffering? Don't you want peace? The Forest gave us magic to share, but because we didn't, it punished us and it created Rhyler. Don't you see? We have to be better than this."

A Low-Born scoffed. "You talk so high and mighty for a High-Born. What do you know of our pain? What do you know about what we've gone through?"

Arla pulled up her tattered sleeves, revealing her scarred arms. Many gasped at how hideously deep they were.

Simion's mouth pressed into a thin line. And for a moment, she wanted to hide them again, but she refused. There was nothing to be ashamed of anymore. This was part of her and she was going to make it a strength rather than a weakness now.

"I know what it's like to feel small and weak and to be treated unfairly." She turned to the High-Borns. "I also know what it's like to gain power. It's addicting. You finally stop feeling so helpless. For once in your life, people listen to you, but then you fear losing that power. You don't want to let go of what you have because you're afraid you will be helpless again, but that's not true. Allowing others to have strength does not diminish your own." She turned to the Low-Borns. "I was angry too, and a part of me wanted revenge. I hurt the people who belittled me, but it only bred more resentment, more hatred. I don't want that anymore. I just want peace. Don't you?" She straightened. "From this day on, there will be no Low-Borns or High-Borns. We are all Ulsanans and that is what we'll call each other."

The crowd did not cheer. Instead, they just looked at each other with doubt and confusion. Not what she had hoped for, but at least they weren't physically fighting anymore. A small change was change nonetheless.

"You may think you are so different, but right now, we have one commonality. We all have people we care about who are still stuck in the city. We have to go back for them, and the only way to do that successfully is to work together. So, put your prejudices aside, because we have work to do."

Arla did not wait for a reaction, instead, she walked through the crowd. "Simion," she called out to him.

Simion went right to her side.

CHAPTER 41

"Well, that was quite bold."

Simion followed her into her tent with amusement written all over his face.

Arla paced the tent. "It was just words to them. It means nothing unless I follow through with the plan."

"Oooo," Simion plopped into a seated position on the ground. "You have a plan?"

She stopped pacing. "I'm going to give them magic."

Simion choked back spit. "You're going to give *magic*? To the Low-Borns?"

She gave him a warning finger. "We're not calling them that anymore."

He raised his hands in innocence. "Alright then. What shall we call them?"

"Ulsanans. We're all Ulsanans. And as Ulsanans they have equal rights to the Whispers, just as The Forest intended. Everyone must have magic. That is the only way everyone will feel equal, not to mention, it'll be more useful to have more of us with magic when we go rescue the others."

Her mind drifted to Rose, unwilling to fully imagine what horrible punishments her friend was going through at this moment.

Just stay alive. I'm coming.

Simion threw his hands back behind his head in a relaxed position. "Ah, so you were serious about that."

She was tired of his laid back attitude. Didn't he understand what was at stake? Or did he simply not care?

"Why are you always opposed to going back for people?" she snapped, getting frustrated again.

Simion frowned. "Because it's dangerous and often unsuccessful."

"The odds are worth facing to save the people you care about, something you don't understand."

That was Simion's problem. He didn't care enough about others, unlike Leo.

Simion sat straight up, no longer nonchalant. "If you cared about them so much, you should have gotten them out in the first place no matter what, like I did."

"How can you say that?" she barked. "It wasn't like I meant to leave Rose behind. She was taken from me!"

Tears burned the back of her eyes as Arla fought to keep them from falling. She didn't want Simion to see her cry, especially when he was being such a jerk again. What was wrong with him? Simion was being so unfair. He had no sympathetic bone in his body.

Simion stood up, all the anger gone from him. "Alright, my Queen, don't cry. I hate your tears." He put his hands on her shoulders. "I'm sorry. I didn't mean it like that."

She shrugged him off. "I think you meant exactly what you said."

"I just... I meant I don't like the idea of you going back there, especially when Rhyler clearly wants you dead. I don't want to see you get hurt."

She scoffed. "You sound like you really care about me."

"What if I do?" Simion responded softly.

Arla paused, not knowing how to respond. Was Simion joking right now?

'You should have gotten them out in the first place no matter what, like I did.'

She had paid little attention to what he said at first because she was so angry, but now that she thought back, Simion had come back for her, and only her, many times.

But he only saved her because he needed her alive to stay on the council, right?

"So, how are you going to give them magic?" Simion finally asked, obviously trying to change the subject.

"I don't know, but we need to figure it out soon."

"Scratching those is not good for you."

Puzzled, Arla looked down at what Simion was staring at and realized she was scratching her arms. "It doesn't hurt as much as it used to," she lied, ignoring the sharp pain of her inflamed scars.

Simion's eyes lingered on her scars. "I cannot believe what he did to you. No one deserves this. How much pain you must have been in..."

He was doing it again. He was trying to trick her with his soft gaze and empathetic tone into believing he cared about her. She pushed it away with a sharp exhale. "I don't need pity. I need that mouth of yours."

Simion blinked at her.

Arla blushed, realizing how that sounded. "I mean, I need you to use your words to convince people to work together and ask around, if anyone knows anything that could help us give magic. You've always been a good talker."

He gave her a sly grin. "Of course. Well, if that is what you command, my Queen, I will gladly do it."

"You will?" She was expecting more resistance from him.

"Of course. I'm in this with you."

Sometimes Simion could be the biggest jerk she knew, and at other times, like this, he seemed so kind. She never knew which version of him she was going to get. And at the center of her confusion was the 'why'. And she needed to know.

"Why are you still here?" she asked.

"Oh, you want me to start now?" Simion turned to go. "Fine, I'll go ask around–"

"No. I mean, why are you still *here*? In this situation. Why did you help me? You could have left or sided with the council to put me away. Things would have been much easier if you had."

"It really would have, wouldn't it?" He bowed low, lower than he ever had to her. "Well, I must be going now."

Arla pinched his sleeve, stopping him. "Don't do that."

Simion crooked his eyebrow in confusion.

"Don't change the subject or try to joke your way out of it. I really want to know, Simion. Why did you choose to stay?"

What did Simion really feel? Whose side was he really on? She was tired of the guessing game.

Simion looked as if he would just continue out of the tent and not answer her, but something changed in his expression and he took a deep, uncomfortable breath. "Do you remember the day we met when I pushed you into that dark hole...?"

Of course, how could I forget?

Simion looked up at the ripped top of the tent. "Would you be surprised to know that I wish that it didn't happen? I wish I had chosen to help you instead. I wish for it everyday now."

Arla only stared at him. What did he just say?

He fiddled with his jacket button, which hung on by its last thread. "The one thing my parents loved most was power, and they believed the best way to get it was through influence. You could imagine their horror when their first child was a bumbling, shy, sensitive thing who could barely complete any physical task without breaking down into tears. Someone who would clearly never gain any respect or prestige. At first, they tried to rectify it by trying to have another child, hopefully more robust than the first, but years of attempts led to nothing and so they had no choice but to rely on their first." He mockingly pointed two thumbs at himself. "So, little Simion, desperate for his parent's approval, did everything he could to make them proud. I knew I would never be the strongest in the room, but I could be the most cunning, and in that way I could gain power. I devoted myself to knowing everything, so I could use it against people. No one would look down on me. No one would accuse me of being undeserving of my family name.

Nevertheless, I feared I was the weakest in the room.

And then I met you. And I saw how weak you were, and it made me feel... relieved. I thought, at least I wasn't as big of a disappointment as you were. At least I was not the heir to the throne with no magic. At least I had friends. I thought putting you down would make me appear stronger, but it just proved I was a coward. You deserved better than that. And I am truly, truly sorry."

Simion waited for her to say something, but Arla did not know what to say.

"Why are you saying this now?" she asked.

"Because I am still a selfish bastard. Because I want your forgiveness. Because I don't want you... to hate me."

He looked at her with a quivering hope so uncharacteristic of him that Arla had a hard time accepting this was truly Simion standing before her.

He wanted her forgiveness so badly that he was willing to appear humanly desperate.

But could she really forgive him? She had never really forgiven the others who had hurt her before. Her father. Ametha. Norendra. They all died before she could, not that they would ask for her forgiveness. She was sure they did not want it, but Simion... did. And he had proven over and over that he was willing to do what it took to make amends. Wasn't that enough?

Is it?

She had asked her people to let go of the past injustices and distrust and move forward. To start over and help each other. If she was asking them to do that, she had to first start with herself.

In the beginning, she hated Simion and truly believed she would always hate him, but somehow, over time, she found herself slowly enjoying his company and relying on him. He had become an important person in her life. And she had learned to trust him. And over time her hope for them grew until at this moment, she realized, it outweighed the pain of their past.

So, even though she would never forget the pain Simion had caused her, in order for Ulsana and herself to heal, she wanted to move on.

And so in the quiet between them, she gave him the words he sought. "I forgive you."

His body relaxed as if her words released him from a prison. He jokingly gave her a smug smile. "I knew you would, because that's who you are. I just wanted to make sure I did enough to deserve your forgiveness."

She rolled her eyes. Of course, he would say something like this.

"I'm afraid you'll have to do even more to continue to earn that forgiveness," she joked, poking his chest.

His smile faded, and his eyes sharpened so drastically it made her heart jump. He gently gripped her wrist and pulled her to him. "Like what?"

Arla gaped up at him, not understanding. "Huh?"

He looked down at her with a burning gaze. "What else do you want me to do to earn your forgiveness?" He was so unnaturally close to her, she swore she could hear his fastening heartbeat. "Whatever it is, I'll do it." His eyes moved to her lips. "If you ask."

She swallowed hard. What was happening?

"I want..." she mumbled. "I want you to help me find a way to give everyone magic."

"Is that all?"

He wanted a different answer, but what, she didn't know.

"Yes."

His face fell as he let her go. "Then I will do that."

She nodded, stepping backward, trying to release the tension with an awkward, unprompted laugh. "See you tomorrow then."

He nodded, oddly gloomy, before disappearing in a sway of smoke..

CHAPTER 42
Simion

It was too dark here and definitely too dusty. Those nasty floating particles were sure to leave a layer of white over his clothes. Simion inwardly sighed. What did it matter anyway? He no longer had any of his fine silk jackets or meticulously pressed pants. They were all abandoned in the castle, and the one he was wearing already was beyond saving.

Arla elbowed him slightly in the ribs. "I think that's her."

The door creaked open, barely hanging onto its hinges as a middle-aged woman with raven tattoos soaring along her neck walked in. Best to make this quick. This disgusting little shack was surely going to collapse on them any minute now. Simion stood close to Arla in case they had to teleport fast.

It was a pain in the ass to get here. For a week, Simion teleported to all the nearby villages, each time landing in places he had never been. A feat he had never done before until recently and it was quite dangerous.

One time he appeared right in the middle of a bathtub with a naked man already in it. Another time he appeared mid-air and landed precariously close to a steel-tipped fence that would have pierced him through. Despite the dangers, he continued his search.

He sweet-talked the locals and flirted with the gossips until he finally procured this meeting. The raven-tattooed woman wasn't anyone special in particular, but a villager told him that his father's friend's uncle had a wife who inherited an ancient text that spoke about The Forest.

The woman closed the door behind her. "Do you have the money?"

Simion tossed the villager's father's friend's uncle's wife a rather heavy bag of coins, which she opened slowly, as if expecting it to be booby-trapped. When she was sure it was safe, she pulled out a coin and bit the edge. "You know, this book has been in my family for generations, it would take a lot to have me let it go."

Simion wanted to roll his eyes. His sources already told him that this woman did not care for the book at all. It had collected dust in a corner for years, but what she did care for, was gold.

Simion tossed another jingling bag at her. "That should suffice."

Satisfied, the woman rummaged through her own bag that hung on her shoulder and pulled out an old crusty book. Arla received it gently with both hands, afraid of damaging it. Something he too would have done. Books were meant to be treasured, which this woman clearly had not done, by how precariously she transported it. The bag was not even leather for Whisper's sake. He was surprised the book's corners were not bent with negligence.

Simion waved the woman off. "That is all."

Arla gave him a look that warned him he was being rude. Ah. His Queen really was too soft sometimes. He gave her a shrug of innocence, like he didn't mean to be unkind.

The woman left quickly, impatient to spend her gold.

Arla patted the book hopefully. "Do you really think this will have our answers?"

"It better." Simion grumbled. "I'm tired of looking."

They had been pouring over book after book searching for an answer to how they could give everyone magic. So far, most of them said the same things that the texts in the royal libraries did. All of which were washed of the truth by the High-Born writers of the past.

Arla plopped herself on the ground and began to read, putting her finger against the page so as not to skip a word. Simion watched her, lingering on her bright and hopeful face, and a familiar feeling tugged at his heart.

His Whisper bobbed like an acorn on a steady stream down from his head to his tongue. It was happening again. His magic was pulling him toward her.

When it first occurred, Simion thought he was losing control of his Whisper. He would go about his life when his Whisper would suddenly demand to be spoken, and when he did, it pulled him straight to her. He feared she was manipulating him somehow with her own strange magic. Unlike the rest of them, she knew The Forest's language.

He thought that maybe her magic reached beyond summoning monsters. It wasn't until he landed in those dark tunnels that he realized what it really was.

He remembered how sad her voice was, and more shockingly, how badly he wanted to hurt that stupid captain for leaving her. Horridly, he found himself wishing that it was him she reached in the dark for. He wanted her to stop thinking of Leo and think of... him.

It turned out his Whispers knew something he did not want to admit. The little jolts of excitement when she entered the room. The willingness to make any joke, no matter how crass or stupid, just to see her smile. The longing to be near her. It was the reason he spent days picking up broken stones and gluing them haphazardly back together.

He cared for her.

As plain as day.

And his Whispers evolved to fulfill his desire to be near her.

But she loved the idiot captain.

His brain kept trying to remind him of this fact over and over again, but then something terrible started to happen to him despite his brain's warnings. He was beginning to hope that maybe the love between the

Queen and the Captain was fragile. That maybe there was room for him to prove that he was the one that should be by her side instead. That someday, on a bright afternoon, she would turn to look at him and realize he was the better choice. Maybe that was why he rarely left her side.

He was waiting.

Simion sat next to her, trying to catch a glimpse of the text. She pushed her long black hair behind her shoulder, releasing a faint scent of roses. Simion leaned a little closer, unable to resist.

Arla's finger stopped, and her hazel eyes grew wide.

"What did you find?" he asked, leaning back again.

She repeated the text. "It is in everything we see and do not see. We breathe it in. We breathe it out. It is the essence of everything. It cannot be created or destroyed. It can only move from one to another and only willingly. It is like letting go." She placed the book slowly on her lap. "She said I couldn't create them..."

"She?" Simion asked.

Arla didn't answer his question, lost in her own thoughts. "But maybe I can't transfer them, just like Rhyler."

"But the High-Borns only have one Whisper each."

"Except me. I have many."

Simion did not like the sound of this. "Arla..."

"I can give them my magic. One by one."

"But don't you need them? And what will happen to you if you give away your Whispers?"

Would she shrivel up and die like Norendra did? His chest constricted with anxiety.

She smiled. "You sound like you're worried."

He was. He really was. "I do, don't I? How strange."

"I think if I give it willingly, it will be fine, but there is only one way to find out." She turned to face him and lifted her hands toward his face.

He jerked back. "You're not doing what I think you're doing, are you?"

"We have to try."

"No." He kept his distance. He wasn't going to be the reason she hurt herself.

"I promise to stop if I feel it draining me."

He gave her a wary look. "I don't trust you."

She laughed. "*You* don't trust *me*? I never thought I would hear that." She scooted closer to him. So close, her knees touched his, and it sent a shot of electricity through him. "Please? I have to try."

She looked at him with such hopeful pleading, he couldn't help but relent. He was quite disappointed in himself for being so weak for her. "The moment it feels strange, you stop."

She nodded, brightening at her win, which only heightened her beauty. He leaned in, and she placed both hands on either side of his cheeks. His body instantly grew hot from the touch. He hoped it was because the magic transfer was already working, but he knew better.

"Are you feeling feverish?" she asked. "You're hot."

"I'm fine," he snapped. "This is a small shack with no air circulation, of course I'm going to be hot. Continue."

Arla gave him a scowl before closing her eyes. Her eyebrows furrowed in concentration, giving him the freedom to stare at her openly without having to make up an excuse.

He watched her long black hair fall perfectly over her shoulders, a few strays sticking to her sweaty forehead. Her face: flushed pink from focus and lack of breathing. Her lips: slightly rosy and fully plump.

"You should breathe. I heard it's good for you."

"I'm trying to focus," she grumbled.

"Focus *and* breathe."

"Simion."

She was getting frustrated with him again. He secretly loved when she did. He wanted to push her further, but he knew she really wanted this to work, so he held himself back.

He could have continued to stare at her for hours, if not for the strange sensation flowing through his face. Like a window had opened, letting in a gentle breeze. And then something powerful rushed into him, knocking him backward onto the ground.

"Simion!" Arla rushed to his side.

His forehead throbbed so intensely he could barely hear or see.

"Are you alright?"

She sounded worried. He liked that.

"Oh." Simion exaggerated his pain, leaning against her for support. "The pain. It hurts so bad."

"I'll get a physician!" Arla was about to get up, but Simion grabbed her wrist to stop her. "You're the only one who can fix me. You just need to put your arms around me and squeeze. The pressure will help."

Catching on, Arla rolled her eyes. "Simion."

Simion grinned. "Alright. Alright."

"So?" Arla helped him sit up. "Do you hear anything?"

Simion closed his eyes reluctantly. He stilled, and through the darkness of his mind, a ping echoed. It was like a raindrop fell into a still lake and from it a Whisper grew. It was small and confused, like it had woken from a deep sleep and realized it was in a new environment. He waited patiently for it to take root. As soon as it did, it grew louder. Too loud.

He twitched. "It's loud. Really loud."

"Then say it," she commanded.

He opened his mouth. "*Mo'tek en rela'io.*"

Mud oozed from the ground beside them, curling on top of itself until it grew into a large lizard-like creature and kept expanding past the size of the hut.

"Oh no. I forgot." Arla covered Simion's body with her own as the mud creature burst through the top of the shack, sending pieces of the wooden roof on top of them.

Simion wrapped his arms around her waist and teleported them just outside.

The creature groaned and shook off wood beams and nails from its back, splashing mud everywhere. Simion gasped at the size of the thing as it lethargically curled into a ball to rest.

This was indeed Arla's magic now in him. How… amazing.

"Simion!" she shouted as she threw her arms around his neck. "We did it!"

He closed his eyes, taking in the curve of her body against his. They fit together perfectly.

She pulled away too quickly. She always did. He longed to bring her back to him.

Isn't this nice? He wanted to say. *Forget about the Captain and stay here with me.*

But he didn't, because it would only drive her away. So he remained still as she avoided looking into his eyes, like she was embarrassed by what she had done. Was it so bad hugging him?

"How did you do it?" he asked, trying to hide his disappointment.

"I imagined the Whisper leaving my head and going through my body into my arms and to you. Like I was passing it along gently. It took some convincing, but it went because I asked it to."

"Funny that no High-Born had ever tried this. Probably because they would never have wanted their Whisper to leave them."

Arla nodded, pressing a gentle hand on the monster, getting mud all over her hand instantly.

Simion admired the monster. "How many of these do you have?"

"A handful," she replied, looking nostalgically at the now half-asleep creature. "This was the first one I could control. I summoned it in the meadow with Leo and Uro... we were really happy then."

Simion frowned.

Stop being so sad. It hurts too much to watch you suffer.

"Who's to say you can't be happy in the future?"

She gave him another sad smile. "It doesn't feel like I can be. Not like I was before."

Simion placed a hand on the mud creature, dangerously close to hers. "You may never recover what you lost, but that doesn't mean you can't gain more. Life is full of changes. Who's to say?"

Tears brimmed her beautiful eyes. "I hope you're right."

Her voice was so soft. He wanted to reach for her chin and point her face to him. Feel if her lips were as soft as her voice right now. He forced himself to pull away.

"Of course I am right. In fact, I'm right most of the time."

Arla smiled. A real smile this time, and it warmed him.

Simion suddenly felt his energy drain from him. No doubt because he was still hanging on to the creature. "Is it this tiring every time?"

"You get used to it."

He could feel the strain on his body rapidly increasing. Unable to hold the creature anymore, he blew out a breath, and the Whisper slipped from him, making the monster disappear. "To hold this much magic and control these huge things must take so much effort. I didn't realize..."

He looked at Arla. It was easy to judge Arla as weak. She was a short, semi-plump young girl who spoke way too kindly, but whoever underestimated her was truly a fool, for she was powerful beyond her magic. The amount of pain she could endure and the energy she could muster were truly unbelievable. Simion did not even know if he could endure what she had gone through.

He offered her his hand. She looked at him quizzically.

"It's my turn to give it back."

The old him would have never offered to give back such power, but he did not need it. He didn't know exactly when, but over time, being powerful didn't matter so much to him anymore. In fact, he wasn't sure if it ever did. He only wanted his parents' love and even that seemed unimportant now. There was only one person whose affection he hopelessly craved for now.

She smiled and took both his hands and put them up to her cheeks. "Try to focus on the Whisper moving through your body."

It was easier said than done, especially when she smiled at him like that. It took everything in his power not to pull her face to his, but somehow he managed.

CHAPTER 43
Leo

Leo laid on the hard ground and wished it would swallow him whole. He wanted it to put him in eternal darkness, where Uro went. At least there, he would not hurt so much anymore.

It wasn't supposed to be this way.

When he had left Ulsana, he had forced Hae-il to track Norendra's magic, which led him straight to Rhyler's camp but not without obstacles. He had to fight more times than he expected. A part of him suspected Hae-il purposefully led him into confrontations hoping Leo would die, but Hae-il was not a lucky man.

When they finally found the camp, they had to hide on the adjacent mountainside. Leo was surprised at how large it was. At least two hundred or so people moved amongst the tents, barking orders and training. No doubt for some type of attack. When did Rhyler recruit so many Low-Borns?

"You got what you wanted now let me go," Hae-il grumbled, rubbing his still-healing hand where Arla stabbed him.

Leo looked down the mountainside they had come from. "200 feet. At that height, you won't feel a thing."

Hae-il looked over the ledge and immediately understood. He paled as he tried to step back, but Leo was blocking his only escape. "No. Please."

Leo moved forward. "You shouldn't have hurt her."

"I was trying to get to you!" Hae-il waved his bandaged hand. "She already stabbed me, isn't that enough?"

Leo stopped to think about Hae-il's question and everything that led him here. "No, it will never be enough."

He shoved Hae-il over the edge.

Hae-il screamed and screamed, flailing his arms. And he kept flailing, even though he never hit the ground. Finally, he blinked and looked down, realizing his heels were still on the rock edge. Only his body leaned out, held there by Leo's fist gripped around his shirt.

Leo held him there for a long, silent few minutes, grappling with himself. He wanted to let go. He wanted to get rid of Hae-il and all the High-Borns in this world.

But all he could see was Arla's face. Those tear-brimmed walnut eyes. What would she think if she saw him now?

He yanked Hae-il back to safety. The tracker shakily fell to his hands and knees. "You really are a monster."

Leo almost burst into a bitter laugh. Even under his mercy, Hae-il was spitting insults, such a noble characteristic.

"Be grateful this monster is letting you live. Now go before I change my mind."

Hae-il did not hesitate. He ran as quickly as his wobbling legs could take him and disappeared over the mountainside.

Not long after, Leo made his way down toward the camp and after a few hours of surveying, he finally found Uro. Much to his unbounded relief, his brother was safe and sound within the encampment. In fact, he was not only just safe, but... thriving. He no longer looked like the frightened, unsure young boy on that platform where he saw him last.

In the shadows, Leo observed his brother laughing with others and helping them sharpen their swords, and teaching them correct fighting positions. The very skills Uro despised when he was forced to practice them with Leo, which he found ironic.

Finally, after an hour or so, Uro entered an empty tent by himself, full of blankets and linens, and that's where Leo followed him in.

Once in the tent, Leo deliberately loudened his footsteps to get his brother to turn around. Uro startled, his hand quickly going for his sword, but then immediately loosened when he recognized him.

"Leo!" Uro exclaimed. His brother welcomed him with open arms. "You finally found me! I knew you would!"

Leo was a little jarred by how nonchalant Uro was being, like they were meeting at a friendly party, rather than in enemy territory.

Still, he hugged Uro tightly. "You gave us a scare, disappearing like that. I'm glad you're safe."

"I'm sorry. I know you must have been worried about me, but Rhyler said it could endanger everyone here if I sent word, especially since... you know." Uro averted his eyes, but Leo knew what he meant. Rhyler was worried that if Uro reached out to them, then Arla would eventually find out. She was Queen of Ulsana, the representation of everything they fought against. "But that doesn't matter anymore. I'm just glad you are here." Uro beamed. "With you on our side, we could really win this."

"Your side?" Leo asked.

"You finally see what we have to do. That's why you came, isn't it?"

"I came to make sure you were safe."

"I'm more than safe."

"Good. Then, let's go." Leo made to grab him.

Uro dodged his grasp. "I'm not going back!"

"We're not going back." The words sounded foreign to him. Was his plan to return to Ulsana? When he left Arla, he only knew two things for sure: that he could not be there anymore and that he had to find Uro. And now that he had accomplished both, he wasn't sure what the next step was, which was not like him at all. He liked order. He liked having a plan. He liked knowing what to do next.

"Then where are we going, Leo?"

Leo paused.

Uro scoffed. "You don't know, do you? Because you know that no matter where we go, we'll be Low-Borns and treated as such, but not here. Not in Rhyler's future."

Rhyler's future. The future where all High-Borns lay dead at his feet.

He looked at Uro's eager face and realized that Uro had looked so happy here because he *was* happy. His little brother believed in Rhyler.

This was bad.

Wasn't it?

Uro smiled. "I told Rhyler about you, you know. He was impressed by what you've done. He was sure you'd come for me eventually and realize that you belong here."

Did he belong here? Leo had to admit he did not disagree with Rhyler. In fact, he understood him, just as many Low-Borns did. The High-Borns did deserve to pay for what they did. But did that punishment warrant their deaths?

Uro must have noticed his hesitation. "Rhyler is going to save us. We'll finally be free to do whatever we want."

Whatever they wanted…?

He just wanted the people he cared about to be safe. He wanted to stop suffering. He wanted the nobles to pay and… a flash of Arla's smiling face crossed his mind. He wanted her. But it did not seem like that was possible now. Somewhere along the way, he had to choose between her and his sanity, and he could not have both. They belonged to two different worlds.

"We can have it all." Uro continued. "As soon as we take Ulsana."

"Take Ulsana? What do you mean by that?"

Uro grinned. "Tomorrow morning, we will attack the city and make it ours."

Uro's eagerness unnerved him. "You're going to capture all the nobles?"

"No, Rhyler said it won't be enough to just imprison them. We have to eliminate them. As many as we can."

Leo's blood ran cold. He had never heard Uro talk like a cold-blooded killer. This was all Rhyler's doing. He had poisoned Uro's mind with hatred.

Rhyler may have been Low-Born, but he was just as power-hungry as the nobles. Rhyler did not want justice, he wanted revenge.

Isn't that what you want too?

Leo paused, shocked at his own inner voice.

Don't you want them to pay for all the hurt they've caused? It's only fair.

A part of him did. The part that raged in anger, but another part of him, felt something wasn't completely right about that. What would the end look like when all the nobles were dead?

'Did it make it go away?' Rose's words still lingered within him.

"And you truly think that will give you your freedom?" Leo asked.

"Of course. Rhyler promised us."

"Uro–" But he never got the chance to finish his sentence, because a group of men entered the tent, each grim-faced and serious. Clearly, they knew an unwanted guest had arrived. The leader spoke for all of them. "Uro, I see you found a guest. Rhyler wants to see him."

They grabbed Leo, putting his hands behind his back. The lackey's grip was shoddy, easy to get out of, but Leo refrained from escaping because he, too, wanted to talk to Rhyler.

Uro frantically circled them. "There's nothing to worry about! He's on our side."

"Rhyler will be the judge of that." The leader said as he dragged Leo out.

"Don't worry!" Uro shouted after him. "Rhyler will see you're with us!"

Of course Uro believed that he had become a worshipper at Rhyler's feet. Leo, on the other hand, was not so sure.

Leo was bound and thrown into a prison wagon, metal bars separating him from the world. He didn't have to wait long before Rhyler appeared. The rebel leader had an odd presence about him. It wasn't one of terror or violence, but even and planned. Which probably made him more dangerous.

"We finally meet face to face," Leo said. "Last time, you had your minions tie me up and force me to watch your little speech."

Rhyler gave him a friendly smile. "Did you like it? You must have if you are here."

Leo leaned forward, determined to get his answers. "What will happen once you kill all the nobles in Ulsana?"

Rhyler chuckled. "I see you are not one for small talk. Very well. I will humor you for Uro's sake. I will create a new kingdom, one where *we* will have the power. No one will ever hurt us ever again."

There was still something about the man that made Leo uneasy. His instinct told him not to trust him.

"You can't possibly think you can actually kill them all?"

"Oh, no. I don't plan to kill them *all*. Some will live. So they can truly understand what they put us through. They will live as we lived. Desperate, hungry, afraid."

Now it made sense why Leo was hesitant in truly believing Rhyler. This man did not want true peace. He wanted death and power.

"Uro told me you switched to our side," Rhyler continued. "I have heard of your adventure in The Forest. What you did for the Queen Regent. I find it hard to believe that someone as bound to her as you are would betray her." Rhyler stepped closer to the bars. "Or did your affection turn to disgust when she found out the truth and did nothing to change it? Were you disappointed when she chose to protect her people over yours?"

Leo looked away and instantly regretted it because Rhyler knew what it meant. "I knew she would. She is a High-Born after all."

Leo did not respond, unwilling to give Rhyler more information.

Rhyler gave a great sigh, like a man burdened by responsibility. "Maybe you have switched sides, but I cannot take that risk. So you will stay here until everything settles. Because tomorrow, the world changes." Rhyler grinned, his eyes bright with desire. "Ulsana's streets will run with the blood of those who have wronged us for too long."

Leo could almost taste Rhyler's blood thirst because he had it too. Rhyler was willing to hurt others to get his revenge and so was Leo. Seeing him now, Leo saw his future reflected back at him if he let his darkness finally consume him. It would be easy to lash out, to destroy, but what would that gain? What would Leo be left with in the end? Another kingdom of the powerful and the powerless.

It all felt the same, whether they were on the top or bottom, the entire thing felt wrong. And he did not want to end up like Rhyler.

Rhyler seemed to sense Leo's resistance because he leaned forward to look straight into Leo's eyes. "You will see I am right, Captain. Just you wait. I will bring you the head of the queen that has oppressed you."

Everything in Leo prickled, and he shot up to his feet. "Stay away from her."

Rhyler chuckled. "I knew you couldn't have come here to join us. You care too much for her." Rhyler backed away. "Just wait, Captain. Just wait."

And wait, he did.

They wheeled the wagon along as they made their way to Ulsana and he saw how they got in: spies on the inside. Low-Borns employed by the crowd working in every section of the castle. It was so easy. And when the attack began, he remained there, helpless. His anxiety spiked, knowing that Arla was in the castle and Rhyler was going to go after her. He had to stop him, but he was not strong enough to bend the bars nor small enough to fit through them. He kept trying to undo his ties, but kept failing, until he caught a lucky break. During the attack, an injured horse crashed into the wagon, tumbling it to its side and releasing the door.

Leo freed himself and grappled a sword out of a noble guard's hands.

The battle raged within the city. Nobles attacked him, believing he was with Rhyler, but he disarmed them quickly. He desperately searched for Arla. He needed to find her and get her away from this place, along with Uro.

His heart stopped when he saw Uro about to kill Arla. What kind of nightmare had he walked into where Uro, who once loved gossiping with Arla, sitting beside her in giggling fits, now was calling his shadows to pierce her heart?

What had happened to them?

When he blocked the attack, he wanted to convince Uro that they didn't have to be a part of this. They could run away and start over somewhere else, but it was too late.

We will never be free.

Uro's last words haunted him. He was right. They would never be free except in death.

And so darkness had found him once again, but it was different this time. Where there was once anger, there was only hopelessness and the stench of failure. Here, in the refugee camp of Ulsanan's leftovers, he had no access to a sword or rope, only isolation, and slowly he thought to starve himself to death.

But Arla would not let him. Often, she came just to feed him. She would try to make small talk, but he couldn't bring himself to say anything. It was like a numbness had taken over him, holding him under water, drowning out everything else.

The only time he felt anything was when he saw Arla's lip quiver. He felt pangs of guilt for making her suffer too. If only she would let him disappear, then her pain would disappear too.

He was failing her, he knew that. He also failed Uro and Rose, and both were dead because of it. And his mother... she had suffered so long while he only managed to pay for her survival. Why hadn't he done something earlier and taken his mother somewhere else?

He failed as a brother, a leader, a friend, and a partner. He was of no use to anyone. What was the point of his life now?

There wasn't. And so he lay there, unmoving, long after Arla left, staring, unblinking at the tent cloth over his head.

"I do not think you should go inside." A voice said from outside the tent. "He could still want to hurt nobles."

"Get out of my way."

A sudden burst of light disturbed Leo from his cathartic state. A flash. And suddenly, a shadow above him winked out the sunray that beamed through the entrance.

Hovering above him was that irritating scholar.

"Leo!" shouted Simion, too loudly for someone so close to him. "Get up! It's Arla! There's been a horrible accident. She's bleeding out!"

Every inch of Leo sparked, launching Leo to his feet. The sudden shift sent him immediately into vertigo, but he refused to fall from the dizziness.

Simion clenched his nose. "Oh Whispers, you smell."

"Where is she?" He was trying to shout, but his voice was unused for so long, it came out like a hoarse gruff.

"Follow me!"

Leo dashed behind Simion as he rushed out of the tent and into the blinding afternoon. Leo could barely see as he struggled to follow Simion weaving through startled Ulsanans.

Are the physicians already with her? Leo's heart raced. *Please don't die, Arla. Stay alive. I can't lose you too.*

Leo skidded to a stop just beside Simion, who pointed ahead of them. "I don't know if she'll make it," he cried out dramatically.

Leo followed where Simion was pointing, ready to run, ready to fight, ready for anything.

But then something stopped him.

Ahead of them in a small clearing was Arla, glowing in the sunlight.

Uninjured. Perfectly fine.

His ears grew hot with rage. This bastard lied to him. He curled his fist, ready to swing.

"Leo!" Arla rushed up to him, beaming with joy. Immediately, all his rage fizzled out. "You're finally outside! I can't believe it! Are you okay? Do you need anything?"

"No," Leo said shyly, suddenly feeling uneasy at her bright attention. "I'm fine."

"What made you come outside today?" she asked, still smiling widely.

Leo threw a hard glance at Simion. "The bastard told me you were dying."

Arla gaped at Simion. "He what?"

Simion shrugged, no guilt to be found. "It worked, didn't it?"

The ground rumbled beneath their feet, and then vines burst from the ground, attacking a grown woman further away. She slashed at the vines with a sword haphazardly, clearly never having taken up the weapon before. Another woman across from her remained still, her forehead covered in sweat, staring at the vines.

"Let the Whisper move freely!" shouted a third woman. Leo squinted and saw that this shouting woman was a noble, judging from her tattered silk dress.

And the one she was shouting at, holding the sword, she was wearing stained cotton and her hands were scarred, the telltale signs of a working servant.

Leo's mouth hung open. "That woman wielding the vines... she's Low-Born."

"We don't call each other Low or High-Borns anymore," Arla replied, beaming with pride at the three women. "But yes."

"How did she get magic?"

"I gave it to her." Arla kept watching the three women practice. "Simion and I figured out how to do it without anyone having to die."

Leo couldn't believe what he was hearing... or seeing. "And that one, shouting the instructions... she's... a noble."

"Yep."

Leo was flabbergasted. A noble helping a Low-Born control their new found magic... What was he seeing?

The vines snapped apart and retreated into the ground. The magic-wielding woman stomped her feet in frustration while the noblewoman shook her head. "This is not going to work."

The magic-wielding woman barked back, "Only because you're a terrible teacher, who doesn't know what they're doing!"

The noblewoman reddened. "How dare you!"

Arla gave a small sigh. ""Everyone is still hesitant in trusting each other and– It's a bit of a mess, as you can see. But we are trying."

The third woman with the sword came between the two who were threatening each other's lives now. "If anyone is going to kill anyone, it's going to be me!"

"Oh, no." Arla ran to them, trying to stop them from ending each other's lives.

He couldn't believe it. Somehow, the two classes were working together... albeit not well, but they were still there, trying. He watched as Arla yanked the sword from one woman and tried to calm them all down.

Leo's mouth still hung open.

Arla returned, looking exhausted, but flushed with hope. "They agreed to try again."

A flicker of hope sparked in his chest, but his heart had not felt it for so long that this feeling threatened to collapse him. Leo shook, feeling like a shadow of his former self.

For days, he had told himself he was a failure. That he was forever broken, with no purpose and no future. Everything he cared about he lost or left. Most days he could barely muster up the energy to open his eyes. The fact that he was standing here under the afternoon sun was a miracle. Everything in front of him now was a miracle.

And it was all because of her.

"I can't believe this. This... is...amazing."

"Well," Simion interjected smugly. "While you were feeling sorry for yourself, some of us have been hard at work."

Arla frowned. "Simion..."

Simion cleared his throat. "I mean. Welcome back Captain. So glad you are with us again."

Arla's frown curved into a teasing smile, which was returned in kind by Simion, an exchange Leo noticed instantly.

A small, worried feeling crept up from the bottom of his stomach. What was this look between them?

CHAPTER 44
Leo

Arla walked Leo back to his tent, along with a few other guards. She remained an arm's length away from him, and he wondered if it was more because she did not trust him or that he stunk.

He hoped it was the latter, although the presence of the guards suggested otherwise.

He inwardly blushed with how disheveled he had let himself become. His hair was uneven and too long, while his beard had grown unwieldy across his chin. But it wasn't just his physical form that had diminished, it was his soul as well. It was like waking up from a bad dream and rediscovering he had limbs. For the first time in a long time, Leo was unsure of himself.

When they finally arrived at the tent, Arla ordered new linens for his cot and dusted off the tent cloth. Coughing, she smiled, "Seems liveable enough. I'll come back later with food. You can rest until then."

Even when he had not spoken to her for weeks, she was still smiling. Still trying to bring light into his life. And he knew it was an act, specifically for him, which only made him feel worse.

The last time he had seen her, she had confessed that she loved him and he didn't say it back, in fact, he just left her. How that must have hurt her...

Leo stopped her before she left.

"I'm sorry I had to leave, I–"

She gave him a gentle smile. "It's okay. You did what you thought was right, and I can't blame you for that. I'm just glad you're alive and willing to go outside and take part in the world again. That's enough for me."

Emotion overcame him. Even though he was a failure and a traitor in her eyes, she still treated him so kindly.

"I know you have the guards there to protect the nobles. You think I might hurt them or myself, but I want you to know that I did not fight for Rhyler."

Arla paused. "I saw you draw your sword on a noble in the city."

"I had to disarm him. I just wanted to find Uro and keep him away from all this." He looked down in shame. "But I failed." His lips quivered, holding back the wave that would surely pull him under again. "I'm sorry I couldn't save him."

Arla hugged him so tightly it almost hurt.

The shock of the sudden warmth overcame him. He thought she would shout at him, tell him he was a failure and that he should have done better, but instead, she embraced him with such... care.

"Please don't blame yourself like that," she said softly into his shoulder. "It wasn't your fault."

"Don't say that," he said, his voice thin.

"It wasn't your fault," she repeated.

"But it was."

"It wasn't your fault."

A part of him wanted her to hate him. To shout and hit him. Tell him he was a failure and that he deserved to be punished.

But she kept repeating, "It wasn't your fault." Over and over again. The words bombarded him until he could not bear it any longer. He pushed them away in his head, but still she repeated, until they broke through.

And he buckled.

He buried his head in the crook of her shoulder and wept, shedding all the pain inside him.

And she held him as he shook in grief.

It felt like hours before the tears eventually dried. And then, surprisingly, he felt a little more like himself again.

Finally, he let her go and wiped the rest of his face with his dirty sleeve. "Thank you," he breathed.

"Of course. Always." Arla gave him such a loving gaze that he couldn't help himself. He leaned forward to kiss her.

She pulled back. A small movement, but it felt monumental. He stopped himself and straightened back. She looked away from him nervously, and his chest constricted.

And then he remembered his appearance. Of course. He was so unkempt that it must be hard even to look at him at this moment. It made sense that she kept her distance.

She forced a sweet smile to hide the awkwardness. "I really am happy you are feeling better."

He smiled at her, but her gaze did not land within his. Instead, she continued to avoid his eye, and suddenly Leo felt it was something less to do with his appearance and more something else. Suddenly, the image of how Arla looked at Simion earlier today burned into his mind.

"What you did today... giving magic to the Low-Borns and training them. It gave me hope that we could really make things better. I'm sorry I doubted you."

"No. You were right. I wasn't making decisions, and that got us into this mess. I just wanted everyone to be happy, but I know now that to get the peace we need, it will mean going through tough times."

And there it was. Like a drop in a lake that rippled to the edges of his soul. He grounded himself in her words. Her goal. Leo had finally found something to grab onto again. Another reason to live.

Leo smirked. "Things are always more complicated than they look."

Arla nodded, still not looking him in the eye. "It is."

"I know... that I'm a mess right now, but whatever I have left of me, I will use to help you. I promise."

She finally looked at him, surprised. "Leo, I don't expect anything from you. I just want you to heal. You've been through so much."

"But so have you."

Arla paused and something in her expression made him think there was something more to her words.

"Do you not believe that I want to help you?" he asked.

"I believe you don't want to hurt me."

Her answer took him aback. Yet, should he have expected anything different? He had left her when she needed him the most. It was one of the hardest decisions he had ever had to make — to choose between staying for her or leaving for Uro. But he had made his choice, and now he was telling her he would help her — a promise maybe she was not ready to believe.

She forced another smile. "You should rest now. I have to go."

He watched her leave without the heart to stop her. There was a time when she used to linger just to be able to spend a few more moments with him, but now she didn't seem so eager to do that.

What was he to her now after everything that had happened?

Was it fair to even ask that question at this moment, when she had so much on her shoulders?

No, he told himself. Arla had a lot on her mind. She had responsibilities. It was not fair to burden her with what he wanted from her right now. The only thing she needed from him was his help. And his help he would give.

CHAPTER 45

When Arla awoke the next morning, she felt a bit guilty. She did not intend to pull so quickly away from Leo the other day. She was shocked that she did that. There was a time when all she wanted was to be near him, but her body moved on its own, as if rejecting the closeness. Leo had clearly noticed.

'I promise.'

She wanted to tell him not to say those things to her. She didn't want to hear him promise her something he would not follow through on. Things may change again, and when they did, she didn't know if he would leave again.

Perhaps that was what it was. She had built a wall to protect herself, in case he were to abandon her again. Not that she blamed him, but it still hurt to be left.

She left the tent, toward the main training arena they had made in the woods, ready to mediate more fighting between the Ulsanans. It made sense why the fights between the classes continued. They were learning how to fight, wield magic and move past old wrongdoings all at once to save their loved ones. It was a lot to ask of them.

But when she got there, she saw something completely unexpected.

In the center were a group of Ulsanans from all backgrounds in perfect formation, practicing defensive positions, and in the front center was Leo, going over the techniques. He bellowed out commands, firm and authoritative, and the others followed without argument.

It seemed Leo was training them so hard that they did not have the energy to fight each other anymore.

It was amazing to watch.

Simion appeared beside her. "I can't believe they are all listening to him." He looked a bit tired. She must have looked the same way. They were both staying up later and later teaching Ulsanans how to wield their newly given magic.

Leo had told her he would help her any way he could, and there he was, following through on that promise. Still, the wall of ice remained.

Simion crossed his arms. "Oh look, he also managed to bathe and cut his hair."

She hit him on the arm.

Simion dramatically rubbed his arm in feigned hurt for much longer than he needed to. "Oh, Queen Arla, how could you hurt me so? I am only your humble servant."

Arla truly did not like it when Simion teased Leo. His lack of empathy bothered her, but she could not help but be amused at his theatrical antics. How silly he could be when he was not cruel. She was about to smile when she saw Leo walking towards them. She bit her lip and grew serious.

Simion noticed the shift and pouted, turning his attention to Leo. "Looking good, Captain."

Leo ignored him completely, only looking at Arla. "They are not battle ready."

Simion snorted. "Obviously."

Arla lightly shoved Simion with her shoulder. She felt Leo's eyes silently observing them.

"But they will be after I'm done with them." Leo continued. Arla beamed, which made Leo perk up. "But these handful of fighters are not going to be enough to take out Rhyler's entire *magic-wielding* army."

"Well, the plan isn't to face the entire army directly. We just need a few of us to sneak into the castle and get the prisoners."

"And if we're discovered?"

"We won't be discovered because we'll have a distraction." Arla grinned mischievously. "I am going to summon an army of monsters."

CHAPTER 46
Leo

"How many?" Leo tried to restrain the shock in his voice, but it came out anyway.

"Fifteen," she said with a confidence that flabbergasted him. So far, Arla had only summoned two creatures at a time, so how could she do fifteen in only a week? "I'll keep practicing until I can get them to stay and fight. While they create a distraction for Rhyler's guards, Simion will teleport a group of us into the tunnels so we can get in unnoticed. Once inside, we'll free the prisoners and bring them back."

The plan seemed solid enough, but Leo worried about the strain this would put on Arla. He wasn't sure whether to bring it up now when she seemed so excited about it.

"We'll get Rose back soon," she said.

Rose. Leo was so sure she was already gone from this world, but Arla seemed to disagree. Her blind hope restrained him from pushing it further. He did not want to discourage her.

A young boy sheepishly approached Arla. "Um. Your Highness? They are ready."

"Oh." Arla startled. "Right." She turned back to the two of them. "I'll be right back."

She followed the boy only a few paces to a small group of people who eagerly waited for her. She waved her hands around, directing them to form a line.

Simion crossed his arms in disapproval. "I keep telling her to limit herself to one every few days, but she insists on more."

Arla held a man's face in her hands and closed her eyes. Her hands glowed as slivers of gold thread inched their way from her hands and to the man's forehead. The boy watched in awe beside her.

"So that is how she transfers her magic?" Leo asked. "Doesn't that mean she has less for herself?"

"So perceptive, Captain. What's it like being a genius?"

Leo really did not understand how anyone tolerated Simion's presence for more than a few breaths. Already he wanted to punch this man in the face.

Simion looked at Arla again, his sarcastic tone turning to genuine worry. "She says she has plenty, but that's a lie. So far she's given away five Whispers. She cannot afford to keep doing this, but she does anyway. Stubborn woman."

"A *selfless*, stubborn woman." Leo corrected.

Simion sighed. "That she is."

Leo noticed how Simion watched her. There was a longing there that Leo would be a fool not to recognize. "You rushed me out of my tent for her, didn't you?"

"Wow. I am shocked that you could piece that together. Maybe you are more than just a sword-wielding brute." Simion continued to watch Arla, concern rimming his amber irises. "If you have to know, I did it because I was tired of hearing her cry."

The idea of Arla crying alone made Leo ache.

"Frankly," Simion continued. "I don't think you are worth the tears. She deserves someone better."

"Someone like you?"

Simion finally turned to face him, at the end of his patience. "*Exactly* like me."

Leo was taken aback by the absurd level of confidence this man had. He could have tackled Simion right then and there, but that would have just played right into his belief that Leo was a brute.

"Her infatuation with you was only because you were the first to give her attention when she had none, but now that she has more options, she'll see who really belongs by her side. And let me be direct with you, Captain, I intend to make that choice very clear for her."

Leo tried to keep his voice level. "You are very sure of yourself."

"I am sure of what she needs. Doesn't it make more sense for her to end up with me? I understand magic. I understand her problems as Queen. I am better equipped to help her bring Ulsana together. You are just a soldier who left her when she needed someone the most. *I* was the one who gave her the support she needed. *I* was there."

The full consequences of his actions hit him like a brick. How utterly abandoned she must have felt, especially from him, the man who told her in the heat of the night that he wanted to protect her and care for her. Those words must have sounded like lies to her now.

Before, he had been so angry with her for not making a choice, but he had put all the responsibility on her to make it. He did not share the burden with her. He didn't understand at the time.

That was what Simion was talking about. He understood where Leo did not.

Was Simion right then?

He remembered the way Arla pulled away from his embrace. The distance she put between them. No, she did not put the distance there, he did. He had left her first.

And in her moment of need, Simion was there for her. How monumental that must have been. How comforting...

He looked at Arla, who was smiling so brightly as the man gave her a hug. Was she able to smile today because of Simion?

What else had bloomed between them in his absence?

He imagined Simion holding Arla in his arms. His heart constricted at the thought of her sighing softly into Simion's chest the way she had with him. Every fiber of his being rejected the thought. He wanted to march up to her and beg for her forgiveness.

But did he deserve it?

CHAPTER 47

Arla kicked the dirt in frustration. Only three. That was the maximum number of monsters she could summon at once and have them moving at the same time. The fourth always appeared and then slipped away, taking the others with it.

She had so confidently boasted she could do fifteen, and now she looked like a fool. How was she possibly going to do this?

She turned her head so as not to let her frustration show too much in front of the boys. She had been out in the woods practicing for three days, and each time Simion and Leo insisted on coming with her. It was strange how attached they had become to her lately. If one was there, the other was sure to be there as well. She often found them bickering on the side so much that she wondered if they had come more for her or for each other.

Wiping the sweat off her brow, she prepared to start again. There really was no other choice. The monsters were key in creating a distraction large enough to divert Rhyler's army away from their search and rescue party without losing any lives.

So far, about seven Ulsanans received magic, so they would come along with the three of them.

She closed her eyes, willing the Whispers to fill her again. There were a lot fewer than before. She did not think giving away a handful of them would already make her feel emptier, but it did. She could hear their echoing absence in her head.

"*Uthred 'el thur-nabu qil-i buthra-dana.*"

A lightning fox-like creature thundered into existence, sending crackles of light around it. She smiled. Of all the Whispers she had, she could not let go of this one. The very creature that had saved Leo from being executed in the arena.

"*Uthred 'el thur-nabu qil-i buthra-dana.*" Another lightening creature exploded into existence beside the first. Already she felt the drain. "*Ceradas bival-ahala.*"

The six-legged insect monster that almost killed her in The Forest crawled from the ground, screeching.

The Whispers wavered in her head, sensing she could not handle summoning another one of them. She willed them to stay and fall onto her tongue. One more. She could do it this time. She had to.

She pulled down another one by force.

"*Ceradas bival-ahala.*"

Another creature of death burst from the ground, slashing the air with its fore-legs, spitting acid near her feet.

Yes! A fourth! Finally!

Her vision blurred from the strain as her body slowly began giving out. *No. Another one.* She pulled the Whispers back to the front of her mind, even as they resisted her. She mentally grabbed one, but it fought back. She growled in frustration and yanked it harder. It twisted as it tumbled onto her tongue and changed shape, flipping over itself until its words were utterly different.

And when she went to say them, it came out strangled. Sounds she had never heard before.

And then the whole world darkened.

Sharp leafless trees burst from the ground, growing tall enough to block out the sky. She knew these trees. Suddenly, she was right in the middle of The Forest once more.

Why was she here again?

She kept finding herself here where it all began. The same dark place. Except it did not instill fear in her like it used to. Instead, it was becoming as familiar as a home would.

A grayish glow formed beside her.

Arla squinted. "Wynera?"

The ancient princess gave her a worried look. *"Be brave."*

A ghastly voice whipped out from the trees, shaking Arla to her bones. *"You defy me, daughter."*

Arla clutched her chest, trying to anchor herself. The voice was so powerful it threatened to burst her eardrums.

Daughter?

"Your champion gives more magic to the unworthy."

Arla shook, realizing whose voice this was.

She was hearing The Forest's voice. The sheer power of it made her knees shake.

Wynera's shimmering form wavered in fear. *"They are not all unworthy. There are some who still wield magic with empathy."*

The Forest rumbled as if laughing. *"After everything they did to you, you still believe? I gave your beloved the power to choose, and instead of freeing himself from me, he chose revenge, giving magic to that human, knowing what he would do. And yet you still believe humans deserve to wield magic?"*

Wynera's eyes watered, making Arla's heart ache.

"That is unfair," Arla interjected.

She felt the entire air shift and pressed against her. The weight almost knocked her backwards. Why did she just anger the most powerful entity in the world? How stupid of her. Still, she could not let it reprimand Wynera unjustly. She tried her best to keep her voice steady. "It is not a bad thing to hope."

"Your champion speaks despite her fear. Is that why you chose her?" The Forest chuckled. *"She is so small. Too frail. She will fail."*

Arla pointed a finger up, trying to politely interject once again. How did one interrupt an all powerful entity properly? "Sorry, but what will I fail at? And why do you keep calling me her champion?"

Wynera placed a ghostly hand on her shoulder. *"Because I chose you to help me stop Rhyler. To stop... Dehen."* Wynera gave her an apologetic look. *"The Forest believes that all humans are unworthy of magic and wanted to prove it by testing Dehen. It gave Dehen the power to grant magic to anyone and Dehen chose the one human who would kill all the nobles."*

Poor Wynera. Arla wondered how disappointed Wynera was when Dehen chose vengence. Did it break her heart all over again?

"You are the last thing that could stand in his way. Because you are the only one who he cannot take magic from he wants to end your life, and if he does... then there will be no stopping him from spreading his hatred."

"He will kill all of them, won't he?" Arla didn't need the answer. Rhyler and Dehen would not stop at just Ulsana. He would want to spill the blood of every noble in the world. She spoke to The Forest. "And when he does, what will you do then?"

The Forest rumbled. *"When the human destroys what he can, I will take the rest."*

Arla couldn't believe it. "You're going to kill us all?"

The Forest roared in anger. *"Humans always destroy precious things with their lust for power. They are a plague."*

"Not all of us are like that."

The Forest chuckled. *"I've watched your kind for thousands of years. I know what you are made of."*

Arla was panicking now. Whether or not she stopped Rhyler was no longer going to matter. The Forest was going to kill them all anyway. It just wanted to see them suffer in a war first. There had to be some other alternative. Some way she could save them. And then the idea came to her.

"What if, instead, I stop Rhyler and take back the kingdom and don't let the power corrupt me, then you won't destroy us."

The Forest flared in anger. *"You dare command me?!"*

Arla flinched back, but stood her ground. "It was a wager. You like those, right?"

The Forest's anger receded and she could feel the curiosity ooze from it. *"Clever. Then, let us see, little champion, what will become of you when you taste what true power is. Either you will succumb to it like the rest of your kind or someone dear to you will betray you for it. Just like your ancestors. You will see."*

The ground opened up beneath her, and she plummeted into eternal darkness. She screamed, but no sound came out as she spun and spun until her body landed on all fours back to the ground.

"Arla!" The boys ran up to her, worry written all over their faces.

"Are you alright?" Leo asked.

"You were speaking in Whispers I've never heard before." Simion said.

Each offered her their hand to take.

She took neither and remained crouched on her hands.

"The Forest," she gasped, trying to take in a breath. "It's watching to see who wins. Me or Rhyler."

"What?" Simion asked. "Why?"

"It wants to destroy us. It thinks humans are corrupt and cannot be trusted with pow–"

'Either you will succumb to the power like the rest of your kind does or someone dear to you will betray you for it.'

Arla gasped. Something cracked open, pouring a flood of Whispers through her. They jammed into her skull filling it until she thought her head might burst. She clutched her head screaming.

She blinked back tears of pain and then, suddenly ropes of light burst through her vision. She saw... *everything*. Every rock. Every leaf. Even her own hands. They all had a stream of light running through them. Each light pulsed with warbled words, beckoning her to say them.

Each of them started with the same phrase. A phrase she had heard before.

Ithrid gu-lia bukami chrek-ek noon-tha. Ther-gul eil dan huy-uq-tha. Loren vuy-i-al-san.

A small beetle scurried past her fingertips, a light beating at its center, repeating over and over, '*inesh*'.

It compelled her to say it, and like a moth to a flame, she could not help but repeat the words.

"*Ithrid gu-lia bukami chrek-ek noon-tha. Ther-gul eil dan huy-uq-tha. Loren vuy-i-al-san... inesh.*"

The beetle froze mid-step. It squirmed in anguish and then sharp black roots shot out from its back, growing larger and larger. Arla scrambled backward as the beetle's back split into infinite black roots until it grew twice her size. The black roots congealed together, forming a monstrous, skeletal-like beetle with tattered wings and a horned head.

It roared, flapping its giant wings.

Leo and Simion shouted in shock, and then quickly went for their weapons.

"Wait!" Arla shouted. "It's mine."

The beetle stood still, waiting for her command.

The other four creatures remained still, also waiting. They were still here... Realization hit her that she had done it. She had five creatures up at the same time!

She felt ecstatic until exhaustion hit her hard, and with one sigh, all her creatures turned to mist.

Except for the beetle. Instead of mist, it crumbled into a pile of ash.

Arla reached over and touched the pile, smearing ash on her fingertips.

Ithrid gu-lia bukami chrek-ek noon-tha. Ther-gul eil dan huy-uq-tha. Loren vuy-i-al-san.

She had used this Whisper before. It was the same phrase she had used to turn her stone statue into a creature, but the last word belonged to the object.

To change the statue was *Ithrid gu-lia bukami chrek-ek noon-tha. Ther-gul eil dan huy-uq-tha. Loren vuy-i-al-san...* ***chryu***.

Whispers that she never heard again, probably because the statue did not exist.

She looked around for the beetle on the ground, but it was gone.

"*Ithrid gu-lia bukami chrek-ek noon-tha. Ther-gul eil dan huy-uq-tha. Loren vuy-i-al-san... **inesh**,*" she repeated, but nothing happened. No giant beetle creature appeared.

And then she realized what this power was.

She pulled back her hand.

The beetle was dead.

Blinked out of existence.

She had turned it into a creature, and when she could not hold its magic, it died. Just like her statue.

"Did you hear a new Whisper?" Leo asked, treading lightly.

She turned to Leo and saw the stream of white pulsing through him too and at the center of his chest beat a light that echoed, '*Mehvar. Mehvar*'

It beckoned her to say it, a pull so strong she was already leaning forward, ready.

She pushed herself away from him. Hurt flashed across his face, but she was too frightened to feel guilty about it.

"What's wrong?" Simion asked.

Arla looked to Simion, but there was no light beating in his heart. She could only hear Leo's, which only grew louder.

She squeezed her eyes closed. "The Forest did this. It wants to corrupt me. To prove that humans don't deserve magic."

It was probably laughing at her now watching her struggle.

"Did what?" Leo was very concerned now. "Arla, talk to us."

"I can see them and hear them. The Whispers that things make. It's too much. I don't want to make a mistake and hurt someone."

Leo gently grasped her hand. "You won't. You can control this."

"How can you know that?" she snapped, pulling her hand away.

The light in his chest dimmed, but still it beat. *'Mehvar. Mehvar.'*

He paused before continuing in a comforting tone. "Because I will help you. Whatever you need, I'm here for you."

"I don't believe you," Arla retorted. "You can't possibly understand."

She did not mean to say it, but it was partially the truth. Leo had no idea what it was like to have magic. How it felt. What it could do to her. To the people around her. Even if it came from good intentions, what could he really help her with when it came to magic? And who knew if he would stay once he understood? He hated High-Borns. He hated magic. He hated everything Arla came from.

Leo withdrew from her.

She wanted to apologize immediately, but Simion was already pulling her away. "For now, just don't use this new magic. Maybe there is something in the books that mentions these new types of Whispers and what could be expected."

Arla nodded, feeling a bit of comfort in the belief that maybe the past would hold some answers.

"Let us go." Simion led Arla away.

The ground pulsed with streams of light that led in every direction, but the light was dulling with every passing second, like her power was wearing off, and yet she could still hear Leo's Whisper thrumming in her ears.

'Mehvar. Mehvar.'

CHAPTER 48
Leo

"This is not good."

Leo grimaced at Simion's comment. *Obviously,* this was not good. They stood a foot apart as they watched Arla from a distance.

She was pulling another creature from the ground. Sweat beaded her brow, and her chest heaved hard up and down, the signs of obvious strain. Arla was already pushing herself before, but the way she was training now was borderline neurotic.

Instead of sleeping like she should, she spent her nights summoning monsters. Ever since she had discovered her new Whispers, she had been acting strange. She stopped coming outside her tent during the day, leaving Leo to continue to teach the volunteers how to fight while Simion taught them how to control their Whispers.

She explained it was because it wasn't safe. He suspected she meant *they* were not safe from her, which still confused him. She had told them she could hear more Whispers, but she never explained what that actually meant. What could she do now that scared her so?

They had discovered she was training by herself in the middle of the night quite by accident, and although she clearly did not want them there, they stubbornly watched over her, worried that she was going to break from the exertion.

She had sped up her monster summoning, going from five to a whopping ten, although she struggled to get them to move in unison. The pressure of getting this to work was high, since they were set to travel to Ulsana tomorrow night.

Unlike Arla, Leo was not so eager to step back into the royal castle. Unlike Arla, Leo did not believe Rose was still alive and to now risk Arla's life to save captured nobles, was not high on his priority list.

Arla swayed as she summoned another creature. He knew that movement. He was running before he knew it.

She collapsed in his arms as Simion caught up quickly, grabbing her other arm. "We need to get to the physician."

Her head rolled to the side, completely unconscious as her nose bled. Panic crept over him as he picked up his pace, his fear malforming to agitation at Simion.

"Move faster," he growled.

The physician woke up with a start as the boys barged into his tent, carrying an unresponsive Arla to the cot. He got to work right away.

"Is she okay?" Leo eagerly leaned over Arla, checking that she was still breathing.

The physician pushed him away. "If you let me get to work, I can tell you soon enough."

Leo and Simion reluctantly kept their distance and waited for the physician to be done.

The physician held onto her wrist. "*Tempe-burlam.*" A wave of light hovered over Arla, returning color to her skin. "Blood pressure is low, but overall she is fine. But there is something else..."

Arla woke up with a start, looking around in confusion. The boys rushed to her side.

"What happened?" she asked, holding her head.

"You collapsed." Leo attempted to touch her shoulder but thought better of it.

She wiped her nose. Seeing the blood on her hand, she did not seem surprised, which was even more concerning. Was this not a new thing? Had she collapsed before? How often was it happening?

Seeing Arla like this drained him. The loss of Uro still left him feeling like a fraction of himself, but day by day he felt a little stronger because he had a reason to get up in the morning. He had something to hope for. But that reason was now lying on a medical cot, fading in front of his eyes, and it was becoming unbearable to watch.

Arla rolled off the cot with some effort and got up to leave. Leo held her down. "Where are you going? You need to rest."

"I'm fine." The dark circles under her eyes made her look almost skeletal, sending a shiver of worry through Leo. Why was she acting like this wasn't harming her?

Arla pushed past him and left the tent.

His hands curled into fists. He wasn't going to let her destroy herself.

He marched after her.

Simion attempted to follow, but the physician stopped him. "I need to speak with you."

Leo called after her, but she ignored him and quickened her pace, although her steps were still wobbly.

"Arla!" he shouted, not caring who heard him.

Still, she did not stop as she ducked into her tent.

He burst in after her. "I know you can hear me. Why are you ignoring me?!"

"I'm not." She did not look him in the eye.

"Yes, you are!" he shouted. "I will not leave until you tell me what is going on. I know you think I can't help you, but you can't go on putting this burden on yourself. Please. Let me help you."

Arla bit her lip, unsure.

Leo paused. *Oh.* It wasn't him she wanted. It was the scholar.

He remembered how Simion was able to comfort her the day she got her new Whispers. Maybe he was right after all. Maybe Simion was what she wanted. Simion knew more about this world than Leo did.

Ignoring the ache in his chest, he said, "I'll go get the scholar."

Arla grabbed his sleeve. "No." Her head drooped. "I'm sorry, I'm just... I'm..." She sighed. "Just when I thought I had a handle on my Whispers, things changed again. Things keep changing all the time, and I'm never ahead of it." She took in a deep breath, still hesitant, and then finally said. "I can hear other's Whispers. It's like everything has a word for itself and if I say them then I can turn them into monsters. Living or non-living it doesn't matter. But once I can't hold them anymore they disappear... forever. That's why I can't look at people, why I turn away. I don't want to see them, I don't want to hear them."

To say he was shocked was an understatement. "You can hear everyone's Whisper?"

He did not know that was possible.

She shook her head. "Not everyone's. Just a few. I can hear the animals and some trees."

"And the people?"

"Just one so far."

"Whose?"

She hesitated again.

"Whose, Arla?" he asked again.

She pointed to his chest.

Leo startled. "Mine?"

It was strange thinking he had his own Whisper. He couldn't help but wonder what it sounded like.

"I don't know why it's just you." She squeezed her eyes shut. "But it's begging me to say it, but if I do then... I don't want to. I don't want to hurt you."

Leo wanted to hold her, but she had pulled away every time he had tried before, so he kept his distance. Instead, he put his hands together to refrain from reaching out. "It's not fair that so much is on you. It must be so scary and so tiring. I want you to know that of all the things you worry about, I am not one of them. Whatever happens, I know the risks and I will not blame you for anything."

She gave him a confused look.

Leo smiled. "What I mean is, it's okay, you can hurt me."

"But I don't want to."

"I'd rather take that risk than have you keep avoiding me."

Arla. I miss you. Don't push me away.

He wanted to say it so badly, but was afraid of what answer she would give. Would she feel obligated to say that she missed him too? Would she say it just to make him feel better?

Instead, he said, "It'll be hard to work together if you keep avoiding me."

"But—"

"No more 'buts'. I am going to help you, so you might as well not fight me about it. Let's just work together, okay?"

In a way he was relieved that her avoidance of him was because of her new found magic. He was afraid it was more related to the scholar.

Arla contemplated what he said for a moment. She really was afraid of hurting him, he could see it in her eyes, but he held his confidence, hoping it would soothe her. And after a few moments of hesitation, it seemed to work.

She nodded slightly. "Okay." He could see how tired she was, barely even able to keep standing or her eyes open.

Arla's knees buckled, and Leo caught her by the waist before she hit the ground. She was unconscious again, and the worry spiked in his chest once more.

She needed to rest.

He picked her up in his arms and relished the contact. It had been so long since he felt her body in his arms, he wanted to linger there just to savor the moment a little longer, but he knew it was wrong to do so, so he carried her over to her cot and gently laid her down.

Just as he was about to completely pull away, she rolled into his chest and let out a sigh that sent shivers down his body. It was the sigh he remembered. The one of contentment and safety.

He wished she had done it on purpose. That she was dreaming of him and wanted him close, but a part of him worried it was actually the scholar she was thinking of. And that thought made him finally let her go.

He covered her with a blanket and forced himself to leave immediately, or else he would have just kept watching her sleep, searching for all the little signs to determine who she was thinking of when she sighed like that.

He found the physician back in the medical tent, speaking to the scholar in a low, concerned voice.

"Doctor," Leo said. "She collapsed again. Can you see if she is alright?"

"Of course," the physician blubbered and scurried out of the tent.

Simion crossed his arms, tapping his forearm with a finger in worry. "The doctor said he doesn't know how much longer Arla can last if she keeps pushing herself like this." He huffed in frustration. "Why is she being so stubborn? There is no way we are going to Ulsana tomorrow with her like that."

"I agree."

Simion blinked, shocked. This was the first time they had agreed on anything. He waited, but Leo did not continue. "Is that it? No explanation? No follow-up?"

"You already said it all. The fewer words I have to exchange with you, the better."

"Good, so then we postpone the rescue."

"I agree," Simion replied.

Now it was Leo's turn to be surprised. The scholar agreed with him? That was a first.

"So then what do we do?" Simion gripped his jacket collar in exasperation. "Strap her down and mute her? How can we stop her from destroying herself?"

"I don't know..." Leo felt just as helpless as Simion.

"You are completely useless, you know that?" Simion said bitingly before marching out of the tent.

Leo was not offended by the scholar. He understood his frustration. He was just as scared, but he couldn't lose his cool, not when Arla was already falling apart. He had to remain steady, even when he felt like a storm threatening to explode.

When he was broken, Arla was strong for him, so now he would be the same for her.

That night, he laid down, knowing he would not get any sleep. He needed to think of how to convince Arla to postpone the rescue, at least until she had enough rest.

And then, a crunching sound of gravel caught his attention just outside his tent. In one motion, he was up, and just when he reached for his sword, the tent flaps billowed open.

"*Kem-et.*"

He saw only a glimpse of a young woman waving her hand in front of his face before the ground shook and trees of black and rot shot up from beneath his feet. In an instant he was in The Forest again. His heart beat fast. He grabbed for a weapon, but there was nothing on his person or nearby.

What was this? Magic? How could he be here again?

A mist billowed around him and through it, a figure appeared in front of him. At first, the figure was all darkness, until it opened its eyes and a silvery gas emanated from them. It stepped from the mist to reveal Rhyler himself.

"You." Leo readied himself for a fight.

Rhyler stood before him, but his eyes were not his. He looked at Leo with a twisted expression, like a man possessed.

Leo squinted. This was most definitely not a dream and it was truly Rhyler standing in front of him. But something was off.

Rhyler grinned, wider than a normal human could. "I was like you once. A Low-Born in love with a noble. A foolish servant."

His voice was distorted, sounding far away even though he stood just in front of Leo. And the way he spoke... It was so different from how Rhyler spoke to him last.

"She told me I was the most precious thing to her, but she lied to me," Rhyler said. "They do that, you know. They hide things. To keep us weak."

This story... It was so different from the one Rhyler told the crowds. He had never mentioned someone he loved before. "You..." Leo said cautiously. "You're not Rhyler are you?"

Rhyler laughed, a sound that was closer to shrieking. "No I am not."

"Then who are you?"

"I am Dehen. I was a Low-Born, killed by the first Seojin King for loving his future Queen. My blood fed the The Forest and created The Darkening."

Leo took in the figure in front of him, understanding. "And you gave Rhyler his magic. You share his body."

"That I do."

There were so many more questions to ask. So many mysteries Leo wanted to unveil, but something told him Dehen was not here to enlighten him. Leo raised his fists. "If you're here to kill me, I must warn you, I won't make it easy for you."

Dehen shook his head. "I am not here to kill you, soldier. I am here to help you. The Queen is slowly withering away, isn't she? She was never meant to have that kind of magic, she cannot handle that kind of power, and it will consume her. The Forest is cruel and gave it to her knowing it would destroy her."

He was lying, Leo was sure of it. "How are you any better? You gave Rhyler magic so he could kill as many High-Borns as he could."

"I gave him what I thought he needed to make things fair." Dehen snapped. "If I had not, do you think anything would have changed? Admit it, without him, Ulsana would not have changed, your Queen would not have attempted to equalize the classes. You cannot have change without pain, there is no greater motivator for us humans."

Uro's dead eyes flashed in Leo's memory, inciting his anger. "How you get somewhere matters. Even if it brought change, it took too much sacrifice. There are other ways it could have been done. Don't pretend you are interested in change and a better future, you just want revenge."

Dehen circled Leo, like a predator. "And you would know, wouldn't you, soldier? You lust for revenge as I do. Don't tell me you did not want to kill the man who beat your father to death. That you wouldn't mind the High-Borns being punished for what they've done."

Leo kept his eyes on Dehen, ready for an attack. "You're right, I do understand it, which is why I know it's not the way."

"Ah. The high and mighty captain, not yet corrupted by enough loss. I wonder how you would change if you were to lose her. What would it do to you?"

Leo froze, the cold depths of fear coursing through his blood.

"It does not have to be that way. I can help you save her. I have the Whispers that will take her magic away, relieve her of her pain."

This was a trick. It must be. He wasn't going to fall for it.

"And why would you do this?"

"I never cared if your precious Queen was alive or dead. I just wanted her power, but now that I know I cannot take it, I just want her out of the way."

"So you can kill all the High-Borns."

"I do, but what do you care for the High-Borns? We both know you only care about her."

It was true. Leo had no love for the nobles, but to let Rhyler win would hurt Arla. And the dream he had sworn he would support.

Dehen put his shadowed hand over his heart. "I promise that we will spare her life, but you must act quickly, there isn't much time left for her. You see it already, don't you? The way it drains her. Soon there will be nothing left of your precious Queen. Could you live with yourself knowing you could have saved her? Do you want to fail at protecting yet another one of your precious people?"

Leo shook, knowing the answer. No, he couldn't live with that. Losing Arla would plunge him into a darkness he knew he would not return from. He couldn't bear even the thought of it. His shoulders slackened in defeat.

Dehen grinned, knowing he had won. "So, then..." He stretched his hand toward Leo's throat. "Shall we begin?"

CHAPTER 49

The camp was abuzz with activity. The sun was setting across the tents, giving an eerie orange tinge to everything, making the entire place look like it was on fire. A fitting image for the current energy of the people. Arla scratched at her scars on her now exposed forearms. The sight of fire still made them sting a little.

It was time.

The ten volunteers of former Low and High-Borns gathered in a circle, each holding a weapon in their hands. Arla could not help but feel proud of how far they had come. A few months ago, if someone were to say that former High and Low Borns would band together for any purpose, they would have been laughed out of the room, yet here they were.

And although they were nervous, they were as ready as they could be. Arla closed her eyes, thinking of Rose.

I am on my way. Please be alive.

"Everything is ready." Simion looked confidently at the rescue crew. He had been tirelessly training them to control their new and old magic and was satisfied with where they were.

Leo hurried toward them, still buttoning his jacket. He was late, which was unusual for a punctual man like himself. And he looked a little disheveled too, like he had not gotten much sleep last night. He didn't even bother to greet anyone before going straight to her. "Arla, I need to talk to you." He pulled her aside. The concern in his eyes was nothing new to see.

He had been looking at her like that a lot recently, afraid she would break at any moment. Did he not have any faith in her?

"We need to postpone the rescue," he said.

"What?"

"You're not in the right state to do this. You're extremely sleep-deprived, and this new magic is clearly draining you. We can find a better way that doesn't require you to spend so much of yourself."

"I can't believe you're saying this right now. Every day we wait is another day Rose and the others suffer. What if they are being tortured? Or publicly hanged one by one? Any more delay and she could be dead! We can't afford to wait any longer! Don't you care about Rose?!"

Leo flushed red. "Of course I care, but we don't even know if she's alive. It's not worth losing you!"

"I'm fine!" she shouted quietly.

"Stop saying that! I'm so sick of hearing you lie. You're not fine."

Arla wanted to cover his mouth. His shouting was going to make the others nervous if they heard him. "We don't have time for this, we have to go. If you feel like you can't come, then don't." She pushed past him, purposefully making sure to look strong in her stride. She was at her wit's end with him. Why would he bring this up moments before they were supposed to leave?

Simion met her with his signature sly smile. At least he was confident in her.

"We're leaving now," she commanded.

He bowed and held out his hand for her to take. "As you wish, my Queen."

The air sucked in around them and then, in an instant, they were in a familiar place that smelled of damp wood and fine mist. The southern end of Ulsana's castle was right at the entrance to a tunnel that she had taken many times to go to the meadow. A place where she had once shared a meal with Uro and Leo.

The memory tugged at her heart. She would never have that again. And that truth buckled her. She forcibly pulled herself from sinking. It was not the time to dwell on what was lost. Her only job now was to make sure she did not lose anyone else.

"I'm going to bring the others." Simion disappeared in a lingering smoke before reappearing with one volunteer and then another and then another. They looked around, surprised to find themselves here.

"How are we going to get into the castle?" one of them asked, clutching his sword tightly, like he was itching to use it.

Arla grazed her hand over the stone before finding the one she was looking for. She leaned her entire body weight on it until it pressed in and then an entire section of rock opened like a door, revealing a cramped tunnel, barely five feet tall.

"There are hidden tunnels all over the castle, and I know this one very well."

The others looked into the tunnel hesitantly.

"It gets wider further in," she assured them. "You should go in first to adjust to the darkness. I'll join you in a few minutes."

They lingered for a moment before one young woman grabbed a torch. "We'll see you soon." She headed inside with her head held high. The others followed quickly after that.

"They really trust you," Simion said.

Did they?

"They *should* trust you," said a voice from behind.

Arla spun around to see Leo. "You're here..."

Simion looked between them. "Oh, was he dis-invited? He didn't tell me that when I brought him here."

She admittedly was glad to see him, but then she quickly became suspicious. "Are you here to help me or stop me?"

By his silence, he still didn't seem sure.

Arla did not wait for his answer, instead, she turned her back to him to face the front of the castle. She scanned the courtyard to the alleyways, looking for a big enough spot to–there! A large courtyard lay beyond the gates, with a fountain at its center. It was the perfect place.

She unleashed her monsters, as many as she could, all at once to create havoc. And just as they planned, Rhyler's guards jumped into action, fighting them off. One defender struck her monster in the chest. It screamed in pain, and Arla heard a sharp pitch in her head that sucked away some of her energy.

She had practiced keeping the monsters alive, but never while battling and never while they were getting injured. Which, in hindsight, she should have. This would take more focus than she had prepared for.

"Go!" she shouted at the boys, straining.

Leo and Simion hopped into the tunnel. They would lead the group to the underground prisons, where they would free everyone and bring them back here as Arla kept the monsters in her view. She could not keep them in existence without seeing them. Rhyler, no doubt, knew she was here.

Time passed as she held the monsters, watching them swing at Rhyler's fighters.

Her body weakened with exhaustion. How long had it been since the group had left? Were they discovered? Were they okay?

Finally, after what felt like hours, Leo and Simion returned with a larger group than before. Keeping one eye on the battle, she pivoted to see the prisoners. They were dirty and skinnier than before, but mostly unharmed. There was much relief among them, but some volunteers looked solemn, and Arla immediately knew why.

The prisoners some had hoped to rescue were already long gone. She felt for them, but her own eyes were searching for a familiar face that also was not in the returning party. Simion looked at her with a tinge of sadness, no doubt knowing who she was looking for.

She grabbed the closest rescued prisoner from the group, an elderly man with a gait in his walk. "Where is Rose?"

"Rose?" the older man repeated, confused.

More shouting in the courtyard diverted her attention back to the battle. A monster was already fading. She re-focused, pouring more of her energy into it.

"She is a soldier." Arla traced an imaginary long braid down the back of her head. "Long black braided hair. Permanent scowl on her face."

"I don't know who that is…" The man looked very sorry that he could not answer her.

Arla let him go. Rose had to be here, where else could she be?

She asked every one of the rescued if they saw Rose all the while keeping her monsters alive longer than she was supposed to, which caused her head to throb. One by one, they shook their heads. Her frustration grew with every 'no' until she grabbed one prisoner in exasperation and shouted, "She must be here somewhere!"

A creature screeched before disappearing into mist.

"Rose?" An older lady stepped out from the group. "I do not know if that was her name, but I overheard that horrid man mention keeping a soldier with him."

Arla ran to her. "What do you mean?"

Arla's desperate tone made the woman hesitate. "Well… I might be wrong, but there was a woman of that description who was very resistant. I thought for sure they were going to kill her until one of them said she must be kept alive."

Arla gripped the woman's shoulders. "Where is she?"

The woman leaned back, afraid of Arla's intensity. "I don't know. They took her somewhere else. They said she would be important later."

He must have known that Arla would come for Rose.

Relief washed over her. Even if Rose was being used as a lure, Arla did not care. Rose was alive, and that's all that mattered.

Leo was in shock. "I was so sure she was…" His face turned red in shame.

Arla shuddered, unable to hold on to the creatures any longer. One by one, they disappeared into mist. Rhyler's guards startled at the sudden disappearances but quickly regained themselves and ran into the castle.

She turned to the group. "Hurry to the meadow. You should find others waiting for you there with horses to take you back to camp."

While this group was meant to get the prisoners, another had traveled earlier in the week to a nearby village and was waiting to guide them back to the camp. That part was actually Simion's idea.

"Wynera," she said out loud, which confused the others. "Are you there?"

Wynera's voice floated up from the abyss. *"I am."*

"Can you help me find her?"

Arla had no idea if Wynera had the ability to find Rose or not, but she was desperate and would try anything. Wynera went silent and for a moment, Arla feared the princess had been pulled away by The Forest again. Just when she was about to call out her name again, Wynera returned.

"She is here."

Relief washed over her. "Can you show me?"

"Yes, but know that I know where she is only because I know where he is."

Rhyler. Rose was with Rhyler.

A wave of Whispers tumbled in her skull, and her vision flashed, revealing a layer of light over everything. The streams were back again, showing everywhere magic pulsed. And then there was one bright one, lightly shaded in gold that pulsed like a beckoning lighthouse. Somehow, Arla knew where this would lead.

She felt it without having to look as it curved and dipped along the wall, out the tunnel, beyond a long hall, down to the right, into the throne room.

"Rose is in the throne room," Arla declared, her voice suddenly hoarse. The magic had taken its toll on her.

"How do you know?" Leo asked.

"I just do, and Rhyler is there too."

Leo thought for a moment. "Okay then. You stay here. Simon and I will create a distraction, get him away from Rose long enough to get her safely out."

"No, he's not going to leave her. He's waiting for *me*, and if I don't show up, he might just kill her to antagonize me. I can't take that chance."

"You're in no condition to fight right now. You've already depleted too much of your energy."

He wasn't wrong. Exhaustion already crept up her body inch by inch.

"It doesn't matter, I have to go."

"You don't have to do anything. Let us get Rose. Arla, just think of your own safety for once!"

"I'm going!"

Leo shut his mouth into a thin line. He did not continue to argue, instead, a strange look crossed his face, like he was deciding something, or rather he had come to a conclusion, which drew him into a gloom of seriousness. The switch unnerved her. Something had changed.

She could see the light beating in his chest again. Even now, she did not know why it was only his Whisper she could hear. What did it mean?

Simion stepped forward. "I can take us to the throne room faster."

She smiled. "And give us the element of surprise."

Simion winked. "Exactly."

At least Simion was on her side.

Simion turned to Leo. "I'll bring you after I set her in a hidden place, and we'll all attack together."

Leo reached out. "Wait."

Simion put his hand on her shoulder, and her body lurched backward into mist. She blinked, expecting to feel the moonlight through the throne room windows, but instead, something pushed her backward against stone.

CHAPTER 50

Coldness hit her back as darkness enveloped her, but she wasn't unconscious. In fact, her heart beat loudly in her ears, and her eyes were wide open.

"Simion?"

A leather strap wrapped around her mouth. Hands gripped her wrists and pressed them on each side of her head. Panic overwhelmed her.

Where was Simion? Was he taken during the teleportation? Was that even possible?

She aimed to kick whoever held her down, but a body pressed against her, preventing her legs from moving. A tiny crack of moonlight through the tunnel barely illuminated his face. She almost choked in shock.

Simion.

Simion was pinning her against the wall. He looked at her so... desperately. An utter contrast between how confident he was just a few seconds ago. She looked around in a panic.

The tunnels. That's where they were right now. Somewhere in the maze of them, Simion had teleported them here to be alone.

She shouted through her muffle.

"I'm sorry." His voice shook. "I truly am... but I can't let you fight Rhyler in this state. I... I can't let you die. Please forgive me... *Peren thi egentha he-han ugrha.*"

Her body lurched as something dug into her chest.

She knew this pain. This was what it felt like when Rhyler was trying to steal her magic, but the Whispers were different.

The Forest rumbled in her ears. *"Did I not tell you, little one?"*

Rage bit at her. Did The Forest do this? Did it give Simion new magic to stop her? Was he possessed? He must be possessed to be doing this. But she looked at his dark brown eyes. There was no sheen of possession, only desperation.

This was Simion, through and through.

How could he?

She wanted to claw out his eyes and crush the fingers that trapped her to the wall.

"Julenthe man iglenthe."

A tidal wave hit her, digging her further into the wall as the invisible force grabbed onto the Whispers in her head. This wasn't like Rhyler's magic. This one felt older, more powerful.

Streams of light burst in her vision as she saw it flow through Simion, except his was not white, but copper. The Whispers desperately clung to her as the force yanked them one by one from her cranium wall and pulled them away.

Anger turned to desperation as she looked at him wide-eyed, begging him to stop.

Tears streamed down Simion's face as he willed himself to keep going. It was almost over. She could feel her magic ebbing. The streams of light faded, leaving her.

"Iru con daime–"

A torch flame clattered to the ground.

Simion shouted, falling to the floor, releasing Arla from the wall. The abandoned torch rolled to her feet, illuminating the tunnel, revealing Leo wrestling Simion on the ground. Simion shouted again before Leo clamped his hand down on Simion's mouth, hard.

"He offered it to you too, didn't he?" Leo growled, sweat beating down his face. He must have sprinted to get here.

"*Too?*" she said as she finished undoing her muffle. "What do you mean? Offered what?"

Simion fought against Leo, who pinned Simion back to the ground. "Dehen, the spirit that possesses Rhyler, offered me the Whispers to take away your magic to save you from being consumed by it. I refused, so I guess he offered it to someone else who was close to you."

Take away my magic? Simion chose to... hurt me?

Rage. Betrayal. Disappointment. They all swirled within her, releasing a wave of emotion. Arla pushed Leo aside and grabbed Simion by his collar. "I can't believe you would do that to me!"

"Arla." Simion pleaded, his hands raised. "Arla, please."

She shoved him to the ground. "After everything you said about forgiveness and being sorry for the past, you do this?! You made me believe you changed! But you're still the selfish bastard you've always been!" She shoved him hard again. "Why?! Why did you betray me?!"

Simion frantically grasped her wrists. "Because I love you!"

The air stilled. Only the fire, flickering against the wall, told her that time had not stopped.

What did he just say?

Simion squeezed her wrists tighter. "I couldn't watch you wither away and die from this magic. I couldn't do it. I'm so sorry. I didn't do it to hurt you. I love you, Arla." Simion tearfully pressed his forehead into her hands. "I love you. I'm sorry."

Arla stood still, tears running down her cheeks. Her heart felt like it was tearing in half. Simion loved her. A part of her knew he did. The countless times he had helped her. The things he did to make her happy... And he *did* make her happy and her heart felt guilty for it because she was supposed to love Leo, the man that now stood behind her watching them cry together in silence, allowing them to have their moment.

She looked down at Simion. The pleading in his eyes made her want to hug him, but her heart felt hollow.

He loved her, and he hurt her.

First Leo and now Simion. Did men only know how to cause her pain?

Simion reached for her again, but she pulled away.

"Arla..." he whimpered.

She did not look at him. She wasn't sure if she could ever look at him the same way again. Instead, she picked up the torch.

"Arla... please." Simion begged.

She turned back to Leo. "Rose needs me."

And without waiting for either of them, she ran down the tunnel.

CHAPTER 51

Arla barely heard Leo catch up to her as she flew through the tunnels. She did not need to know exactly where she was because the pulse of light guided her to where she needed to go and soon in a matter of minutes, she emerged from the darkness into the light of a hallway, where she took off running again until she got the hall that led straight the gold-gilded doors of the throne room. Which was...oddly empty. Usually, guards stood every six feet across each side, but today, there was no one to stop them as they approached. Arla exchanged looks with Leo, both knowing full well this meant that Rhyler was expecting them. They had to prepare for anything that would be behind these doors.

Leo drew his sword. Arla took a long breath before she grabbed the handle with both hands and pulled it open.

The door groaned open to reveal an empty throne room, or rather, almost empty, except for the four people that occupied the platform at the end where the jeweled encrusted throne chair sat.

Arla's attention went immediately to the only person who mattered on that platform.

Rose was being held forcibly on her knees by two burly men, who looked as if they had never bathed in their lives.

A bulbous black bruise completely shut Rose's right eye, while various cuts were still bleeding on her arms and legs. Rage flared within Arla as she imagined what other injuries Rose had that she could not see.

She looked for the person responsible, and there he was, sitting arrogantly on Ulsana's throne.

All her life, Arla had only seen her father on that throne. His enormous frame filled it so much he made it look small. Rhyler, on the other hand, looked so... ordinary.

He sat on its edge, his chest pulled out and his spine straight, like he knew he did not quite fit.

Rhyler pressed a finger into the arm of the throne chair, as if testing its sturdiness. "What about this chair makes someone want power so badly? Or is it only the greedy and cruel that make it to this seat?"

"Ironic you say that when you are the one sitting in it now," she practically spat.

Rhyler smiled sadly. "Only those with power can enact change. It is a burden I must bear."

Arla wanted to laugh. "You really don't see it, do you? You are no better than anyone else who sat on that throne. You're not making things better for Low-Borns. The only thing you're doing is changing whose foot is pressing on whose neck."

"A princess like you would never understand," he said dismissively.

A Queen, Arla wanted to correct. Rhyler was trying to make her feel small by calling her by a different title, as if she did not rule Ulsana.

"You're delusional," Leo retorted.

Rhyler's eyes drifted to the captain. "You shame Uro's memory by siding with the enemy."

Leo pointed his sword directly at Rhyler. "Uro is dead because you filled his head with ultimatums."

"This world makes you choose, Captain."

Arla grew tired of the talk. She only came here to get Rose out safely, and she was already quite drained of energy. Arla opened her mouth to release her Whispers, but Rhyler shot up a finger, wagging it back and forth. "Ah, ah, ah."

One of the burly men pressed a curved knife to Rose's throat.

Arla's blood ran cold. All traces of her Whispers pulled back. "What do you want?"

"A trade. The soldier for the princess."

She should have expected this. A life for a life. It was like Wynera had said, Rhyler wanted her dead because Rhyler was afraid… of her. She was the only person in the world whose magic he could not take. Someone who could stop him. Never in her life did Arla think someone would view her as such a formidable threat. And for the first time in her life, she knew she was.

Rhyler grew impatient. "What is your answer, Princess?"

The other burly man grabbed Rose by her braid and yanked her head back, exposing her neck even more. He pressed the edge of his knife deeper, drawing a bubble of blood. Rose bit her lip to stop herself from yelling.

"Stop!" Arla shouted.

Leo remained frozen beside her. She could tell he was playing out all the moves it would take to get to Rose and all of their consequences. He probably knew what she already did. They would not get to her in time.

"How can I trust you'll keep your word?" she asked.

Rhyler scoffed. "Do I look like a High-Born to you? I will release her, and they will both walk free."

She really didn't know if she could trust him, but she knew it was her only option if she wanted to save Rose. The gravity of her next decision was dawning on her. If she did this, she would not wake up tomorrow and see the sun rise over the trees. She would never again feel the breeze against her skin or taste the sweetness of pastries.

She turned to Leo, trying to memorize every line of his face. The way his wavy dark hair always seemed to fall perfectly over his forehead. The crease between his eyebrows from frowning too much in his life. Her heart shriveled. Could she really do this? Could she face death so that Rose didn't have to?

Rose's eyes burned with fierce defiance. This was the woman who always treated her like she were a nuisance. The one that attacked her in that Underground shop. The one that demanded she leave them alone.

But she came to Norendra's funeral.

Not to pay homage to the late advisor, but so that Arla did not have to face her grief alone.

Arla locked eyes with Leo. "When they let her go, promise me you'll get her out."

Leo's eyes widened in fear. "Arla, don't."

"You would have made the same choice, and you would have asked me the same thing." She gave him a pleading look. *Please don't make this harder than it needs to be.*

Leo looked so devastated it made Arla almost second-guess her decision.

He also faced an impossible choice. The life of someone he considered his sister and the life of... well, what were they now? She didn't know exactly, but she knew he still cared for her.

Arla put up her hands as a sign of surrender. "You have me."

"Don't be an idiot!" Rose shouted. One of the men punched her in the mouth, making her spit blood.

Arla held back her Whispers, even though she wanted to make the man pay.

Rhyler grinned as the air thickened with electricity. Arla could almost feel his Whispers dropping to his tongue.

I'm sorry, she silently said to Wynera. *I didn't do what you needed me to do. I hope the next person you choose can do what I couldn't.*

She looked at Rose one last time and almost gasped.

Light beat around Rose's chest, echoing. *"Inai. Inai."*

There it was again. These Whispers. Why was she hearing Rose's now?

Her eyes met Rose's and then something snapped into place.

An understanding. A realization. And a bone-deep fear.

She suddenly felt so sick. Arla sprinted to Rose. "No!"

Rose gave her a grim smile and then she shouted so loud it shook Arla to the core.

It was a cry of determination. Of will. Of goodbye.

Rose thrust herself forward right into the edge of the blade and twisted her neck.

Blood sprayed across the marble floor.

Rose fell.

Her head hit the ground with a sickening crack.

An inaudible cry erupted from Arla's own throat.

And then chaos erupted.

Stone and wood burst from the ground. A creature of bone and ash as large as the room itself pulled its molten form from the floor. It shot out its bone fingers and impaled the two men straight through their chests.

No. No. No.

Rose remained limp, facedown on the cold stone floor. Blood pooled below Rose, soaking through her shirt.

Get up Rose.

Arla took a shaky step forward.

I came here to save you.

Rose did not move. Her back did not rise or fall with breath. And Arla knew then that her friend was gone.

All feeling left Arla then. Her fingers went numb. She was neither cold nor warm. No longer a being with a beating heart, but something more... hollow.

Why did you do this?

The room flooded with more of Rhyler's followers, armed to the teeth.

And the empty void in her chest filled with something hot. A burning sensation that could have consumed the world.

Arla turned to look at them all, hatred in her soul.

Let them come.

Let them all die.

She summoned another monster of darkness that burst from the ceiling this time. It lashed at several fighters with its giant talons.

Still, more funneled into the room, but Arla did not let them distract her from her true target.

"I saw your monsters," Rhyler said, unaffected by the surrounding chaos. "Calling so many must have exhausted you. How many more do you think you have left? Three? Four?"

"Shut up!" Arla screamed. She willed her monster to go after Rhyler.

Rhyler spread out his hands and Whispered. Metal seeped from his pores and covered his arms. Her skeletal creature swung at Rhyler, but he blocked the attack with his impenetrable steel arms, saving himself. But those arms did not stop him from being flung back.

She took a quick look back to check on Leo. He hastened from one assailant to another, cutting them down, becoming an invisible wall that protected her back. His eyes burned with the same rage that filled her own soul.

Rhyler coughed as he got up, his arms returning to normal again. "Come now, Arla. Isn't this exhausting? Why keep fighting the coming tide? You know I will win in the end."

The strain of holding her two creatures was bearing down on her. Already, her legs felt so heavy even though her rage still fueled her to keep going.

Rhyler looked over at Rose's body. "You know, I asked her about you, and she gave up nothing. A Low-Born so willing to protect their oppressor." He clicked his tongue in disappointment. "It is fitting that she died on her knees."

Arla yelled out, summoning another creature.

He's a monster. He deserves to die.

Just like my father.

He needs to die.

Die. Die. Die!

A wave of exhaustion hit her so hard it sent her to her knees.

All her creatures whisked away in grey vapor.

She called upon her Whispers in frustration, but her head was silent, and her body depleted.

Rhyler grinned and looked to where the last creature had disappeared. "Looks like four was the limit."

And that's when she knew she had made a mistake. The rage had blinded her. She had become too brash. Too impatient. Too eager. And now she had fallen into his trap.

He was just waiting for her to exhaust herself.

"I told you," Rhyler said smugly. "This was only going to end my way."

A streak of crackling black came for her. Its jagged tip, like death's hand, drove toward her heart.

So this was how she would die. On her knees, just like Rose.

Hands pushed her shoulders. Her body flew to the side.

The entire room flashed darkness for a moment and then daylight broke out again through the window.

Arla gasped in horror.

Leo lay on his back, his shirt tattered as black and red cut across his chest. Blood poured from him like a river.

No. No. No. No

Arla crawled to him and pressed her palms against the wound, desperately trying to stop the bleeding, but it just seeped through her fingers, puddling between them.

"It's no use," Leo groaned.

"Don't say that." Blinking back tears, she pressed her other hand on top of the first. Leo cried out in pain, which made Arla retract.

Footsteps approached them. Electricity sparked in the air. Rhyler was going to attack again.

Seeing Rhyler, Leo grabbed her hand. "Can you still hear it?"

Confused at first, Arla did not know how to respond, and then a familiar beat drummed in her ears. A small flicker of light throbbed in the center of Leo's chest. *'Mehvar. Mehvar'*

Arla nodded.

"Good. Turn me into one of your monsters."

She pulled her hand away from him. "What?"

He cracked a half-smile that did not reach his eyes. "I'm dying, anyway. Might as well be a useful death."

Tears streamed from her face, puddling on the floor, mixing with his blood. Why was he always facing death for her? Why did the world always keep taking from him? It wasn't fair.

She pressed her forehead into his. "You're not dying. You're going to be okay."

"Arla..." He lightly pulled her face up by the chin to look at him. Already his face was pale with death. "I love you. I wanted to say it to you first and every time after, but it did not turn out that way, did it?" He took a haggard breath, trying not to show the pain he was in. "I've loved you since you climbed that tree in The Forest and I'll love you long after I'm gone."

If her heart had broken because of Simion, then it was shattering now because of Leo. She did not know she could feel this kind of pain that howled through her bones.

"Use me to end him."

She shook her head, refusing. "I can't."

She couldn't do this. She didn't have the will, nor the energy left. This was the end for both of them.

The light was fading from his eyes. "You have to. It's the only way to stop him now. I know you can do this. Just one last one." He wiped her tears from her face. "It's okay."

She couldn't breathe, her lungs withered from sorrow, and yet she knew he was right. If they did not stop Rhyler now, so many more would die. So, she had to use everything she had left, of Leo and herself.

I can't.

A louder voice bubbled up within her. *You must.*

She squeezed Leo's hand. "I love you too."

She breathed in and, with the last of her magic, she spoke the words that would destroy her. "*Ithrid gu-lia bukami chrek-ek noon-tha. Ther-gul eil dan huy-uq-tha. Loren vuy-i-al-san...*" The word beat to the rhythm of Leo's slowing heart. "*Mehvar.*"

She screamed when Leo's head snapped back. His dark pupils spread until both his eyes were black as scales of silver and darkness spread across his skin. He cried out in pain as his spine snapped along its ridges and widened, growing in size until Leo was no longer human, but a massive creature of scales and wings, like a majestic force of the night.

For a moment, he stood still, his scaled nostrils breathing out hot steam in a huff.

A trio of men charged at her. In one turn, Leo's tail slammed into them, sending them flying back. He turned his body to shield her from the back, taking on the magic and swords that were meant for her.

Rhyler stood only a few feet away. He broke into hysterical laughter. "Did you just sacrifice him to help you?" He laughed harder, doubling over. "There is nothing you High-Borns won't do to gain power! Nothing!"

She no longer felt the hot rod of rage boiling within her. This feeling now in the essence of her soul was much colder, like ice.

Slowly she got up, Leo's blood still on her hands. "I'm going to kill you slowly and then destroy everything you ever worked for. By the end, no one will remember you even existed."

She could hear The Forest chuckling. *'Let us see, little champion, what will become of you when you taste what true power is.'*

Leo roared as he barreled into the last remaining guards, leaving only Arla and Rhyler to face each other.

Rhyler sent another strike of lightning, but Arla dodged it, rolling into a nearby body. For a sickening moment, she thought it might be Rose's, but no, it was someone she did not recognize. She felt something cold and sharp below her. A dagger. Quickly, she grabbed it.

She willed Leo to swing his scaled tail at Rhyler, who immediately ducked out of the way. She did not know where all this newfound energy came from. It was from a place beyond exhaustion, where her entire self was numb to her.

She sped forward and threw the dagger as hard as she could.

The dagger pathetically clattered to the ground beside Rhyler's feet.

Rhyler barely held back his laughter as he stared down at the blade. "You misse–"

Before he even finished that sentence, Arla already had the cloth out. In his distraction, Rhyler failed to notice Arla ripping the ends of her shirt, giving her a long ribbon of cotton.

She twisted behind him and threw the cloth around his mouth and yanked as hard as she could with her entire body. Rhyler gagged as the cloth went into his mouth, pressing his tongue to the back of his throat. Arla quickly tied the cloth.

"Leo!"

Leo's monstrous form tossed the last remaining guard away and swooped down to them. Arla lunged out of the way. Leo's claws grabbed each of Rhyler's wrists and crushed him to the ground, breaking the bones that held his hands to his arms. Rhyler screamed in agony.

Arla slowly got up and walked over to the writhing Rhyler, picking up the dagger.

She crouched over him, feeling neither joy nor horror at Rhyler's pain.

She placed the tip of the blade at his throat and pressed.

A dribble of blood made its way up to the surface.

Rhyler shouted behind the gag, his eyes bloodshot in rage.

"I told you." She lifted the dagger. "I am going to kill you slowly."

She thrust the dagger into his shoulder.

His scream startled her. Like waking her from a dream. It was a horrible sound that brought her no joy, and yet, she did not relent. Instead, she yanked the dagger out and stabbed him in his other shoulder.

The feeling of tearing through skin and muscle made her skin recoil, but she did not let go of the dagger as Rhyler's blood poured from him.

Shouldn't he bleed? Just like Rose did?

Rhyler seized beneath her and then a mist of black erupted from his eyes. A ghostly form enveloped him, like an outer layer, revealing the translucent face of Dehen, whose teary screams echoed with Rhyler's.

"How dare you do this?!" Dehen's eyes bulged like a madman's. "You should be the one suffering! It is what you deserve! You all need to be punished!"

Dehen and Rhyler thrashed frantically.

Arla let go of the dagger, leaving it in his shoulder.

Seeing him this way, Rhyler didn't seem like the sinister villain she made him out to be.

He looked... like a scared child.

He was just... in pain, and he wanted everyone to suffer like he did.

Something she knew well.

Hadn't she also felt the thrill of dominating over the council that belittled her before? Over Ametha? Hadn't she felt justified in doing it?

Yes, she had known that type of anger. That type of pain.

Her hatred withered away until what remained was regret.

How could she have let herself go this far?

How could she have hurt someone so purposefully?

Wasn't Rhyler just as hurt as she was?

A resounding sound, like the ringing of a glass bell, echoed in her head.

From Rhyler's chest, a glow revealed itself slowly, like light pouring out from a newly opened door.

It did not beat like Leo's, but rather scratched inconsistency, like crackles of lightning.

And like a distant echo, it Whispered.

Hinam. Hinam.

And then, all at once, it made sense to her now what her new magic was.

"I know your pain," she said. "I hear it, because I understand you. I know what it's like to be treated like you are lower than dirt. I know how angry it can make you feel. You think that the only way to be safe again is to be more powerful, more cruel than the people who hurt you." She looked at Leo's dried blood on her hands. "Monsters create more monsters."

She remembered The Forest was watching. A part of her still wanted to torturously kill Rhyler and avenge those she lost, but another part knew that if she did, it would only spread more pain. She had to prove The Forest wrong. They could be good. They could have power and wield it with kindness. They could choose to heal.

"Let's stop this, Rhyler. This pain you feel doesn't need to last. It doesn't need to destroy others."

Dehen and Rhyler cackled. "You don't understand me at all, Princess. I *want* to destroy them. They deserve it."

Her heart dropped watching the last thread of hope fall from her hands. Rhyler was not going to stop.

Rhyler's chest beat with a light, *Hinam. Hinam.*

She could see its red hue as clear as day. Which made her all the sadder to do what she had to do now.

"*Ithrid gu-lia bukami chrek-ek noon-tha.*"

Rhyler cocked his head in mock curiosity, while Dehen spoke. "Will you summon another creature, Princess?"

"*Ther-gul eil dan huy-uq-tha.*"

Dehen gave a guttural gasp. "What are you doing?"

"*Loren vuy-i-al-san chryu.*"

"No!" Dehen's ephemeral form shuttered. "Stop!"

"... *hinam.*"

Rhyler screamed as his chest expanded, gobbing into mud and bone. His skin misted away, leaving only a skeleton of spotted black and white and smoking horns. Even as a monster, he looked vengeful.

He roared, spitting fire and ash, his mind gone from this world.

He raised his skeletal hand, ready to strike her, but then realized he could not. He struggled against it, but he was Arla's creature now, and he would do what she commanded. She didn't want to see him struggle, it was too much like the pain he had to endure so long as a Low-Born.

"I'm sorry it ended up this way."

Rhyler's monstrous form continued to struggle and screech along with Dehen as Arla let out her breath, releasing the monster from this world. Slowly, Rhyler misted into nothingness, giving Arla one last look of pure hatred until nothing remained.

Arla fell to the floor, but she could not completely let herself lose consciousness. She held onto an invisible thread of light. The last of her Whispers she could not let go.

Leo's winged form curled his tail around her to keep her warm.

"We did it." She tried to smile, unsure if it was to comfort herself or Leo. She placed a hand on his scaled tail. "I'm not sure how much longer I can hold on to you."

He looked at her deeply with his black eyes, as if to say it was alright. She leaned her body against him. Her eyes struggled to stay open.

She was so, so tired.

He nuzzled her with his nose and closed his eyes, unbothered.

A tear fell down her cheek. "Can't we just hang on a little bit longer?"

There was no answer.

Her mind started to fog.

No, I can't let go just yet. Just a little longer. Please.

But her body did not listen to her, and she sank into the abyss.

CHAPTER 52

It was like falling slowly, forever in suspended nothingness.

And it was... so peaceful.

There was no pain here. No past or present.

She curled into a ball. *I can stay here forever.*

The fight had cost her everything. She had no more friends left in the world. No one else to laugh with or dine with. No one who cared about her. No one to pour her love into.

Regret mercilessly shoved itself between her ribs.

She should have sent them all away the day Uro asked to leave the army. She should have smuggled them all to a new life somewhere far away from the chains of Ulsana's past.

I'm sorry.

The sound of a water droplet hitting the surface of a lake shook her. It rippled like a high-pitched whirring of glass.

She curled tighter, not at all curious.

Leave me alone.

Another droplet pinged into the water.

She covered her ears.

I don't want to wake up.

Another ping.

She did not know how she could still hear them with her ears covered, but they were so loud and all around her.

Another ping. Then another. Like rain, except every splash of a droplet created new pitches until a melody formed. A song of the morning spring. Bright and playful.

The joy of it disgusted her. How could such a sound exist after everything that had happened?

A droplet landed on her shoulder and slid down her arm until it rested on her tucked knees. It wriggled underneath her chin, trying to get her attention.

She turned away, but the water droplet persisted until she opened her eyes to shout at it. "Go away!"

The water droplet squinted in glee back at her, round and innocent, unaffected by her yelling.

Was it the same one she met in The Forest? She did not know. She did not care.

The droplet rolled around her knees playfully.

She resisted the urge to shake the droplet off of her. "How can you act like that when you know what happened?"

This was too cruel.

"Don't make me go back," she begged. "Wherever they went, send me there too."

The water droplet stopped rolling and stared at her. In its dark black pupils, she saw The Forest, stretching endlessly across time and worlds.

And from the eternal distance in its eyes, came the ancient voice. *"It is not over yet."*

A force struck her so hard her head thrust back. Eons of magic passed through her, stretching her body across all existence.

A glowing raindrop fell on dead earth. A seedling of gold sprouted from the ground. Trees of such beauty grew, it made Arla's soul swell. Water droplets hung from the branches, vibrating an endless song. A scream echoed. Blood showered from above. Sharp trees devoid of color pierced up from the crimson floor. Light streams cast out from its roots, going through everything.

And then they all converged underneath Arla's feet.

Light beamed around her, blinding her. It was too much. She was going to splinter into pieces, she was sure of it. She was going to turn into shards of herself and never be whole again. She was going to –

Her eyes fluttered open, gasping. She grabbed her chest and arms instinctively.

She was... intact.

The morning sun beamed through the shattered window, its rays in her eyes.

She didn't want this. She didn't want to be awake, because that meant... the flood of emotions hit her again.

She couldn't be here, she couldn't do this, she –

She blinked. Once. Twice. Three times. To make sure she was seeing clearly.

Because there, lying next to her, unconscious... was Leo.

In all his aliveness.

Joy, elation, every possible happy feeling in the world enveloped her. She wanted to shake him awake, but then her breath halted, finally realizing that in her blind joy, she did not realize that Leo was completely naked.

Heat flared up her cheeks. Arla quickly shot her eyes back up to Leo's face.

Do not look. Do not look.

Leo's eyes opened slowly, like he was waking from a peaceful dream. Arla couldn't help it. She threw her arms around him. "Leo!"

Leo grinned and returned the embrace fully with... his entire body. Arla became rigid. Leo pulled away and looked down. Crimson spread across his cheeks. "I guess the clothes don't return with me."

Arla laughed while trying very hard to keep her eyes on his beautiful face.

It was unbelievable, he was alive! How could this be? She tried not to think too much about it, afraid that it would reveal that this was all a dream. Because if it was, she did not want to wake herself.

She pulled the jacket off a nearby unconscious man and gave it to Leo.

Leo tied the jacket around his waist and twisted it to the side so that it hid most of his front pelvis and his butt. He did not look completely satisfied with the coverage.

And just as they glowed in their joy, more of Rhyler's followers funneled into the broken room.

CHAPTER 53

Arla fully expected Rhyler's followers to attack immediately, but instead, they just stared at her. Before they could raise their weapons at them, she spoke first. "I am not your enemy. I do not want to fight you. I want to help you. I want to be equals. I want... peace."

They did not respond. They just kept staring.

Strange...

It was then that Arla realized it was not her they were staring at, but something behind her. When she followed their gaze, her jaw dropped.

Jutting up through the stone was a lone tree, its lush green leaves glowing like no regular tree could. This was the type of tree that only lived in The Forest before The Darkening. Just like in her vision.

And it was exactly in the spot where Rose's body used to lie.

Arla looked across the room for Rose. Did she return from the dead too?

One of Rhyler's guards pointed to it. "It came from you."

Arla looked back at the guard then pointed to herself in confusion as if to say, 'Me?'

The guard nodded. "It grew beside you and curved its branches over both of you, like it was trying to protect you."

Looking down at the base of the tree, Arla could still see the pool of Rose's dried blood.

Arla reached over and touched the bark of the tree.

A lone tear fell from her eye.

Rose was not coming back, was she?

Which also meant, this wasn't a dream. Because in her dream, Rose would be leaning against the doorframe, frowning and telling her she was an idiot.

"It didn't come from me," Arla said so softly the others could not hear her.

Another of Rhyler's followers muttered to the others. "The Forest chose her."

Some of Rhyler's guards exchanged looks of doubt, but others were looking at her with awe. Something she was not comfortable with.

"What does that mean?" another asked someone else in the crowd.

"She is a High-Born," someone reminded another. "She is the enemy."

Eventually, one of Rhyler's followers stepped forward. Arla readied herself for a fight, but the woman did not swing her sword, instead she asked, "Will you fight with us?"

"No," Arla replied calmly. "But I will fight *for* you. For everyone. I promise."

The warrior searched Arla's face for the truth and then pulled out her sword. Leo moved forward, ready to defend Arla.

But the woman did not swing her weapon, instead she placed it on the ground at Arla's feet and then stepped back. "I believe you."

One by one, the others followed and put down their weapons.

And at that moment, Arla was once again Queen Regent of Ulsana.

CHAPTER 54

The next few weeks were a blur of unending change. Arla and Leo remained in the castle and the others from the camp returned only a week later, reuniting tearfully with their loved ones. Nobles that did not survive Rhyler's revolt were sent across the river properly and parts of the castle were already starting to be re-built.

Leo was miraculously uninjured from his time as a monster, but could not remember much of what happened during his transformed state. "I didn't really have thoughts, I was just instinct." Leo replied when asked about it. "The only thing I knew was that I had to help you." He paused before asking. "Do you think you'll be able to turn anything back from a monster again?"

"No. I don't think so."

She was pretty sure that Leo only returned by the mercy of The Forest, which... did not even exist anymore. News came to them a few days after Leo was transformed back, that it had mysteriously disappeared, leaving behind a lush meadow. One would have never known it used to be a land of darkness and death. Many wondered if that meant magic was completely gone from this world, but Arla doubted it, there was still that tree in the throne room...

'It is not over yet.'

She had made a bet that was not yet complete and The Forest would not let her perish without finishing it. But then, why did it disappear?

Whispers squiggled playfully in her head, which caused a flare of light to catch her eye in the corner. A light stream curved along the lines of a branch up to the feet of a perched bird.

The sight of magic did not leave her, in fact it had become more common. There was not a day that went by now that she did not see them. Slowly, she was adjusting to their movements so that they were less distracting.

A new council was quickly formed that included former Low and High-Borns along with those that used to follow Rhyler. A true representation of Ulsana as a whole. She thought that if each group felt equally heard then it would prevent future rebellion.

Leo remained head of her guard where he said he felt most comfortable. Jun was returned to his nursery safe and sound and Linuth was placed as his primary caregiver.

Arla still had not addressed the people as the returned Queen Regent yet, but she knew she would have to soon. The public was eager to know what future lay ahead of them, but first, she needed to rest. Alone in her room, she sat at the vanity whose mirror was cracked. She did not bother to fix it, instead she appreciated its damaged form. In its imperfection it showed what it had survived and still it reflected beautifully.

That afternoon sun shone in its fullness, splaying rays of brightness across the floor. The wind picked up even when the window was closed and swirled around her before it settled into Wynera's glowing form.

"Wynera," Arla moved closer. "Thank the Whispers, you're still here."

Wynera looked around the room and then through the window, where a group of people that used to be from different classes helped each other lift a wooden column onto a cart.

Wynera gave a contented smile. *"I never believed this could ever happen."*

"Is this what you wanted from the beginning? For us to work together?"

"No. I wanted you all to die."

Arla pulled back, shocked.

Wynera held her soft smile. *"I was there, when Dehen chose vengeance with Rhyler and I wanted the same too. So I waited and soon enough your carriage came along with all those soldiers. Seeing that crest on their armor again... I could not control my rage. I sought to kill you all. I sent the trees and the monsters, but then I saw you..."* Wynera softly grazed Arla's hair, like a mother would a daughter. *"You were so kind. You cared so much. Unlike the Seojins before you. You reminded me of myself and it made me hope again. You made me think that maybe I did not have to hold onto this hate anymore. But The Forest sought to kill you all. It didn't believe your kind could be forgiven. The only way I could save you was to give you a part of myself. And in doing so, I chose you to stop Rhyler from destroying everything."*

Arla was honored that Wynera had believed in her so much, even though she still did not know if she deserved it. "I hope I live up to your belief. I haven't always made the right decisions."

Wynera gave her a playful smile. *"How human of you."*

Arla couldn't help but smile back at the Princess. This was the first time Wynera looked so happy. She was always slightly floating in the air, but she seemed higher off the ground today. Arla was glad that Wynera was finally feeling a little lighter.

"Wynera," Arla felt hesitant to ask this question, for it might have brought down Wynera's mood, but there was no one else she could ask that might know the answer. "There was news that The Forest has disappeared. Do you know where it went?"

"Despite our best efforts, The Forest is still bitter towards humanity and no longer wants to exist along with it, so it went away to a different world, but it left something," Wynera whispered over to Arla's side and hovered her translucent hand over Arla's chest. *"A gift."*

Arla felt the entire world shift inside her chest. Everything sung with Whispers of life itself.

She gasped. "What is that?"

"It gave you a piece of itself. A sliver of its power. To give magic like it could to others."

"But – !" Arla tried not to get too worried, but this was a monumental thing. A piece of The Forest was alive in her. "That's too dangerous!" Arla started pacing, no longer able to keep calm. "This could easily turn into another way to separate people. What if I accidentally favor some people over others and I don't even realize it? No. This is too much for a person to have. I don't want it."

"It is precisely because you worry about being fair and uncorrupted that I believe you deserve it. And I think The Forest believes it too, deep down. It hates humans so much, but you cannot hate something so vehemently without having loved it so fiercely first. I think The Forest wanted to give humanity a chance to prove itself, it just needed the right person to come along."

So The Forest was hopeful, but also testing her. It gave her the ultimate power and wanted to see what she would do with it.

"So the wager is still going," Arla said.

Wynera nodded. *"It will be watching."*

Arla straightened, fully encompassing the weight of everything she had to carry now. The Forest was going to watch her for the rest of her life and generations after her of whether they would let power corrupt them once again and surprisingly, Arla felt up to the task. She was no longer the girl that did not believe in herself. She was a Queen.

And then she thought about what Wynera had said again. That one cannot hate something without having loved it so fiercely first.

"I think you're right. I think deep down, The Forest wants me to win the bet. Because it gave Leo back to me. It allowed him to live for no reason other than to give me hope. To keep me going."

Wynera smiled. *"The Forest is a complicated entity."*

"And what about you? What will you do now that this is all over?" Arla thought of all that Wynera had lost. "... I'm sorry we couldn't change his mind."

Wynera shook her head. *"He is finally at peace now and because of that so am I. I have done what I could here, it is time for me to leave this place."*

In some way, Arla knew their time together would not be forever. Wynera came to her for a purpose and once that was fulfilled, she would move on. In fact, Arla wished that she would. Being tied to a realm you did not belong to was a lonely existence.

"Will I ever see you again?" Arla asked, quietly.

Wynera smiled sadly. *"Maybe when it is your time, but I hope that will be years from now."* She reached over and cupped her hand on Arla's cheek just as she had done the first time they met in The Forest. *"Thank you, Arla Seojin. I am so proud of everything you've done."*

Tears burned the back of her eyes as Arla tried to keep herself together. Words she never thought she would ever hear, finally met her when she thought she no longer needed them.

"Goodbye, Wynera."

The sunlight flowed across the room and in the bright light Wynera shimmered like the sun itself. And then the light faded and she was gone.

CHAPTER 55

Arla stood under the tree in the throne room. Rubble and dust remained and the fragments of the throne itself still lay scattered all over the floor. Only the tree stood magnificently alone in the destroyed room.

The leaves sparkled like diamonds against the sunlight, each one bordered with a shade of blushing pink. She took in its beauty, letting it calm her.

Today was the day she would finally address her people. It would be the first time Arla would speak to them since she regained her title, and admittedly, she was nervous. She really wanted to say the right things so that the Ulsanans felt safe under her leadership. She had practiced her speech over and over, swapping and adding words, only to get rid of entire sections of the speech altogether.

And even now she was still adjusting what she would say.

"Are you ready?" Leo appeared behind her.

"I'm as ready as I will ever be."

Leo looked up at the tree, admiring it.

"Do you think she's in there?" she asked.

They had never found Rose's body after the fight, which devastated Arla at first, but then slowly, she believed that maybe they couldn't find her because she was here, bound to the magical tree.

Leo smiled. "Definitely. And she's probably saying something like, 'There is nothing to be nervous about today, idiot.'"

Arla gave a small laugh and placed a gentle hand on the bark of the trunk, which felt more velvet than coarse. "I'm not the idiot. You're the idiot." She stepped back from the tree. "I just want them to know I am on their side."

The tree (or Rose?) did not answer.

"Did you ask Simion to help you with your speech?" Leo asked.

"Why would I do that?" she almost spat, the memory of him still bitter.

Leo showed genuine surprise. "You haven't talked to him yet?"

Simion had disappeared after being abandoned in the tunnel. What he did after that, she did not care to know. Instead, she had focused all her energy on rebuilding Ulsana and creating a new council.

But then, one day out of the blue, someone discovered him in the castle's dungeons, where he had self-imprisoned himself in a windowless cell.

Knowing she was still angry, Leo went to the dungeons instead and reported back that Simion refused to leave or even speak to him. He just stared silently at the wall. She could tell from Leo's tone that he felt sorry for the former councilman, but Arla had no tears left to shed for the traitor. Yet, she couldn't help but send him regular meals to make sure he was well fed at least, which made her even angrier at herself.

"I don't think I can even look at him now, or ever, after what he did. It's just too...hard."

"Arla..."

Arla knew that tone. It was the one Leo used to soften something she did not want to hear.

"He was important to you. I think you owe it to yourself to at least talk to him."

"And say what? What could he possibly say now that would make me forgive him?"

"Maybe you don't need to forgive him, but you at least need some closure. I can tell it bothers you. I see how sad you get when anyone mentions his name."

"I'm not sad, I'm angry."

"You're angry because you're sad."

She huffed, crossing her arms. "Why can't you just blindly be angry with me?"

"Because I know what it's like to have done something wrong. And I also know that people do crazy things to protect the people they love. Simion isn't a bad man, he's just a fool in love. Just like me."

She looked at him. Leo took her hands in his, a little nervously.

"Arla, this may not be the right time, but I need to get this off my chest. I know I broke your heart when I left... but I hope you know that it never changed the way I feel about you." He squeezed her hands. "I love you." He cleared his throat as he nervously rubbed her knuckles with his fingers. "And I know you love me too, but I also know just because you love someone does not mean you want to be with them... I don't know much about being a royal. I don't always know the right thing to say or do. And I am not educated in politics or magic like Simion is, so I am not much help to you, but I am a quick learner and will do anything I can to help you, but... if you decide I am not the one you want to be with, that I may not be the right... choice, I will understand and I will not get in your way."

Arla did not expect Leo to bare his heart right now like this. Maybe a part of her was avoiding it, because she herself did not know the answer. He was right that he didn't have the skills of a politician or a royal, but did that really matter? She thought deeply of what was truly important.

"Leo... when Dehen offered you the chance to take away my magic, why did you refuse?"

Leo was not offended or surprised by the question, instead, he answered her in a steady voice. "Honestly, I almost took the offer, but at the end of the day, I couldn't do it. It wasn't my choice to make. You needed to make your own decision, and I could only be there for you, just like how you let me make my own choice to leave Ulsana. Even if I disagree with you, I can only voice my opinion, but I will not force my decision onto you. No matter how painful it is to watch you suffer."

She paused, taking in what he said.

And then the solidity of knowing spread over her.

The rumble of the crowd echoed beyond the archway, itching for Arla to present herself.

Leo looked to the end of the corridor. "Regardless, you have more important matters to attend to. I should go."

Arla grabbed his hand. "Come with me."

"What are you–"

"Just come!" She pulled him out of the room and down the narrow stairways until they stepped onto the square stage that faced the waiting crowd.

They had agreed that her first speech should be on the same level as the courtyard rather than the tall balcony that overlooked it. It was an appropriate symbol of equality that Arla sought.

Leo stared awkwardly at the people, and they returned his expression, equally confused.

"People of Ulsana," Arla spoke. "I know there has been a lot of pain in our past and a lot of injustices, and I am truly sorry for that. But I know from personal experience that the only way to start healing is to move forward. We will not forget the past, but it doesn't mean it has to define us anymore. I want a future where we can all flourish and be free to pursue what makes us happy. And we can only have that if we are fair to each other. That is why from now on we will treat each other as equals and we will bring in a new era of peace together. And we will do that by giving everyone magic."

The crowd murmured in confusion. How could she give *everyone* magic?

She paused letting the full moment seep in of what she was about to reveal. "I have been given a gift by The Forest. I can grant magic to anyone just like it did."

There was a hesitancy of distrust across the crowd.

"And I know having one person with so much power can be... an issue, which is why I want to share it with all of you. From this moment on, Ulsana will open up a school for everyone, regardless of their background, and they will be granted magic and learn how to use the Whispers."

There was silence at first, like they were not sure whether or not to believe her, but then came a slow clap by a noble who Arla recognized as one that she freed before, followed by another who Arla also recognized as the man she forced apart in the fight in the camp and another and soon half the crowd cheered in excitement while the other half only looked grim and skeptical.

Arla knew she had her work ahead of her, but believed one day they would all agree.

Arla waited for the crowd to quell before she said the next thing. The most important thing. "There is another secret I have been keeping from you for a very long time. I kept it hidden because I was told it was wrong, but there was never anything wrong about it." She noticed Leo inching his way off the stage. She grabbed his hand again and pulled him back. "This is Captain Leo Treterra. And..." she took in a breath. "I love him. I have for some time now and I no longer want to hide that anymore."

The crowd silenced.

She smiled at Leo, who only stared back at her, paying the crowd no attention. "I love you, and I choose you."

"Are you sure?" he asked quietly.

Leo was a good man, and he always did what he felt was right, even at great sacrifice to himself. He loved deeply and loyally and cared for her without trying to control her. He made her feel like she could be all versions of herself. Weak. Strong. Vengeful. Caring. No matter what mistakes she made, he accepted her as she was. And that was a man worth everything.

She smiled. "I am."

He looped his arm around her waist and brought her to him, pressing his lips against hers in an instant.

She heard a garble of noise from the crowd, with no idea if they were shouting in shock, joy or disgust. She did not care. All she felt was Leo pressed against her, kissing her like he had missed her for a thousand years, and that's all she needed to feel.

CHAPTER 56

The dungeon was damper than she expected. No place for anyone to live as long as he had. She moved along the cells of the underground prison, filled with hope and disdain. She turned the corner and saw what she had come for.

Simion was asleep against the damp stone wall, arms crossed, beard fully wild, dark circles under his eyes. He looked quite a mess. What happened to the man who complained about even a smidge of dust on his coat?

She was sure he would have lost his resolve and teleported himself away to a fancy inn with a comfortable bed by now, but her guards told her he had stayed the entire month. Looking at him now, she did not doubt it.

"Simion." Uttering his name brought up emotions she thought she had already thrown away. Why did she let Leo talk her into coming here?

Simion slowly opened his eyes, still sleep-deprived, until he recognized who was staring at him and shot straight up. "Arla."

She stood rigid, suddenly unsure of what she was going to say.

Simion swept dirt off his tattered pants, completely embarrassed. "Sorry for my appearance. The amenities in prison are quite subpar."

"You should be sorry for much worse," she grumbled.

Simion looked down. "I'm surprised you didn't let me starve to death."

"You can thank Leo for that. He did not think you should die down here."

That was a lie. Sending him food was her idea, but he didn't need to know that.

A long silence dragged between them until Arla began to wonder if she was ready for this conversation. Maybe she should just leave.

"I know that you probably hate me," Simion quickly said. "But you have to know that I did it for you."

"So you're not sorry for what you did."

"Of course I'm sorry. I'm sorry that I believed the only way to protect you was to take from you. It was wrong of me. And as you've proven, I was wrong to even doubt you were in danger in the first place." He rested his head against the bars. "It seems like I keep needing your forgiveness, and I'm sorry for that too. I'm sorry for everything."

What does one do in this situation?

She had just asked the people of Ulsana to let go of the past and look toward the future. Now she had to ask herself, what type of future did she want with Simion? Should she hold onto her bitterness and cast him away? Vow never to forgive him? But was that really what she wanted?

No, I want to laugh with him again. I want to trust him. I want to judge him for all the good he has done and not for the one mistake he made.

Because after all, hadn't she made mistakes too that had dire consequences?

"I do not know if I can forgive you just yet, but I do know that you care for me and you are truly sorry. So, I think you can earn your forgiveness instead."

He looked up, hopeful. "Oh?"

"I want to offer you the role of First Advisor." She shot up a finger to silence him before he could say anything. "But you must promise to never make a decision on my behalf ever again."

Simion did not beam with excitement like she thought he would. Instead, a slow bittersweet smile drew from his lips. "I promise I never will.

Thank you for offering me your forgiveness and a seat by your side, but I only need the forgiveness. I cannot take the role."

Arla tilted her head. "I thought that was all you ever wanted. This is the most powerful seat in Ulsana, second only to the crown."

"It was what I wanted up until just recently, then something else became more important."

His eyes bore into hers so intensely, Arla almost had to look away, but she didn't.

"But it seems I am not as important to her as she is to me. At least not compared to a certain captain."

She felt guilty for some reason, like she had made a wrong choice. Even though she knew she didn't. "How did you know?"

"I know everything, remember? Even in here, I have eyes and ears to the outside." Simion shook his head and chuckled sadly to himself. "I must admit, I knew I never had a chance against the him, but still, I dreamed. I am truly happy for you. I am. But the last thing I want to do is stay and watch it. I only chose to stay long enough until you forgave me, however long that took. I promised I would remain here until you did."

The pain he was trying so hard to cover up made her ache. Arla fought the urge to reach over and touch Simion's hand. She wished she wasn't the one that caused the look on his face right now. She wished there was a Whisper that would take away his feelings for her and allow him to return to the humorous snake he used to be. The one whose heart didn't know how to crack, but she knew she could not. So instead, she gave him the words that he wanted to hear.

"I understand. You don't have to stay here anymore. I forgive you."

It was like a weight lifted from him. Simion stepped back from the bars, standing proud. "Thank you, Arla."

"Thank you, Simion, for helping me through the hardest moments of my life and being there when I needed you. I will never forget that." Now she was the one with her hands on the bars, leaning toward him. "Wherever you go, please take care of yourself."

He gave her a sad smile. "You know, this all would have been so much easier if you pretended you didn't care for me at all."

His heartbroken face lingered in Arla's mind long after that moment because it was the last expression of his she ever saw before he disappeared in a puff of smoke in front of her. No one knew where he went or whether he would return.

"I hope he is okay," she said to Leo as they sat together in the gardens the next day. The breeze picked up ever so lightly against her cheeks.

"I understand why he left so fast." Leo's fingers grazed the top of her hand. "If you had chosen him, I would have left too. As far away from here as possible. Although..." He lifted her chin to look into her eyes. "I don't think any distance would have been far enough to wash my soul of you."

She giggled. "And you say you aren't an eloquent man."

She rested her head on his shoulder and looked onward to the surrounding rumble in the garden. It was a mess of a place, but they did not pay attention to what was broken, instead they looked to a lone rose bush, fully bloomed in vibrant gold.

The End

LEAVE A REVIEW

Have thoughts on what just happened?

Reviews are the life blood of authors, and the more I get, the more incentive I have to write more. So please take some time to write a review of what you thought of my book! I will greatly appreciate it!

And be sure to reach out to me via email or social media to let me know you wrote a review! I would love to see your opinions!

Acknowledgements

To be honest, this was a story I really didn't think I would finish.

I originally wrote the first draft two years ago, but after the initial feedback, I realized something was off about the story. So, I furiously rewrote it and rewrote it and rewrote it again, and still it did not work.

So, I left it alone for a while as my life became busy with moving across the country, getting married and buying our first home. And when I returned, I wasn't sure if I would find Arla's voice again or if the story would ever work, but my friends and family would not let me quit.

They kept asking when the story would be done, which kept me motivated to finish it. Their words were encouraging during the times of doubt and tough during the times I was just avoiding the work.

And so I am dedicating this acknowledgment to them. You all pushed me to finish, and I am so grateful you did. You are the reason this book ever got done. So thank you, thank you, thank you.

And a big thank you to my beta readers, who gave me the feedback I needed to make this story work. I am nothing without you all.

About the Author

Jyna Maeng
(pronounced Gina Mang ← rhymes with Bang)

Jyna considers herself a multi-potentialite with many careers as a retail worker, swim instructor, actor, software engineer, and now author. She has an overactive imagination and a worrying addiction to chocolate and often wonders what it would be like to taste feelings. Her greatest dream is to wake up one day with a superhuman power that lets her eat whatever she wants at any quantity without consequences.

Join her in these places:
Newsletter: www.jynamaengbooks.com/backmatternewsletter
Tiktok: @jynamaengbooks
Instagram: @jynamaengbooks

www.ingramcontent.com/pod-product-compliance
Lightning Source LLC
LaVergne TN
LVHW091709070526
838199LV00050B/2319